It Tolls For Thee

James Williams

Alternative Book Press
2 Timber Lane
Suite 301
Marlboro, NJ 07746
www.alternativebookpress.com

2014 Paperback Edition
Cover Illustration by CL Smith
Book Design by Alternative Book Press
Published in the United States of America by
Alternative Book Press
Originally published in electronic form in the United States by Alternative Book Press.
Publication Data
James Williams, [date]
It Tolls for Thee/ by James Williams.—1st ed.
p. cm.
1. General (Fiction). I Title.
PS1-3576.J36W555   2014
813'.6—dc23

ISBN 978-1-940122-17-5
Printed in the United States of America
10 9 8 7 6 5 4 3 2 1

Table of Contents:

I

For Staff Sergeant Dan Ross and the men of First Squad, it is not a question of if they will get hit, the only question is when. Stalled on their way up a hill in Zabul Province, Afghanistan, the soldiers find themselves trapped with rocket-propelled grenades exploding all around. As the men scramble for cover, churned up clods of dirt and pulverized stones rain down upon them. The airborne rocks deflect off of their helmets sending a reverberated ruckus into their brains. They squat behind boulders or belly flop into swales, anything to get out of the line of fire. Smoke and dust have mixed to form a haze making it difficult to see more than a few feet. The trailing winds from enemy rifle rounds send unnerving chills through their bodies. Uncertainty over which bullet is destined to find them floods their veins with adrenaline causing involuntary twitching of their hands and feet. Their teeth vibrate at each ground shaking explosion and a tremor pulsates down each of their spines. Their senses are further confused by the light from each blast. The detonated explosives illuminate the hillside with brilliant flashes that obliterate the haze for split seconds at a time. The soldiers' instincts tell them to force the issue rather than wait for the inevitable, but Sergeant Ross gives the orders and they struggle to remain calm until those orders come.

The Taliban hold the high ground and Dan Ross and his men are running out of options. Kneeling behind a boulder, Dan eases his head around the edge to get a look at the hilltop. After a quick glance, he pulls his head back to the tenuous security provided by the rock. He grits his teeth and slams his fist against the top of his thigh. Getting mad will not get him out of this jam, but Dan is feeling guilty for getting his men in this deep. Taking time to clear his head, he leans his forehead against the stone and stares down at the red tinted soil. His mind progresses through the short list of alternatives with the well being of other squad members complicating his thought process. He takes another look at the summit in an attempt to assess enemy strength. The radio attached to Pfc. Bailey's pack can be heard amid the chaos, "Ross, Ross, come in Ross. This is Blake. What's your situation? Do you copy?"

"Give me that radio, Z," Dan yells, "And keep your head down." Dan stands hunched over with his back to the boulder. He looks to his left and squints, straining to see his men spread across the width of the hill. Dan shouts into the mouthpiece, "Lieutenant Blake, this is Ross. We're stuck about 200 yards from the top. Those Hajis are really laying it on thick, over."

"I understand that Sergeant," Blake says, "Some of their rockets are hitting this road. What's your head count?"

"I have seven men left. Lester's hit and his leg's pretty bad. He can't go any farther, over."

"What can you see at the top? How many of them are up there?"

"All I see is lots of muzzle flashes, smoke and dust. Judging from the fire they're layin down, I'd guess maybe thirty Hajis are up there. Look Lieutenant, we need a medic for Lester, right away. Can you send Doc up and can we get any air support?"

"Negative on the air support, there's no way. Captain Craig has them tied up. I hate to tell you Dan, but it's your hill. You have to take it. Do you copy?"

The hand with which Dan holds the mouthpiece drops and falls to his side. He hangs his head for a moment, before he lifts the handset and says, "We know that. We copy." Dan rubs his chin with the back of the hand holding the transmitter and he thinks for a moment. An idea pops into his head and he flips the handset back around. He asks, "Hey Lieutenant, do we have any mortars in the logistics truck?"

"Affirmative on the mortars, Sergeant. We've got about two minutes worth, that's it. We'll get them ready. Second Squad is about 300 meters to your right, but they're cut off, they can't catch up with you. I'll have them set up to provide suppression fire. Third Squad is moving around to the back of the hill, only it's going to take a while for them to get to the other side."

Dan yells over the battlefield noise, "If you think we're gonna sit here and wait on Third Squad, you're crazy. We gotta get moving or there won't be any of us left. Do you copy?"

"Calm down Dan, just calm down," Blake says, "We'll hit the top with these mortars. When the bombardment stops, Second Squad will open up with the machine guns. That's when you go. Is that clear?"

"Affirmative, but tell Combs to give it all he has with those machine guns while we get started. When we get close to the top, he can shut 'em down. We don't need to dodge his bullets too, over."

"Roger, we copyBlake says, "I'm sending Doc up to see about Lester. You have about four minutes until you go, over."

Dan hands the radio back to Pfc. Bailey, who goes by "Z". Dan says, "Pass the word. When I get up, we all move to the top. Tell everyone to keep their eyes on me. If they can't see me, tell them to watch the guy next to them. We all go at the same time. Is that clear? And tell them to use their grenades when the suppression fire stops, then tell them to shoot anything that moves up there. You got all that?"

"Yes sir, Sergeant. I'll let 'em know." Z says, as he tightens his chin strap and sticks the butt of his rifle into the ground to pry himself from his squatting position. He works his way down the line from one man to the next.

Dan squints into the haze and yells to the closest soldier he can see, "Little Al. Get over here with Lester."

Specialist Albert Sandoval carefully moves around the rocks and dried up bushes to get to Pfc. Lester, who is lying next to Dan. Lester's right leg has been torn open above his knee by a piece of shrapnel. His pant leg is sopping with blood all the way down to his boot. The hot metal is protruding from his leg. A few minutes earlier Dan applied a field tourniquet above the wound. After seeing Lester up close, Sandoval is in shock. He is sure Lester is dying. Sandoval's eyes are wide open and he begins to shake. He screams, "What am I supposed to do Sergeant? I don't know what to do. I can't help him."

Dan backhands Sandoval in the sternum and yells, "Snap out of it and get your celox on him." Dan is referring to gauze the soldiers carry to help with bleeding. Dan says, "Doc is on the way up. Stay with him until Doc gets here and don't tighten that tourniquet too much, just enough to slow the bleeding."

Dan is young to be a squad leader, but he has a natural take charge disposition that his men admire. He has no compassion for the enemy nor does he pretend otherwise. On the other hand, the the welfare of his men is his first priority. After passing the word to the rest of the squad, Z scampers back to Dan's side. He never gets too far from Dan because he carries the radio. He squats down and runs a hand down each of his arms and he pats his sleeves, raising a cloud of dust from his uniform. He looks at Dan and says, "Everybody's ready, Sergeant."

While mortar shells are screaming overhead. Dan puts his hand on Lester's shoulder. "Hang in there. Pete. Doc is on the way. You'll be OK."

Lester is calm despite the alarming loss of blood. His face is pale and he is exhausted from the whole ordeal. As he winces to cope with the pain, he hands Dan a note he scribbled on the thin brown wrapper from a MRE. It is a letter to his parents, neatly folded and addressed.

Dan examines the blood stained letter and he stashes it in one of his pockets. Dan says, "You'll be home before this gets there."

Lester coils from the pain. He shakes his head in disagreement and says, "No, I don't think so. Go get those SOB's for me, would ya Sergeant?"

Dan nods his head and clutches the wounded man's shoulder and gives it a squeeze. His body language serves to reassure Pete that those Hajis are going to pay for hurting one of Dan Ross' men. It was not supposed to be this way. Blake's platoon was assigned to cut off the trails going into the valley. They were supposed to pick up any stragglers trying to escape from Captain Craig's main assault. Craig has three platoons and air support attacking a hill about four miles north of Blake's position. The last of the mortars explode at the top of the hill. Dan hears machine gun fire erupt on the right flank and he knows it is his cue to move out. He closes his eyes and recites a Hail Mary out loud. After the quick prayer, he takes a breath to fill his lungs with enough air and confidence to lead the charge. Next, he stands with his rifle in one hand and he waves his other arm forward. He shouts, "Let's go." As Dan leads First Squad the final 200 yards up the hill, he notices the American artillery has diminished the enemy rifle fire, but the remaining volleys are no less lethal. The insurgents are lying low, yet they continue to mount a gallant defense. The men of First Squad serpentine around boulders and bushes, running hunched over with their 40 pound packs pointing into the air. They are undaunted by the hail of bullets and the sporadic explosions from Taliban rockets. First Squad climbs straight into the teeth of the enemy defense. The terrain is steep, but they are able to remain on their feet. The young GIs trained for this sort of combat in the rugged mountains of west Texas. These hills in Afghanistan are similar to those in Texas. They are steep and rocky with little vegetation, but the surrounding mountains reach high altitudes and are densely forested. This is where the training pays off. Second Squad's machine guns go quiet as the men approach the summit. Each of the attacking soldiers throws grenades over the rocks at the top of the hill. The ensuing explosions further reduce the enemy resistance. The remnants of the hilltop defenders rise up to fire at the oncoming Americans, but they are cut down by the dominant firepower from First Squad. Having worked his way to the left side of the summit, Dan flanks the Talibs. He slips around a big rock and finds three of them shooting downhill into the haze. He squeezes off a burst from his rifle, striking and killing the three insurgents. Z and Pfc. Darius Green, who goes by "Cuz", are right behind Dan.

"Damn Sergeant," Cuz says. "You nailed them Hajis." Cuz looks around. His eyes widen and he points to an opening in the ground. He yells, "Hey look, what's that big hole? It looks like a cave or somethin."

"It might be one of their hideouts," Dan says. "Cuz, you stay here and watch that hole. Stay covered behind this rock, but don't let anybody in or out of there." Dan turns to Z, "Come on, let's catch up with the others."

Dan and Z scale a boulder and find themselves at the highest point of the hill. They survey the scene through the dust and smoke that is swirling in the breeze. The pungent smell of burnt flesh and gunpowder permeates the air. Their nostrils burn from inhaling the sulfur in the air and the chemical residue leaves a bitter taste with every swallow. It would be enough to gag most men, but these soldiers are too preoccupied with finishing the job to notice air quality. Dan scans the dead bodies of Taliban fighters littered over the hilltop. The dismembered limbs and gashed remains are evidence that many were killed by shrapnel from mortars or grenades. The gruesome scene barely registers in his mind, when he sees his men huddled around a wounded member of First Squad. Dan and Z hurry down to check on the wounded man. It's Pfc. Albert Jones, "Big Al", as he known by his buddies.

"How bad is it?" Dan asks.

"It's his shoulder," Corporal Paul Larson says. "I think he's gonna be OK, but he's definitely going home."

Dan turns to Z. "Let Lieutenant Blake know what's going on. Tell him we need another medic. Martinez, you stay with Big Al. Paul, Hambone, let's check out these Hajis watch the ones that are still moving. Get their weapons away from them. The other squads should be here soon."

Most of the insurgents are dead, but some are moaning, "Kumak, kumak." which means, "Help, help," in the Dari language. Breaking the short lived calm, shots ring out from the direction of the hole Cuz is watching. Dan runs toward the sound of the gun fire. Cuz had seen someone try to get out of the hole he is watching and he fired a few shots to keep the enemy in place.

As Dan approaches, he can hear a man's voice coming from the hole, "Lutfan, lutfan, please do not shoot."

Cuz is still positioned by the rock. He is shaking and so is the weapon in his hands. Without taking his eyes off of the hole, he shouts, "Sergeant Ross, I got a live one."

From atop a rock overlooking the hole, Dan orders the man to come out of the hole. "Do you speak English?"

The man speaks decent English with a heavy middle eastern accent. He says, "Yes, some."

Dan points at the hole with his rifle, "How many others are in there?"

"I am alone."

"Then come on out with your hands in the air and take off your clothes, now."

The man peels off a top layer of clothing. Like all American soldiers, Dan is wary of suicide bombers, so he has to be sure this guy is clean. "Everything, everything comes off," Dan says. "Including that goofy onesie outfit and those damned rags on your head. Hurry up."

The man complies with the order. He appears to be about 40 years old, although it is hard to tell, because exposure to the elements causes these guerilla fighters to age quicker than normal. He looks at Dan and says, "I am hurt."

Dan jumps down from the rock and inspects the man's clothes and wounds. His arms are bleeding from minor cuts and scrapes. In his haste to find cover from the shelling, he fell head long on the rocky hilltop and used his arms to break the fall. "You're not hurt bad." Dan grumbles, as though he is disappointed the wounds are not worse.

By this time, the entire platoon has converged upon the summit, including Lieutenant Blake. Looking at a photo that he has taken from a front pocket on his fatigues, Blake says, "Hey, I think this is the guy Captain Craig was after." Blake stuffs the photo back in his pocket and says, "Okay, he's clean. Give 'em his clothes back."

Sergeant Combs from Second Squad asks, "Are you sure you want to do that, Lieutenant? Captain Craig may not recognize him with his clothes on."

The men laugh, but Blake is not amused. He says, "That will be enough, Sergeant. You guys may not know it, but this is a big deal. If he's who I think he is, the Army's been trying to get this guy for five years. Okay, let's make sure this hill is secured. Captain Craig is on his way up." The squad sergeants begin barking out orders and some of the men administer aid to the wounded insurgents. Others descend into the hole to see what else may be inside.

Dan is worried about Lester. He asks Lieutenant Blake if he can go down and check on his wounded men. Blake knows there is a lot of work to do, but First Squad has done their share. He raises his voice so all of the men can hear. He announces, "First Squad may return to the vehicles. As for everybody else, let's get to work."

The remainder of Blake's platoon fans out over the hilltop. They search for any hidden Taliban fighters. Those searching the hole from which their prisoner emerged, use flashlights to examine the contents. It turns out to be a cave that is being used as a Taliban command center. There are maps, cell phones, explosives, weapons, food and ammunition stored inside. There are enough supplies to sustain forty or fifty men for a month or so.

A handful of men from First Squad unfold a stretcher and carry Big Al down the hill. The closer they get to the road, the better the air quality becomes. After getting back to the road, they find Lester lying in the back of a truck. The soldiers set the stretcher containing Big Al next to Lester. Two medics immediately go to work on their newest patient. After exchanging the blood soaked celox on Pete's leg for a tightly wound bandage, another medic begins packing unused supplies into his bag. He tells Dan, "We've called for air evac. The chopper should be here soon."

Dan kneels between the two men. He says, "Looks like the flag football will have to wait awhile. We can't do without our two star players." The two wounded men have little reaction. It is either the pain killers or the shock that has left them numb. As the helicopters come roaring in, Dan yells above the whoofing sounds churned out by the whirling rotors, "Tell the folks back home hello for us." The helicopters land near the crossroads, stirring up a miniature sandstorm, and their engines howl making it difficult to hear. Dan squeezes the men's hands and smiles. He jumps down from the truck and watches each of the wounded soldiers give a thumbs up signal as they are carried away. He continues to stare until his view is obscured by the veil of dust surrounding the helicopter.

The medic packs the last of his equipment. He hops down from the truck and looks toward the hill. He slings the canvas bag over his shoulder and asks, "Sergeant, should we wait for the wounded Taliban to get down here?"

"Hell no," Dan says, "We can pack them in on the back of donkeys for all I care. Now get going. Get my men to a hospital, now."

First Squad gathers around a truck to get some water and collect their thoughts. They see the command vehicle heading toward them with the rest of Bravo Company not far behind. The commanding officer, Captain Craig, starts yelling before his humvee rolls to a stop, "Is this area secured? Where is Lieutenant Blake?"

Dan says, "We have pickets out from Fourth Squad Captain. Lieutenant Blake is at the top of the hill."

Craig glares at Dan and says, "Well Sergeant, it looks like you came through it allright." Craig turns toward the helicopter containing the two wounded soldiers and says, "But we can't say that about everybody, can we?"

Without hesitation Dan says, "There are about twenty insurgents at the top of this hill that are through saying anything."

Craig whips his head back around and he glares at Dan. He says, "But at what price, soldier?" Craig slowly nods his head, but his frown and intense eye contact with Dan indicate his displeasure. Craig bites his lower lip and says, "Allright Sergeant, set up a perimeter and double the pickets. I am going to the top. I understand we have uncovered some interesting items up there."

Captain Craig, First Sergeant Hayes and Lieutenant Ashby, from First Platoon, begin the twelve hundred yard climb. There is a steady stream of men carrying dead and wounded Taliban down the hill. It is a busy scene at the crossroads as medics from the entire company attend the wounded. The dead are loaded into a truck. Maps and other contraband from the cave are brought down to be taken back to the post. Intelligence will want to examine everything. After a few minutes, a second helicopter lifts off carrying the wounded insurgents. Three sergeants from other platoons approach Dan to find out what happened.

With the screeching sounds of helicopter engines fading over the horizon, a sergeant says, "Hey Dan, you were right in the middle of it. What was it like?"

15

Dan lifts his arm and wipes his brow with his sleeve smearing the sweat and dust across his forehead. He shakes his head and says, "Intense. How about you guys?"

"We didn't see anything." The sergeant says, "We attacked the hill, just like we planned, but there was no return fire and we never saw anybody up there."

Another sergeant confirms the remarkable story, "Yeah, we kept firing. We even had air support, but we didn't need it. Hell, there wasn't anything for the jets to shoot at."

At first, Dan is dismayed by the reports from the other soldiers. His mouth falls open and he says, "You didn't see any Hajis or take any enemy fire? Why didn't you withdraw and come help us?"

The third of the three noncomms replies to Dan's questions, "Captain Craig ordered us to keep firing. Lieutenant Ashby asked him about that, but he was convinced there was something there."

The sergeants shrug their shoulders and shake their heads. After giving it some thought, Dan realizes he should not be surprised by the Captain's actions. After all, Dan has seen some unusual tactics from Captain Craig before, but this time First Squad paid the price. Eventually, Lieutenant Blake makes his way back down to the road. He barks out some orders and the soldiers disperse. Blake pulls Dan aside and asks, "How did all of this get started? How did you know they were up there? You were just supposed to be watching the crossroads."

The crossroads are the intersection of the battered path that winds through the foothills back to Combat Outpost (COP) Geronimo and the main road that leads through a mountain pass into

16

a valley with farms and a small town named Murzani. "We were watching the roads." Dan explains, "Then that kid that hangs around the COP. You know, he interprets for us. Jahen is his name. Anyway, Jahen and his brother were riding in a wagon pulled by an old man on a tractor. I sent Lester and Cuz over to tell them to get off of the roads and go home. When my men ran toward the wagon, Paul and Hambone saw some guys moving around at the top of the hill. I guess those Hajis thought we were flanking them, but we wouldn't even have known they were there if they would'a kept still. We figured it was only a few stragglers, that's when I asked for permission to start up the hill."

Blake nods his head, "Very well Sergeant, good work." The Lieutenant turns to the men of First Squad and says, "You all did a good job."

"What about the prisoner, Lieutenant?" Cuz asks, "Is he the dude we wanted?"

"The Captain thinks so," Blake says, "The Captain thinks he is Amir Sadiq Nurzai, second in command among the Taliban in this province. He's some kind of Muslim cleric, but he spends more time fighting than preaching. If he is Nurzai, he's the man the Captain was after all along."

Dan and Blake walk side by side twenty yards away from the rest of the men. "John, there is something I have to ask you about. I talked to some guys from the other platoons and they didn't run into any insurgents, at all. Yet the Captain didn't stop and come to help us. He didn't even redirect the air support. Do you know anything about that?"

"Look Dan, Captain Craig was going by the intelligence reports that he had. It turned out, that information led him to attack the wrong hill, but we found what he was looking for." Judging from Dan's reaction, Blake knows that his explanation is lacking. In fact, Blake feels like he is making excuses for Craig which never appeases a guy who is as down to earth as Dan.

The last soldiers from Bravo Company return from the hill except for a demolition team that is preparing to blow the entrance to the cave. The entire Company snaps into action stowing equipment and lining up trucks for the trip back to the COP. Bravo Company consists of one hundred and twenty men who dismantle the staging area at the behest of their noncommissioned officers who are howling step by step instructions. Their movement stirs the dust that has yet to settle after being raised by the helicopter traffic.

All of the trucks are loaded and ready to roll except one truck stays behind to transport the demolition team and their equipment. Captain Craig's slow southern drawl is heard over radios in every truck, "Let's button up and get back to the COP. Let's get moving." Sergeant Combs drives the point humvee. The Bravo Company vehicles, loaded with contraband and their trophy prisoner, line up behind the point vehicle and start back to COP Geronimo.

II

COP Geronimo is a four mile trek through the foothills of Zabul Province. The roads are really just rocky trails with lots of pot holes. Dan hears an explosion from the top of the hill. He is pleased that another cave has been sealed, but it was a close call for his squad. He looks around at the faces of his men as they are jostled around in the truck. Bumpy rides take a little getting used to, but it is better than walking. This was the first live fire for most of his squad and Dan is satisfied with their performance. The men do not talk much at the beginning of the short ride back to Geronimo. Most of them stare at the barren foothills and think about home.

Dan Ross is twenty two years old from Quincy, Illinois. He is thinner than most soldiers and right around six feet tall. His shoulders are so broad, it looks like he is walking around with the hanger still in his shirt. He is not married nor does he have a steady girlfriend. Most people would describe him as an all American boy. He is prone to sarcasm and when it comes to the Afghan people, he is more than just a little cynical. Some would say he is jaded. Most members of Bravo

Company consider Dan to be a rebel, but he deplores that reputation. He does not see himself as a trouble maker even though he has had his share of runins with Captain Craig. Dan is both stubborn and tenacious, especially when it comes to interjecting common sense into situations. Dan has learned the hard way that common sense and the Army do not mix, but whether they are solicited or not, he cannot help voicing his opinions. Dan has not always been this way. Growing up, he was a happy-go-lucky kid, but the Army experience has changed him. He could have done better in school, but he was a bit of a dreamer. However, he has earned an associate degree by attending a community college near Fort Polk, Louisiana. That is where their battalion is permanently stationed. Dan plans on finishing school when he gets back home. He wants to study mechanical engineering and build things like bridges or highways. The Army has provided plenty of opportunities for him to destroy those things. This is it for him, as far as combat goes. His hitch is up when they get back to the States. It has only been three weeks since their battalion has been deployed in Zabul Province and they have the better part of a year left on their current tour. The voice in Dan's head says, "If we have many more days like this, it's going to be a long year." This is his second combat tour in Afghanistan and from his perspective things only seem to get worse.

Besides Dan, the remaining six members of First Squad are Corporal Paul Larson, Pfc. Eric Simms and Pfc. Oscar Martinez to go along with Little Al, Cuz and Z. Paul is Dan's best friend and brother-in-law. He is twenty five years old from Billings, Montana. Paul is a quiet, studious man. He is just under six feet tall with a slight frame and he wears wire rim glasses when he is not wearing combat goggles. He doesn't talk much, because he likes to analyze things and choose his words carefully. About two years ago, Dan took Paul home to Quincy on leave. Dan introduced Paul to his sister, Katie. Paul and Katie fell in love and were married about six months ago. Simms is from a little farming community in Tennessee. He talks slowly with a country twang in his voice. His folks raise hogs for a living. He compares most everything to tending animals. The other members of the squad are amazed at his ability to find so many similarities in their everyday duties to hog farming. Consequently, they all call him "Hambone". Martinez is from Los Angeles. He was raised by a single mom who supported the family by giving dancing lessons. He has almost all of his pay sent directly to his mom. When he is in the right mood or just acting goofy, Martinez will break into a samba dance, giving all of the guys something to smile about. They call him "Chi Chi". "Little Al" Sandoval is from Rufrigio, Texas. He is the son of migrant farm workers in the Rio Grande Valley, where a good amount of the nation's fruits and vegetables are produced. His brown skin is further darkened from exposure to the Texas sun. He has been working in the fields and orchards as long as he can remember. "Cuz" Green is from Crockett, Texas. It is a small town in the piney woods of east Texas. In his mind that town is a nowhere place and he could not wait to graduate from high school and get out of that town. After a fire fight like the one in which he just participated, Crockett, Texas is looking better and better. Zach Bailey is a baby faced young man from Albuquerque, New Mexico. They are all just wide eyed kids. Paul is the oldest in the squad and at nineteen years old, Z is the youngest. Only Dan and Paul had seen live fire before today.

The soldiers look at each other as though they would like to get something off of their chests, but none of them speak until Z says, "Sergeant Ross, is it always like this? It seems like there was a little bit of confusion out there."

Dan says, "What do you mean?"

"Captain Craig and the whole company were nowhere near us," Z says, "Where were they?"

Hambone joins in, "Yeah no kiddin, we were outnumbered big time out there. What was that?"

Even laid back Cuz is bothered by the turn of events. He says, "I talked to some guys from other platoons, and they didn't see nobody. The Captain had them firin at nothin but the thin air."

Little Al shakes his head and says, "The Captain had to hear our chatter on the radio. He had to know what was happening with us."

The men begin talking all at once. They hash out the incident and try to make sense of the whole plan. In the back of his mind, Dan is concerned too, but he has to keep his men calm and confident for their sake. He lifts his hands with the palms out and says, "Calm down guys, calm down. It's not that simple. Just because you hear chatter on the radio doesn't mean anything. The chatter may not necessarily provide a clear picture of what's going on. Captain Craig had a plan and he stuck to it. It's not always like that. The Captain knows what he is doing." For the remainder of the short trip, the men are awkwardly silent.

The vehicles carrying Bravo Company pull into COP Geronimo about four o'clock in the afternoon. In Afghanistan, battalion headquarters are at Forward Operating Base (FOB) Apache. It is ninety miles north of the COP. Geronimo is a new combat outpost, in fact, it is so new it is unfinished. The perimeter of the post is supposed to be made up of Hesco Bastions. Hescos, as the men call them, are large canvas bags filled with sand or dirt. After they are filled, they are about seven feet tall and two feet thick. Two hescos butted against one another can provide defense against grenades and small rockets. There are also coils of razor wire stretched along the top of the hescos. Since the post is not finished, there are sections of the perimeter that are only wire. The combat engineers that were working on this post, were called away to repair an air base that was attacked. They should be back in a week. A National Guard company of truck drivers delivers equipment and supplies to the post two or three days a week. Large tents are used for most everything that requires cover, such as the soldier's quarters and the mess hall. There are some of those storage containers, those that are found on cargo ships or eighteen wheelers, that have been converted into offices and living quarters for the officers. The latrines are port-a-cans with hescos stacked two high around them. The showers are fortified the same way. There is the constant threat of sniper fire from the hills, so men are careful moving around open areas of the post. The snipers are not especially good shots, but a stray bullet is as deadly as a well aimed one. There is a guard tower at the southeast corner of the perimeter. The front gate faces east, that is the direction the road from the hills leads into the post. Geronimo is situated on an open plain with foothills about a thousand yards out on either side of the road. The hills to the rear of the post are much closer, but they are considered secure.

Bravo Company is the only permanent resident of COP Geronimo, for now. Although there is a twelve man detachment of ANA (Afghanistan National Army) that has been assigned to Captain Craig for training. The plans are to finish the COP and bring in more ANA. They will eventually take responsibility for security in this section of the province. The men leap out of the truck and get right to work. Dan shouts, "Allright guys, get your gear cleaned and repacked. See you for chow in a couple of hours."

Dan and Paul are bunk mates. Their portion of the tent is partitioned off from the remainder of the squad. The two soldiers, who happen to be brothers-in-law, talk while they are getting their gear squared away. Paul removes his fatigue shirt and holds it up for inspection, "I tell you Dan, I didn't know there could be so much dust. It's like walking around on the moon out here. I'm going to take these clothes outside and give them a shake."

Dan removes his top shirt and tosses it to Paul. He says, "Do this one too, while you're out there."

When Paul returns with the freshly shaken uniforms, he and Dan begin to disassemble their rifles to get them clean and ready for the next patrol. While they are working on their weapons, Paul begins to think out loud. "You know, that was a little strange out there today."

Dan had been waiting for an opportunity to vent about Captain Craig and he knows it is safe to confide in Paul. "You talking about the fact that Craig attacked the wrong hill and was no help to us, at all?"

"Yeah, I guess. It seems like such a waste to have all of those men and fire power over there, while we were getting slammed."

Dan snaps the trigger mechanism back into place. "Between his crazy ideas and our lousy intelligence, it's a wonder we get anything done. Craig relies too heavily on the intel. He should use it, but he should take some of that stuff with a grain of salt."

Paul rams a cleaning rod down the barrel of his M-16 and says, "Maybe he should use a little more common sense, or maybe be little more flexible to react."

Dan jumps to his feet and says, "Exactly, that's what I'm talking about. Nothing is what it seems to be out here and things can change real quick."

Leon Hayes, the Company First Sergeant, is making his rounds with news from Captain Craig. Hayes is a short muscular man who has made the Army his career. He is forty two years old with not one ounce of fat on his body. The chevrons on his uniforms have to be custom made to stretch across his large upper arms. He speaks in a quick staccato pace and he seldom wastes time on pleasantries like good afternoon, or even hello. He is outside the door of Dan's quarters, he sticks his head inside and says, "Ross, there is a debriefing on today's action scheduled for eighteen hundred. All officers and squad leaders are requested to attend. Don't be late." He leaves without waiting for an answer. Dan looks at Paul and rolls his eyes.

It is eighteen hundred. There are folding chairs assembled beneath an open ended tent in an area surrounded by double stacked hescos. There are guards posted to keep unauthorized personnel out of ear shot of the proceedings. Lieutenant Blake sits with Dan and other noncomms from Fourth Platoon. Captain Craig stands in front and waits impatiently for the last invitees to take their seats. Craig is a reservist from Conyers, Georgia. He is married and has two young daughters. His family lives very near Fort Polk. He is a short wiry man, with a reputation of being a "red ass". In other words, he gets ticked off easily and his reactions are quite punitive. Craig is meticulous when it comes to the little things. For example, his uniforms are always freshly starched to perfection and he insists his men to dress strictly by the book. He was activated ten years ago and has not received a promotion in those ten years. He is frustrated that he will never get above his current rank and he believes it is because he is not a West Point graduate. However, his superiors will tell you that he is a brown noser with no stomach for combat. For an officer that is prone to make questionable battlefield decisions, he possesses an air of infallibility, like that of a Roman emperor or an American politician. He would be better suited for a desk job, but the Army is a thin on experienced company commanders. Craig begins the debriefing trying to mask his drawl for this official occasion, but his southern accent still comes through. "First of all, I want to congratulate ya'll on a successful operation this morning. As you know, we captured Amir Sadiq Nurzai. He is a Muslim cleric that uses his religion to get these insurgents fired up and he is number two on our most wanted list in this province. The Army has had this guy in their sights lots of times, but he has always managed to get away. I don't mind telling you that this is a feather in Bravo Company's hat. Colonel Willis has already called to express his approval for a job well done. In fact, he indicated that he will look into a company citation for this action."

The men remain stoic with little reaction as Craig continues his remarks. "I would like to recognize Lieutenant Blake and Fourth

Platoon for sealing off the escape route and apprehending the high priority target." Craig nods his head in the direction of Blake and says, "Well done, Lieutenant. Now at this time, I will turn it over to Lieutenant Ashby for the casualty report."

Ashby steps up to the front of the assembly while flipping through some pages fastened to the clip board in his hand. He begins his report by saying, "Thank you Captain. We have confirmed twenty one Taliban were killed and four others were wounded, in addition to the one prisoner taken. The wounded insurgents were transported to the field surgical center at FOB Apache. Chances are good that the enemy fatality count will rise. Two of our men were wounded, both from First Squad, Fourth Platoon. The initial prognosis for each of our wounded men is good. However, the two soldiers will be transported back home for extended medical treatment. Captain..."

"Thank you, Lieutenant." Captain Craig says, "Our thoughts and prayers certainly are with Privates Jones and Lester and their families, as they recover." The Captain glares at Dan as he talks about the wounded soldiers. "The prisoner will remain here, at Geronimo, until an intelligence detail from FOB Apache arrives. They have indicated they would like to interrogate the Amir and examine the captured material before sending the prisoner through the system. We will convert one of the supply tents into a temporary stockade to accommodate the Amir. There will be double guards 24/7, as long as the Amir is with us. Once again, I want to thank you for your hard work. That is all."

The abrupt ending to the meeting leaves Dan annoyed that there is no mention of the inaccurate intelligence. Nor is there any mention of firing on the wrong hill or Fourth Platoon being hung out with no support from the rest of the Company. As men file out of the tent, they shuffle around the rows of chairs. Dan waves his hand and raises his voice above the background noise to get Blake's attention. He says, "Lieutenant Blake, what about attacking the wrong hill?"

Blake is very near Captain Craig and he knows not to say anything that will get a rise out of his commanding officer. So, he ignores the question, but Craig hears it loud and clear.

Craig steps in front of Blake and faces Dan. "Sergeant Ross, if you have any questions, you may ask me."

Dan finally makes his way over to Craig. He says, "Sir, do you know why the intelligence reports were so wrong?"

"Who said they were wrong?" Craig says, "We got our man."

"But Sir, the Talibs could have easily gotten away scot free. We were just lucky to have seen some movement at the top of that hill."

"I don't believe in luck Sergeant. Your job was to pick up any insurgents retreating from our assault. I believe it worked and so does the Colonel."

"But they weren't retreating. They were dug in. We could have lost a lot of men up there."

Craig raises his voice and says, "Quit whining Sergeant. You could have waited before attacking that cave. You should have coordinated the attack with the rest of the platoon. We have two men in the hospital because of your impatience."

Torn between evoking the rage of his superior and backing up one his squad sergeants, Lieutenant Blake uses his forearm to nudge Dan away from Craig. He steps between the two men and says, "I agree with Sergeant Ross, Sir. We saw the enemy and we attacked. We initially thought they were retreating, but their robust defense combined with the captured supplies suggests they were prepared for an attack, maybe even expecting one. If we wait in that situation, they probably disperse and assimilate. The whole operation would have been just another walk in the countryside."

Captain Craig snaps his head away from Dan and is now confronting Blake, "You are out of line, Lieutenant. Your job is to take orders from me, not question them. Now, unless they're teaching something else at West Point, I suggest you both remember who you are working for. Is that understood?"

Lieutenant Blake looks down at the ground and belts out a loud response. "Yes sir, Captain." John Blake is a West Point graduate, a detail Craig never discounts. Craig seems to revel in his ability to exert his authority over the young officer, because deep down he knows it is only temporary. Craig knows with a West Point pedigree, Blake will soon get promoted right up the ladder, while Craig is topped out at his current level. Blake is fresh out of the Academy, only twenty two years old and experiencing his first combat tour. He is from Terra Haute, Indiana. Blake is married and he and his wife have a newborn baby girl. Dan likes Blake and feels fortunate to have him as his platoon leader. Maybe it is because they are both midwesterners, but they get along well. They have their hands full with the tempestuous Craig as their company commander.

Blake and Dan leave the meeting and talk while walking back to their area of the COP. "Dan, I am putting your entire squad in for silver stars." Blake says, "You guys took hell up there and didn't back

29

down one bit. The Company may get a citation, but you guys did all of the heavy lifting."

"You don't have to do that, John. We're not interested in medals. We just want to get home in one piece. Although, I'm beginning to wonder if that's possible with Captain Craig in charge."

Blake chuckles under his breath and says, "I'll pretend I didn't hear that." He pats Dan on the back as the two men split up to return to their respective quarters.

III

The next day is scheduled to be a light one for the members of Fourth Platoon. There are no patrols unless something pops up. Before daylight, the men run through their early morning callisthenics. After working out, they take showers and then go to breakfast. One advantage to working out of a COP is that there is a mess tent and cooked food, as opposed to sleeping in a fighting hole and eating MREs. The food is not the best, but it's usually hot. Dan, Paul and other members of Fourth Platoon carry their trays down a cafeteria style line and shove them toward the civilian servers. Dan thinks the food is second rate and it is. For example, the scrambled eggs are made from powdered eggs. COP Geronimo has a refrigerated truck, but that space is limited to meat and other highly perishable items. After getting their trays filled with eggs, biscuits and sausage, Dan and some of the guys from First Squad sit at a long table next to Sergeant Combs and others from their platoon. Combs says, "Do you guys have to sit so close to me? I'm not sure I should be seen with Ross' Renegades." That is a moniker members of Fourth Platoon use to refer to First

Squad. Dan does not like the name. In his mind, it promotes his misunderstood reputation. Combs is a light hearted guy that likes to take friendly jabs at people. He says, "Ross, you really got yourself in a jam yesterday. It's not like you to stick your neck out like that."

"Yeah, well just how am I supposed to stick it out? Besides, we got out of it, that's all that matters. By the way, thanks for your help, but you really didn't have to stay so far away. You could've come a little closer. You could've joined the party. It's allowed."

Combs takes a bite of sausage and answers while chewing, "We got cut off by a giant crevasse in the ground. We ended up having to go almost all the way back down to the road to get around it."

"Excuses, excuses." Dan says, playfully razzing his friend. "But that crevasse probably kept those Hajis hemmed in. They had to stand and fight it out."

Hambone gets a puzzled look on his face and says, "Those guys were bottled up like pigs in a chute, why didn't they surrender?"

Combs playfully mocks Hambone's country twang by repeating the question in a not so flattering impersonation, "Sarinda?" Most of the soldiers get a kick out of the harmless jeering. Combs proceeds in his normal voice, "Those guys don't give up. Anyway, they had the high ground and all of the advantages. They were probably surprised you guys kept coming."

Dan jumps into the conversation, "That's what we're trained to do, because with those Hajis, it's kill or be killed."

Hambone digs into his eggs and says, "This is a lot different than I thought it'd be. I know we trained for some of this, but I just figured they were just tryin to scare us with all that trainin. I figured we'd be

32

kind'a corrallin them Hajis around, you know, like gettin hogs from one pen to another. But this stuff we're doin, it's pretty harsh."

Dan knew his men did not know what it was going to be like, even though he described it in as much detail as he could. No one really knows until the shooting starts. Dan responds to Hambone, "It's a harsh job, but that's all it is, a job. I'm just counting the days until we get out of this God forsaken hole and back to the good old USA."

Combs, always the one to stir the pot, says, "I heard it's bad luck to count the days."

"I heard that, too," Hambone says, "But, I'm not superstitious."

Cuz has been listening to his buddies and he decides to throw in his two cents worth, "I ain't superstitious or nothin, but I ain't countin the days neither, just in case."

"Well I am. I can't wait until I get out of this man's Army," Dan says, "With the GI Bill, I got my college paid for. In a couple of years after we get home, I'll be working 9 to 5 and watching Monday Night Football. I'll be like everybody else in America, the war will be the farthest thing from my mind."

Hambone is surprised by his sergeant's comment. He says, "You think the folks back home don't care about this war?"

Dan says, "Huh, most people in America don't even know there is a war. They're too busy chasing the almighty dollar to worry about anything else."

Cuz says, "I'm glad we're helpin these here people. They really need it."

Dan is in one of his worst moods, one he rarely shows to his men, but now that they have had a dose of reality, he decides to give them his side of the story. He says, "These people are just trying to see how much money they can scam from our government. Whether they are insurgent fighters or farmers, it doesn't matter. Given the chance, they would cut your throat in your sleep. My motto is, 'Don't let other people's problems become my problems'."

Combs rests his hand beside his plate with a firm grasp on his fork, he looks at Dan and says, "The Army's the wrong business for that kind of attitude. We're making this place safer"

Cuz joins Combs in denouncing Dan's viewpoint, "That's right Sergeant, most of these here people are farmers, just tryin to get by. They don't know nothin about no politics."

"Sure Dan, they're taking what they can get," Combs says, "But, how does that make them any different from you? You joined the Army just to get the GI Bill. You're nothing but a taker, too."

Dan says, "Oh really, and I suppose you joined up for the noble cause, huh Combs? Besides, I'm not getting anything easy. I've had to put up with clowns like you for three years and I still have one more year to go. And I'll tell you something else. All Afghans despise us. You can't change these people no matter how many Americans die for them and you can't trust them either."

Combs shakes his head and turns to Paul, who has been listening to the talk, but has yet to offer his point of view. Combs says, "Larson, you sure don't talk much and now that Ross is in the family, you'll be lucky to get a word in edgewise. What do you think about all of this?"

Paul looks up from his plate to see all of the men awaiting his response. He adjusts his glasses and looks back down. He says, "I don't talk politics. I'm just taking it one day at a time."

Dan defends Paul's brevity by saying, "He's going to be a school teacher. He'll get plenty of chance to talk."

"Hey Paul," Cuz asks, "What subject are you goin to teach?"

Paul looks up again. This time he exhibits more enthusiasm and he says, "Oh, I don't know, history I guess. I've always liked history."

"You're in it," Hambone says, "I remember in school, history class was nothin but studyin one war after another. From ancient times to this one, we had to remember the dates and what they were fightin about. It's like wars are the only things worth rememberin."

Paul focuses in on Hambone and asks, "What did they teach you about this war? What's this war about?"

Hambone seems astonished that Paul would ask a question that has such an obvious answer. He chortles out his response as though it is a universal truth. He says, "The war on terror, of course, so there won't be another 9/11."

Paul sits back in his chair and takes a sip of coffee and says, "Do you really believe that? Well I don't. I think it's all about money. Keeping the war going, keeps the economy afloat. Otherwise, there would be a depression in America and the whole world."

Combs leans back and drops his hands in his lap. He says, "Whoa man, for a guy that doesn't talk politics, you just jumped in with both feet."

Paul stretches his arms apart with his palms up. He says, "Well it's true. Look at the money they're spending. The uniforms, the planes, the bombs, there's no end to it. Somebody is selling all of this stuff to the Army. Keeping us supplied keeps a lot of people working."

Combs finishes off the last of his fruit juice, he crushes the plastic bottle in his hand and tosses it on his tray. He responds to Paul's theory by saying, "I guess I never thought of it like that."

The soldiers are finishing up their breakfast when Jahen, the little twelve year old boy from the valley, comes into the mess tent. He is looking for Dan. "Sergeant Ross, I have something for you," Jahen says, "My brother made this for you. He wants to thank you for helping us get away from danger, yesterday."

Dan accepts the small paper bag from Jahen and asks, "What is it?"

"It is sheer payra. A treat made with pistachio nuts."

"Your brother made this? Is he some kind of a cook or something?"

"He is a very good cook. He wants to go to America some day and open a restaurant."

Combs grabs the bag from Dan and says, "Watch out, Ross. It might be poisoned. Better let me taste it first, just in case." The soldiers all laugh and pass the candy around.

Dan pushes Combs' shoulder and asks, "Hey food tester, where were you on these eggs?" Dan turns to Jahen and says, "This is very good. Tell your brother thank you for me."

"I will tell him. He will be happy that you liked it."

Dan and Paul start back for their quarters. With the constant threat of sniper fire, the soldiers spend most of their down time indoors. They listen to music, read books, write letters or sleep. As they walk across the COP, Ross spots Sergeant Nassir, the ANA squad leader, and two other ANA soldiers walking by the make shift stockade. Dan sees something that really bothers him. The Amir is looking out of the tent and makes eye contact with the ANA soldiers. The ANA soldiers each bow their heads to the Amir. They do it discreetly, but Dan sees it.

"Did you see that?" Dan asks, "Hey Paul, those ANA guys just bowed their heads to the prisoner."

"What are you talking about?" Paul says, "I missed that."

"I mean they bowed down to him like he was the Pope or something. I don't trust those guys, do you?"

"You're paranoid Dan. You need to get some sleep. They probably weren't bowing to him."

Dan stares long and hard at the ANA soldiers and then he looks at the prisoner. Dan notices the Amir is now staring straight at him and it sends a chill down his spine. He speaks to Paul while making eye contact with the Amir, "Oh yes they were. I'm sure of it."

IV

Dan and Paul flop down on their cots to take advantage of the well earned time off. Paul props a pad of paper on his knee and starts writing a letter to his folks. His parents are not the text message type, so he communicates with them the old fashioned way. He can text any news to Katie and he does so regularly. Like Dan, Paul is anxious to get out of the Army and on with his life. Dan lies down and stretches out with his feet extended well off the end of the cot. He dozes off for a while before waking to the thoughts of the confrontation with Captain Craig. He wonders why Craig is so pig headed, but he also knows he needs to be less rebellious. If not, Craig will make Dan's last year more miserable than it already is. Dan drifts into a sound sleep, but is awakened by the booming voice of First Sergeant Hayes, "Ross, the Captain is having another meeting today at seventeen hundred. It's important."

The meeting is in the same place as yesterday's debriefing. Only this time, instead of the smug, satisfied demeanor he displayed at the debriefing, Captain Craig is nervously pacing at the front of the assembly. The men take their seats and Craig begins the meeting by saying, "This is very serious, so I'm going to get right to the point. Battalion has informed me that our intelligence operatives have discovered a Taliban plan to attack this COP. The attack is planned for tomorrow morning. Intel seems to think the Talibs want their Amir back and they are willing to do just about anything to make it happen" There is a lot of moving around in chairs and murmuring among the men in the meeting. Craig continues, "From what they are telling me, this is a concentrated Taliban force of up to two hundred enemy fighters. It constitutes a big percentage of the total number of insurgents in this entire district. If we are successful in inflicting heavy casualties on this attack force, it will decimate the Taliban in this whole sector. We will finally gain the upper hand and have easy going the rest of the way."

Lieutenant Ashby, who is the most senior among the platoon leaders, stands in the front row and asks, "Did Intel have any idea of the enemy strategy for the attack, or is that something we have to guess at?"

The Captain shakes his head and talks while he continues to pace back and forth at the front of the tent. "No need to guess. As you know, Geronimo is pretty much out in the open, except for the foothills. Intel has them coming out of the hills on the main road. Their plan is to overwhelm us with sheer numbers."

Like everyone else in the meeting, Lieutenant Blake has lots of questions. He stands and asks, "Are you talking about a full frontal attack? That would be risky for them."

Craig nods as if to agree, then he offers an explanation for the unlikely scenario. He says, "They are counting on surprising us at daylight with a force twice our size. They think they have all of the aces."

Thinking out loud, Ashby says, "Captain, why don't we transfer the Amir? If he is not here, maybe they won't attack."

Craig shrugs his shoulders and says, "It's too late. Even if we move him now, they may not know it and they would attack anyway. Besides, if they don't attack, we don't get the opportunity to wipe out the Taliban in Zabul Province."

Ever the skeptic, Dan stands and makes his feelings known, "Captain, Sir. This doesn't add up. The Taliban don't mount frontal attacks and seldom are there two hundred insurgents involved in a single attack."

"On the contrary, Intel says the command center we uncovered yesterday is further evidence of a build up. They walk out of the towns to one of those caves. They get outfitted with weapons and ammunition and they are ready to go. It would be easy for them to get two hundred or more men together."

Dan would be better off sitting down and keeping his thoughts to himself, but something inside keeps him from doing that. He asks, "Captain, do you think our intelligence may be off on this?"

The question upsets Craig. He says, "Sergeant Ross. It is not my job to question my superiors. I'm just a simple soldier. When Battalion says jump, I say how high. Now, this is the information they have given me. I will assume it is accurate and plan accordingly. I am not as enamored with the Taliban military tactics as you are."

Dan refuses to back down. He says, "I have no love for them, Sir. But, I respect their ability to mislead, manipulate and make fools of us."

Craig lifts his eyes and speaks to the entire assembly, "Look fellas, this is the golden opportunity we have been waiting for. They are obviously desperate now that we are making progress in destroying their command centers and capturing their leaders. In desperation, they are making a fatal mistake."

Ashby asks, "Captain, how do you plan on defending the COP?"

"We are still working out the details. Get with all of your platoons and make sure they get rested. Have them ready to deploy at zero four hundred. We will reconvene here an hour before that to finalize our plans. If there are no more questions, get some rest. I will see you at three o'clock. That is all."

When Dan returns to his quarters, he is still seething at the exchange he had with Craig. Without looking at Paul, he goes straight to his bunk and falls down on his cot. Six springs pop off of the bed frame and fly into the air. The missing springs cause his mattress to sag almost all the way to the ground. He stares at the ceiling and shakes his head. Paul has been watching his friend storm into the tent. After letting Dan stew in silence for a few more moments, Paul cannot stand it any longer. He says, "Well? Are you going to tell me what happened?"

"Yeah. I'll tell you," Dan says, "Intel gave Craig some nutty story about an attack on this post. Tell the guys to get plenty of rest. We're movin out at four o'clock in the morning."

"Sounds serious. Sure, I'll let them know, but why are you so upset?"

"Because nothing in the report makes any sense. It all sounds fishy to me and Craig seems fine with the whole thing." Dan shakes his head again and says, "You better tell the guys to get everything they need from the armory. After supper, we'll check their gear and make sure they're ready." Paul disappears into the portion of the tent that houses the rest of the squad. Dan lies on his back and thinks. He fears Captain Craig will get them in a real bind someday.

V

After going to supper and inspecting the men's gear, Dan is lying in his bunk, but he is unable to sleep. It is unlikely that anyone on the post is sleeping very well. He checks his watch over and over, but the time moves slowly. His mind drifts to thoughts of home. It's mid afternoon in Quincy, Illinois. His mom is deciding what to cook for supper and his dad is still at work. Even though he is thousands of miles away, Dan can almost smell the aroma of his mom's cooking. He misses seeing his Dad pull up in the driveway with that ear to ear grin. He misses teasing his sister, Katie, about the goofy boys that would come by to see her. His thoughts of home are interrupted by an outburst of laughter on the opposite side of the partition. It is the rest of the squad laughing and cutting up. Dan hops up from his cot and pulls open the partition to find Hambone standing in the middle of the tent in his shorts and t-shirt trying to do some kind of dance. All of the other guys are sitting on the edge of their cots and letting out side splitting howls. Cuz slaps his thigh and yells, "Just give up man. Give up."

Hambone spreads out his arms and says, "No, no, I got this. Hey Cheech, show me one more time. I know I can do it."

Chi Chi stands up, but he is laughing so hard he has trouble straightening up. He says, "Just loosen up man. You're way too stiff. Try it like this." Chi Chi stands in place and lightly bounces on the balls of his feet. He holds one hand close to his abdomen and he holds his other hand out to his side. He swivels his hips and takes one step forward and one step back and switches his hands and his feet, all while making it look effortless. "That's all you got do man, just loosen up."

Hambone immediately tries to follow the instructions, but his feet get tangled and he almost falls. The guys laugh hysterically and start throwing pillows at the frustrated soldier. Dan and Paul are both watching from their end of the tent. Dan walks toward the soldiers and says, "Allright, allright, you guys have to get some sleep. We're getting up early tomorrow, remember."

Little Al says, "Oh Dan, we remember. We're just having a little fun. None of us can sleep anyway. Heck, we rested all day long."

Hambone runs over to get in front of Dan. "Sarge, you saw me dancin. I wasn't that bad was I?"

Dan thinks for a moment and looks at all the guys that are hanging on his next words. He says, "Hambone, let me put this in a way I know you'll understand. You looked like a pig on roller skates." The rest of the guys start rolling on the ground with laughter. Dan turns around to see Paul smiling and chuckling along with everybody else. Dan straightens up and orders, "Come on guys, quiet down. The

Lieutenant will be wondering what we're doing in here, if we don't shut up."

After order is restored Dan and Paul return to their cots. They both lie awake for a long time before falling to sleep. After what seems like only a few seconds to him, Dan's cell phone alarm sounds. It is two thirty, time to get ready.

"Dan, I'll get the squad up and ready," Paul says, "I didn't sleep much, How about you?"

"Not much," Dan says, "We'll get the plans from the Captain. I'll see you at four."

Craig is standing near a large dry erase board in the meeting tent. There are men huddled all around him looking at the board. Craig scans the group to make sure everyone is accounted for before detailing his plan. "We have decided to set up an ambush on the road leading to the COP. Intel has them moving through the hills along the road. We will deploy on both sides of the road at the base of the hills." Craig uses an unlit cigar for a pointer, as the men examine the drawing. He says, "I will be with First and Second Platoons, here, on the right side of the road." He moves the cigar from one side to the other of the scribbled lines that are supposed to be a map. "Third and Fourth Platoons will be along here, on the left."

"Captain, isn't there a chance they may come from these hills?" Lieutenant Ashby asks, as he points to the drawing. "That would put them behind us."

"No Lieutenant, that's not the way Intel has this going down."

"But, if they did, that would create a crossfire with the COP caught in the middle."

45

Craig's shoulders slump and he turns slowly away from the drawing. He says, "Lieutenant Ashby, we will be flanking them, it's not gonna be the other way around. They will be caught in the crossfire, not us. It will be like shooting fish in a barrel." Losing his patience with the frivalous questions, Craig asks the group, "Now, can we move on here?"

Ignoring Craig's plea, Lieutenant Blake says, "It looks to me like the COP is being set up as bait."

"That's exactly what it is," Craig says, "We want everything to look as normal as possible around the post."

Thinking slightly ahead, Blake asks, "Who will guard the post and the prisoner, Captain?"

"That is part of your responsibility, Lieutenant. Leave one squad here along with the Afghan squad and the support personnel."

Blake stares at the drawing and looks at Craig. He says, "Pulling that much of the company out of the post seems a little unorthodox, Sir."

"Well Lieutenant," Craig says, "You always tell me how unorthodox the Taliban is. We'll give them a taste of their own medicine." Craig does not like Blake's body language. He says, "Lieutenant, if you can't figure out how to defend this post with the personnel I have given you, perhaps I should find someone who can."

"That's not necessary, Sir."

As usual, Dan pipes up with a suggestion that is sure to rile Craig, "Captain, Sir, with all due respect, we're 10th Mountain. We don't wait for the enemy to come to us. If Intel says they are coming down that road, they have to be coming from somewhere. Let's go find them."

Craig looks at Lieutenant Blake and says, "Are you going to put a muzzle on that soldier, or do I?"

Blake grabs Dan by an arm and pulls. Dan loses his balance and deflects off some of the other men on his way to the back of the group. When he regains his footing, he looks up to find Sergeant Nassir laughing. The Afghan soldier is amused by Dan's antics. Craig waits for the commotion to subside. He cranes his head and glares at the men in the back. The Captain regains his train of thought and says, "If I may be permitted to continue, the key to this operation is surprise. Do not fire until the enemy is fully exposed. We don't want to scare them off and blow our chance to cripple this insurgency. I will give the order to fire. Do not fire without my permission. Is that clear?"

In unison, the men reply with a hearty, "Yes Sir."

The Captain stuffs the cigar between his teeth and says, "Good luck and goodhunting."As Blake and his platoon sergeants exit the meeting, he turns to Dan and says, "Dan, Iam leaving your squad here to cover the COP. You're my most experienced man."

"Yes sir Lieutenant. But, will you take those Afghans with you. I don't trust them." Blake looks at the ground and paws at the sand with his boots, "I'd like to Dan, but Craig says they stay here. You are two men short and that's twelve guys you can reallyuse. Put two of them on the stockade." Dan removes his helmet and runs his fingers through his hair. He lets out a big sigh and says, "Will do."

When Dan gets back to the tent, Paul has the squad outside and ready to go. Dan takes a minute to explain First Squad's role in Craig's scheme. A few minutes later, the Company moves out of Geronimo on foot, leaving First Squad and the Afghan soldiers behind. Bravo Company takes only enough trucks for the heavy equipment. Dan watches as they split up about 1500 yards out. Half of them go to the hills on the left and half go to the hills on the right. First Squad and the Afghans meet in front of the stockade. Dan figures the most fortified section of the unfinished post is the front wall. Without much faith in the competence of the Afghan soldiers, Dan figures it would be best to position them on the fortified front wall, leaving First Squad to defend the open wire sections of the perimeter. He says, "Sergeant Nassir, put two of your men here at the stockade tent. Put one in the guard tower and the remainder along the front wall."

Before Dan can finish handing out assignments, Nassir interrupts, "I am sorry Sergeant Ross. The stockade and tower are fine, but my men would rather guard the unfinished section at the rear of the post."

Dan is annoyed by the Afghan's request. He rolls his eyes and exhales before asking, "And uh, just why is that, Sergeant?"

"My men are very young. They have not been in battle. They will be more comfortable in reserve."

Dan is in no mood to argue. He just wants to get everybody ready to defend the COP as quickly as possible, so he decides to give in. Dan gets right in Nassir's face and glares into his eyes. After a sufficient amount of time to convey his displeasure, "Allright, but keep your people the hell out of our way. We don't want to have to work around em."

Nassir cracks a wry grin and says, "Thank you, we will be ready."

Paul can sense that Dan is put out with Nassir. He decides to get this thing back on track, "We'll take the front wall. Hambone and Cuz to the right of the gate, Chi Chi and I will be over there, on the left."

"Sounds good, Paul. Z, Al and I will cover the exposed wire on the north end. We can see quite a bit from there."

Hambone picks up his rifle that had been leaning against a post. He reaches both of his arms above his head to stretch and says, "This reminds me of those early mornins back home when we would take our pigs to the auction. We'd get up way before dawn and babysit them pigs all day long, 'till the last one sold. Those were some long days."

Cuz checks all of his pockets to make sure he knows where he has stored everything. He says, "Seems like all the days are long at Geronimo. Why should today be any different?"

It is time for the men to take their positions, Dan says, "Allright guys, let's spread out and get ready." As the men disperse, Dan takes Little Al to the side and talks a little more quietly, "Al, can I talk to you for a minute?"

Little Al is unsure why Dan is being so discreet, He says, "Sure Sergeant, what is it?"

"I want you to keep an eye on those ANA boys. Whatever happens, don't let them out of your sight. If they start running off or something, let me know. Don't worry about the road, we got that covered. Just watch those guys real close."

"No problem, Sergeant."

Nassir checks the positioning of his men at the rear of the post. He carefully places each man and gives them final instructions. He joins two other Afghan soldiers near the stockade.

The sun rises over the foothills. It looks like a giant basketball sitting on the horizon. The road leading into the COP is now illuminated and Bravo Company is pretty well concealed over a mile outside of the post. They are so well hidden that Dan cannot see a trace of them from his vantage point on the north end of the post. There is some chatter on the radio, but it is just the men checking off on their repositioning. To the surprise of everyone, Jahen, the little interpreter, emerges from a supply tent. He had fallen asleep in the tent and spent the night at the COP.

Little Al points to Jahen and yells, "Hey Sarge, look who's here."

Dan rolls his eyes and mumbles under his breath, "Oh great, now I've seen everything." He waves his arm and yells, "Jahen, get over here."

Dan leads the young boy over to the front gate. Paul wonders what Dan will do about the boy, so he gets down from the wall and joins Dan, Z and Jahen near the gate. Dan says, "Paul, open the gate. We have to send Jahen on a very important mission." Paul and Z open the gate. Dan kneels down to get to eye level with Jahen. "I want you to take a message to Lieutenant Blake. You know him, don't you?"

Jahen says, "Yes Sergeant Ross, I know him."

Dan points out to the hills on the left side of the road. "He is over there, about a mile out. Just walk over to the base of the hills and go out until you find the Lieutenant, got it?"

"Yes, I understand it, but what is the message?

Dan does not have a good answer, so he stammers out something to get the boy moving, "Oh, uhhh, tell him uhhh, just tell him we're ready. Now get going."

Jahen takes off running toward Fourth Platoon's position. Paul and Z close the gate behind him. Paul looks at Dan and nods with approval. He says, "That was a real important message. I think you just wanted to get him out of here."

Dan watches Jahen run away, "There's no reason for a twelve year old kid to get caught up in this. Hey Z, get on that radio and let Blake know Jahen is heading his way."

The soldiers on the wall are perched on a catwalk that allows them to stay low and see outside the wire by peeking over the multi stacked hescos. If they stand up they are taller than the wall and can be seen from outside the post. An annoyed Cuz stands straight up from his crouched position and throws his hands in the air, "Caught up in what? We've been starin at that there road for two hours. I don't think they're comin."

Dan can tell the men are getting fidgety, "If anybody wants to get up and stretch their legs, it's OK with me. It's OK to smoke, if you want. Just take about 10 minutes and relax." Dan walks over to the stockade to speak with Nassir. It is hard for him to cooperate with the ANA. He gets uneasy just being near them, but he is curious as to how they are doing. He says, "Hey Sergeant, welcome to the American Army. It's hurry up and wait, but mostly it's just wait. You're guys can get up and move around, if they want to. Maybe get a little circulation going."

Nassir responds with no emotion in his voice. He says, "You must not be concerned with my men. They will be ready." Dan is surprised by the terse words from the Afghan soldier. After all, Dan was just trying to be civil, but everything about those people gives him the creeps.

VI

The men walk around to get their blood pumping. The guys stationed on the wall back down the ladder from the catwalk to the ground. Paul looks at Dan and says, "That was a nice thing you did for Jahen. You know, underneath that gruff exterior, you really are a softie. You're going to make a terrific uncle."

Dan tilts his head and says, "Uncle? What are you talking about? Is there something you haven't told me?"

"Katie told me on the phone last night. You were so busy I didn't get a chance to tell you. She's pregnant. She's already 3 months along."

Dan is ecstatic at the news. He slaps Paul on the back and says, "What? That's great. Congratulations. Wow, you and Katie, parents? Hey wait, I'm too young to be anybody's uncle. Aren't they always the old guys?"

Paul smiles and says, "They come in all ages."

"That's the best news I've had in a long time. Katie will be terrific mom and you're gonna make a great dad. A school teacher and a dad,

I'm happy for you. It looks like you and Katie have your future all mapped out. Hey, maybe we can talk Craig out of some of his cigars to celebrate."

Paul laughs and shakes his head. He says, "I think the tradition is to wait until the baby is actually born, before handing out cigars."

The men assigned to the wall climb the ladders to get back to their positions. Dan and Z return to the north end of the post. Another hour goes by and the men start getting restless, again. They start moving around and stretching for a second time, when the radio on Z's pack comes to life. "Sergeant Ross, come in Ross. This is Blake. Do you copy?"

Without waiting for the order, Z passes the handset to Dan, who answers, "Yes sir, we copy, go for Ross."

"There is a single vehicle heading you're your way. Can you make it out?"

Dan takes a look from the exposed wire on the north end of the COP, but he cannot see around the hescos to get a good view of the road. Dan and Z run over to the front wall, Dan looks up at the catwalk and hollers, "Paul, get some field glasses on the road. Tell me if you see anything."

Paul unhooks the binoculars from his belt and he shakes the dust from the lenses. He holds them up to his eyes, "Yeah Dan, I see it. It's one of those old Toyota trucks. I can see a driver, but nobody else. That thing has to be a mile out. It's right in front of Captain Craig and the rest of the Company."

Dan holds the handset to his mouth and says, "Lieutenant Blake, this is Ross, affirmative on that truck. It's about 2000 yards out. What do want us to do? "

The radio crackles, again, "This is Captain Craig. Do not fire on that truck. There will be more. Repeat. Do not fire. We need to wait on the full force to arrive. I don't want anybody getting jumpy. Wait for my order, over."

It is one of those old beat up trucks that are very popular among insurgents. There are thousands of them just like it in Afghanistan. The truck is moving eerily slow, but it keeps coming down the road, right toward the COP. Dan moves over, closer the gate. He turns back to Paul and hollers, "Hey Paul, Craig says not to fire on the truck. He is waiting for a large force to show up."

Paul is surprised by the instructions. He hands the glasses to Chi Chi. He looks down at Dan and says, "Large force? These guys don't come out in large forces. That truck looks mighty suspicious."

Dan and Z open the gate enough to get a look at the vehicle in question. They are just inside the gate and the rest of the guys are on the catwalk with their eyes fixated on the truck. Without taking his eyes off of the truck and speaking to no one in particular, Z blurts out, "Wonder why he's going so slow? Those guys usually drive like maniacs."

Cuz is on the catwalk on the opposite side of the gate from Paul. He heard Z's question and it makes him chuckle. Cuz says, "That's because they are maniacs, but that's probably as fast as that old thing will go."

As the truck draws nearer to the post, Dan is growing more and more uncomfortable. He rubs his hand over the back of his neck and takes a brief moment to analyze the situation. He turns around to look for Nassir and the ANA detachment. He observes that all of the Afghan soldiers are still in place along the wire at the rear of the COP. He scans over to the stockade and makes eye contact with Nassir, who happens to be staring right at Dan. After a few more seconds of thought, Dan says, "I don't like it, not one bit. Give me that radio, Z." Pfc. Bailey hands him the radio. "Captain Craig. This is Ross, do you copy?" Dan presses the handset against his cheek and waits for the Captain to acknowledge.

Soon, Craig can be heard above the static that accompanies his reply. "This is Craig, I read you. Go ahead."

Dan cannot hold it any longer. He has to try to force Craig's hand. "Captain, that truck's getting too close. We need to stop him at 500 yards out."

The noticeably perturbed commanding officer answers in a slow southern drawl, "Negative Ross. Do not fire until I give the order. Do you read me?"

A hyper Dan says, "Affirmative. We copy, but this is not standard procedure. Any other time, we'd have blown that piece of crap off the road by now."

In an anxious and quick paced retort, Craig says, "Sergeant Ross, follow my orders. That's a farmer in that truck. Are we clear?" Cuz yells down from his perch on the wall, "Sergeant Ross, we got to stop that guy. Farmers don't drive those trucks. This guy is crazy. He's way too close."

Dan has to do something, so he pushes Z in the back and says, "Everybody, move away from the gate. Move down the wall. Make it quick and get ready to shoot if we need to."

The soldiers on the catwalks shuffle down the wall away from the gate, but they keep their rifles trained on the truck. Little Al stops watching the ANA and he runs up to the wall to see what all of the commotion is about. The truck is now only 100 yards from the gate. Instantly, the truck speeds up and dashes for the COP at full speed. Dan's suspicions prove to be right. Paul yells to Dan that truck is speeding toward them. Dan hollers at the top of his lungs, "Open up. Stop that truck."

The men of First Squad begin shooting at the truck. Even though the driver is hit, the truck's momentum propels it into the front gate. Upon contact, the truck explodes, sending a huge ball of fire rolling through the post. At the same time, Nassir and the ANA soldiers, who have moved up from the rear, begin firing at the American soldiers, hitting them in their backs. Most of First Squad is immediately cut down before they know what is happening. Nassir lets the prisoner out of the stockade. The two of them hurry to the rear of the post. Dan and his wounded men turn to return fire. A knifing pain shoots up Dan's leg. He looks down to see blood spurting from his left calf. With each beat of his heart, more blood squirts out. He rips his belt off and ties it off below his knee. Dan yells, "I'm hit."

Dan can hear Hambone's shrieking voice. The young farmer hollers, "Me too. It's them ANA."

Dan looks to his left and sees multiple bullets ripping through Hambone's blood soaked uniform. Dan wants to reach out to the

57

young man, but he has to keep shooting at the turncoats that have ambushed his squad. Paul directs his fire toward the guard tower, hoping to relieve the deadly torrent of bullets raining down from above. The traitor occupying the tower is riddled with bullets, he falls to the debris covered ground and lands in a mangled heap. In spite of their efforts, First Squad is overwhelmed by the surprise enemy outburst. Each of the American soldiers keeps shooting until they are too severely wounded to continue. Out of the corner of his eye, Dan can see Chi Chi and Cuz lying face down with blood oozing from their bodies. At the rear of the post, another Toyota truck appears with two Taliban fighters in the cab. They quickly exit the vehicle and set off an explosion that blows open a breach in the wire. Nassir and the Amir run through the breach and jump in the truck with the other men. The truck speeds off into the hills.

Dan and Paul are pinned against the front wall, desperately firing at the remaining Afghans. Spent shell casings ejecting from their rifles fill the air around the two friends, along with sweat and blood flying from their faces. Even though they are wounded and facing an insurmountable enemy barrage, they replace empty magazines with cool proficiency in order to continue their desperate resistance. Dan feels an intense pain in the small of his back. He flinches and falls to his knees, but he keeps shooting. A spray of bullets slash open Paul's abdomen, he falls into the sand with blood streaming from his mouth.

Still wearing their aprons, some cooks emerge from the mess tent firing rifles. They proceed to blast the remaining traitors from the opposite direction. Without taking his eyes off of his targets, Dan implores his friend to keep up the fight. "Just hold on Paul. Blake will be here." The exchange of rifle fire, from the time the truck exploded until the guns fall silent, lasts less than three minutes. "Paul, Paul, can you talk, Paul?" There is no response. Dan repeatedly yells to his friend, "I can't move Paul, I can't move my legs." Paul can't move either, nor can he speak. Dan surveys the gory scene that features both American and Afghan bodies strewn all over the post.

The smoke from the explosion blocks out the morning sun and there is trash swirling in the wind. He sees Blake leading some men through what was once the front gate, but he can no longer hear and his vision is blurry. Dan cannot even hear his own voice as he calls out for Paul, over and over, until everything goes to black.

Dust and debris fill the air around Blake and his platoon as they file into the COP. In full crisis management mode, Blake orders some men to secure the post and he allocates others to check for wounded soldiers. Combs brings two of the civilian cooks over to Blake. Their excitement borders on shock, as they rant about the incident with wild inflections in their voices and their arms flailing in all directions. Amid the turmoil, Blake deciphers their report and surmises that it was a coordinated attack carried out by the ANA in conjunction with the Taliban. The truck bomber was an elaborate diversion and it worked. Captain Craig has finally entered the post and the crowd abandons Blake and rushes to surround Craig.

Blake is momentarily alone with his thoughts. He sees charred pieces of the gate blackened by the fiery explosion. There are entire sides blown off of the converted shipping containers and papers flapping in the breeze. Everything is covered in dust and ash. There is one soldier digging through the rubble and lamenting out loud that everyone is dead. One of the squad sergeants approaches Blake with a report that the prisoner is unaccounted for and that there appears to be a hole blown in the wire on the west end of the post. The enraged Blake launches into a tirade, "What about my men? Have we accounted for them? Dammit Sergeant, I want a head count on First Squad and I want it now. The Taliban can wait. Now get moving." Even as he rips into the sergeant, Blake notices a wounded American moving among the rubble. Leaping over smoldering debris, Blake shouts for medics as he runs toward the GI. Oblivious to all other activity, his focus is solely on the wounded man. He continues to yell for medics after he reaches the man. It is Z struggling to get someone's attention. Blake squats down beside Z and cradles the young man's head in his arms. Blake wants to turn away when he makes the grisly discovery that one of Z's legs is hanging by a thread. Three medics converge on Z and they slip the wounded man out of Blake's arms. Two of the medics work furiously on Z, while another radios for medevac.

Only ten yards from where Blake is standing, another soldier is combing through the trash near the hescos that make up the front wall. He rises up and shouts, "Hey, over here. It's Sergeant Ross. I think he's still breathing."

Just a hint that Dan may be alive crates a rush of adrenaline pulsing through Blake's veins. He orders the medic on the radio to tell Battalion that we need medevac for at least two men, maybe more. Blake hurries over to find Dan's fatigues are soaked with blood from the waist down. Even Dan's dusty boots are lined with the trails of blood running off of his legs. Blake is horrified by the sight of his friend clinging to life. He prays the choppers get there in time.

After being carried to a medevac helicopter, the personnel aboard the aircraft work feverishly on Dan and Z. Before taking off, the medical staff makes some progress on Dan. A medic yells over the noise of the engines and rotors, "Sergeant Ross, Sergeant Ross, can you hear me?"

Dan realizes that he is on a medevac helicopter. There are I V bags attached to his arms and he is surrounded by medics. He opens his eyes and tries to raise his head, but he cannot move. He says, "Yeah, I hear you." He tries again to move, but he cannot.

"Hold on there, Sergeant. Just lie still." The medic says, "It's all over. We are taking you to the hospital."

"What about my men? Where are my men?" The medics ignore the question, but then Dan hears a familiar voice. It is Blake moving into Dan's view.

"Can you see me allright, Dan?" Blake asks, as he steps over by the bed. "It's nice to see your eyes open. I knew you were too stubborn to stay unconscious much longer."

Dan continues his struggle to sit up, but he has no luck. He says, "John, what the hell happened?"

Blake was expecting that question. He shrugs and says, "Green on blue. Nassir and his men turned on you."

Dan swallows hard and says, "What about the squad?"

"Z made it, he's the only one that did."

In a weak voice, Dan asks, "What about Paul? Where's Paul?"

Blake shakes his head and says, "I'm sorry, Dan."

Dan closes his eyes and grimaces, "It's all my fault. I knew Nassir was no good. Do you know Paul just found out that he is going to be a father? Yeah, my sister's pregnant."

"No, I didn't know that. Look Dan, don't blame yourself. They had it planned. You guys killed most of them."

"What about Nassir and that prisoner, the Amir? Did we get them?"

Blake looks through the helicopter door and stares at the hills. He says, "They got away."

VII

A heavy dose of morphine is making Dan drowsy, but he really does not feel much pain. He continues to come and go, in and out of consciousness on the flight to the hospital. Upon arrival at Bagram Air Force Base, Dan is rushed over to the hospital and immediately taken into the operating room. After hours of surgery and recovery, Dan awakens in the recovery ward. To him, everything is a blur and all movement is in slow motion. He cannot feel anything. It is as though he is suspended in air rather than lying on a bed. As the cobwebs begin to shake loose inside his head, the whole scene feels surreal. Dan lies quiet and still while he struggles to get his bearings. It takes a few minutes, but he determines that he is in a large room containing a dozen or more beds. There are machines with blinking lights that are emitting rhythmic beeping sounds. Nurses and others dressed in hospital blue scrubs are busily administering to a handful of wounded men occupying some of the beds. Nobody appears to be paying any attention to Dan. He feels like he is on the outside looking in. It is like a dream in which each character is doing their own thing with no regard for Dan. When he first attempts to speak, he is unable to muster any power in his voice. Eventually, the words do come out. He says, "Where am I?" Following up his first question with another, he asks, "A hospital?"

A nurse turns from another bed and says, "That's right soldier." She picks up a chart at the foot of his bed and makes some notations. She says, "You've been asleep for quite a while."

"What happened?"

From the foot of the bed, she says, "The doctors worked on you for three hours."

"Surgery? It's over? I didn't feel a thing."

"It's over. You'll be feeling it soon enough." The nurse adjusts the I V bottle hanging near the bed, she asks, "How do you feel? Can you feel any pain?"

"No. no pain." Dan stretches his arms and fidgets in the bed. He is unable to move his legs to roll over, but he thinks he is too weak for that anyway. He says, "I feel good. I haven't slept this well since I joined the Army. What time is it, anyway?"

The nurse glances at a clock on the wall. She says, "It's 6:30 am., Now try to be still, you had a lot of lead in you."

"How much?"

She steps over to the side of the bed and lays her hand on Dan's forearm, "You were wounded in three places, both of your legs and your lower back. It's the back wound that is really tender. That's why it's so important to lie still."

"How long have I been here?"

"You went into surgery yesterday afternoon, around 2pm, I believe. The surgery lasted three hours and you have been in this recovery ward since then."

"The last thing I remember was being on the helicopter, but I don't remember the flight."

"That's good. Those chopper rides are pretty bumpy."

"What happens next?"

"You need to lie still and continue resting." The nurse says, "The doctors will be around to answer your questions. There is pain medicine in this I V. If you feel too much pain push this button and it will release more medicine. If you need anything at all, let me or one of the other nurses know. Remember, lie still and you'll get better."

Dan thinks out loud, "Pain? I don't feel anything, right now." For the moment, he cannot feel physical pain, but his mind is in overdrive. He is trying to figure out what exactly happened. He thinks to himself, "Lieutenant Blake said something about "green on blue". That means Nassir and the rest of those Afghans turned their guns on us, he reasons. How can that happen? It's bad enough trying to figure out which of the Afghan civilians are on our side, now we find out their army is infiltrated with Taliban, too. This whole deal is all screwed up."

The nurse who had been attending Dan steps out of the recovery ward. The images of Paul and the others in the squad are clear in Dan's mind. He closes his eyes and can see Paul's face. It is the face of an excited father to be and subsequently, the face of a lifeless soldier lying in the gritty sand at the COP. He thinks about Hambone, Cuz and the others. The voice in his head says, "You let them all down. They're all

65

dead and you're still alive, it doesn't seem right. You're no better than those guys, in fact those guys were all better than you. They were trying to make a good life for themselves. They enjoyed their jobs and were happy to help the Afghan people. Sergeant Combs was right about you, you're a taker that only joined the Army to get money for college. You don't have anything in common with those hardscrabble farmers nor do you care what happens to them. At least you didn't have any feelings for them, but you do now".

Hate begins to simmer within his soul. In his mind, he can see Nassir's lying face. He is ashamed that he let Nassir sucker him into letting the Afghan soldiers deploy behind First Squad. He remembers seeing those ANA bowing to the prisoner, that Amir or whatever he is. Another thing clear in Dan's mind is the cleric's face sporting that smug demeanor and that devilish smirk. Although Dan cannot move, the rage within forces him to scream loud enough to be heard outside of the ward. A nurse rushes in to see about him.

The concerned nurse asks, "Sergeant Ross? Are you allright?" She begins to go through the same progression of checking the monitors and the I V bag. Once she is satisfied that Dan is ok, she takes a deep breath and lets out a sigh of relief. She says, "You gave me a little scare there."

Dan is sorry that he frightened the nurse, but he is also feeling sorry for himself. He tells the nurse, "I'm lying here unable to move. My whole squad is wiped out and you want to know if I'm allright. Hell no. I'm not allright."

The nurse is a sensitive woman that has only been in Afghanistan for two days. She is getting her first taste of patients fresh off of the battlefield and she has her hands full with Dan. She lays her hands on his chest and tries to calm him down, "Please Sergeant, please settle down. You've been through a lot, but you have to lie still and let the wounds heal. It's all over now. There is nothing left to do."

Dan can sense the stress in her voice. He attempts to apologize, but his mind will not let him rest. He says, "I'm sorry. I just can't help it. I keep thinking about what happened. It's my fault, it has to be my fault. Everybody's dead. Why am I alive?"

The nurse prepares a sedative injection, she says, "It's not your fault, Sergeant. You didn't start this crazy war. You just got mixed up in it like all of the rest of us." She swabs a spot on the underside of his forearm with alcohol and inserts the needle.

Dan is so preoccupied with his thoughts that he does not even feel the injection. As the nurse inspects the syringe to ensure the drugs fully deplete into his veins, Dan asks, "What's that for?"

The nurse withdraws the needle and she places a patch of gauze over the mark on Dan's arm. She replies, "It's something to help you rest and be still."

"It'll have to be awfully strong. I'm wound up pretty good."

She slides on hand under Dan's head and lifts, then she uses her other hand to fluff up Dan's pillow. She lays his head back down and reassures him, "It's strong enough. Now, lie still as much as possible."

Dan tries to make eye contact without moving his head, "When do I get to see the doctor?"

The nurse drops the used supplies onto a rolling cart and she pushes it toward the door. Before exiting the ward, she turns and says, "He'll be around, soon. Please call me if you need anything."

The nurse leaves the ward, but Dan cannot stop rehashing the attack. Whether his eyes are closed or open, he sees bullets tearing open his friends' flesh and blood spurting into the air around them. He hears their voices as clearly as if they were in the same room. In moments, the drugs take over and Dan falls asleep. The drugs are powerful and he is able to sleep without the interruptions of flashbacks. The next sounds he hears are those of nurses attending another soldier in the ward a few feet away from him. He is unable to see the patient, only the medical staff scurrying around, efficiently going about their business. Still another nurse comes over to Dan and begins adjusting I V's and updating charts. The nurse looks down and says, "I see you're awake. How are you feeling?"

"Useless," Dan says, "When can I get up and walk?" The nurse ignores the question, so Dan changes the subject. He nods his head toward the new patient and asks, "What happened to him?"

She looks over at the commotion surrounding the next bed and she frowns. Dan can tell from her expression that she is troubled by the endless procession of boys that are shuffled through this hospital. While staring at the new patient's face, she says, "He just got out of surgery. He lost a leg, but he's lucky, the doctors saved the other one."

With shortsightedness that is, no doubt, a symptom of Dan's own frustration, he questions her consolatory attitude, "Do you call that lucky? Lucky to have only one leg left? That's not my idea of luck." The nurse has learned to ignore such remarks. She hears plenty of ramblings in her line of work and she knows it's better not to engage the patient. Any reponse will get Dan even more excited.

"I'll tell the doctor you're awake," she says, "He would like to see you."

"Thanks, I'd like to see him too. I need to find out when I'm getting outta here. What time is it anyway?"

The nurse knows Dan is not getting out of hospitals any time soon, but she keeps that information to herself and she glances over at the clock on the wall. She says, "It's 5:15."

Dan is amazed, he says, "Wow, I slept almost half a day."

"You slept almost a whole day," she says, "It's 5:15... am."

Dan's mouth opens wide and he does some calculating in his head. "That means I've been here for two nights. It's been two days since the attack."

The nurse finishes her poking and prodding and eventually leaves the ward. Dan watches the activity around the new patient and he begins to think about home. He wonders if his mom has heard the news. He hopes she hasn't, she'd be worried sick. He thinks about Katie. Surely, she knows by now, it's been almost 48 hours. He needs to call home. The door flies open and a doctor walks over to Dan. As he picks up a chart and begins to read, he says, "You slept a long time. That's good. Those are some nasty wounds and you lost a lot of blood. The rest is good for you."

Dan stirs around in his bed and tries to straighten up, "Did you do the surgery on me?"

"I was on the team," the doctor says, "There were two doctors. I'm Colonel Cochrane. We removed bullets from both of your legs. We changed the dressings last night. You shouldn't have any complications from those wounds because the bullets missed the bones."

Dan is relieved at the news, but he has some questions for the doctor, "Why can't I move my legs? I'm trying, but nothing moves."

The Doctor hangs the chart at the foot of the bed and steps to the head of the bed. He looks Dan in the eyes and says, "Sergeant, you still have one bullet lodged in your lower back. It's pressing against your spinal cord and the pressure is causing paralysis from your waist down."

"Paralysis? Does that mean I'm paralyzed? Is that why I can't move my legs?"

"That's right, Sergeant. You are paralyzed, but it may not be long term. We're flying you back to the States for more surgery. They have better equipment and the doctors are more experienced with this sort of procedure. It's a risky surgery and an inexperienced doctor could do more damage than the bullet. They will remove the bullet and that should relieve the pressure on your spinal cord. Consequently, the paralysis may lessen."

In the back of his mind, Dan had a suspicion that something was wrong, over and above the bullet holes he sustained. He does not even take time to let the gravity of the situation sink in, before his mind races forward. He is eager to get this medical setback behind him. He asks, "When do I leave?"

Dr. Cochrane examines the read outs on the monitors providing constant updates on Dan's condition. He turns back to Dan and says, "Now that you are stabilized and out of danger, we will probably send you out tomorrow."

"Good, I have to get back on my feet as soon as possible. Sir, is there a telephone I can use? I need to call my folks."

"Of course, the nurse will bring one in, right away."

Finally, Dan is getting concerned about the paralysis. He looks away from the doctor and says, "You should have let me die. I'm probably not gonna be much good to anyone, now. But thanks for what you did."

"You 10th Mountain guys are pretty tough. I'm sure you'll do a lot before you're through. Besides it's my privilege to help out."

"Have you seen others from 10th Mountain?"

Dr. Cochrane nods his head and says, "Too many. There's another one here now. A Pfc. Bailey, he'll be going out with you tomorrow."

The doctor leaves and soon afterward, a nurse enters with a cell phone. "Would you like me to dial it for you, Sergeant?"

Dan tries to straighten up, "I think I can dial, if you help me sit up."

Between the medication and the paralysis, Dan is fairly pain free, but he is unable to move very well. With a little help, he finally gets situated and dials the phone. Dan's parents are both in their late fifties. They had their two children later in life than most people. His mom's name is Mary Margaret, but she has always gone by Peggy. His dad, Jerry, is a hard working, hot tempered man of Irish descent. Jerry grew up on a farm and he met Peggy when he left the farm and rented a room from her parents. An anxious voice comes on the line, "Hello," Peggy says.

Dan hears his mom's voice. He never thought it could sound so good. He says, "Mom, it's me, Dan" A lump in his throat makes it hard to speak and his eyes well up with tears.

This is the call Peggy has been praying for and Dan can picture his mom's face complete with tears rolling down her cheeks. Her voice is clear, so clear Dan can tell she is struggling to speak above her sobbing, "Oh Danny, are you OK?" Peggy asks, "Where are you?"

"I'm in the hospital and Paul's dead."

"I know," Peggy says, "Katie called this morning. I'm so sorry. How bad are you hurt?"

Not wanting to alarm his mom any more than necessary, he says, "It's not too bad. I'll be allright. You don't have to worry, because these guys know what they're doing. They get lots of practice. Guess what? They're flying me back to the States tomorrow."

"What about your wounds, Dan? We've been lighting candles and praying all day. Your Dad stayed home from work. He's been calling Fort Polk trying to find out something. He finally got a hold of someone who said you were in surgery, but that was yesterday."

"I've been sleeping more than anything and they're keeping me on morphine, so I don't feel much pain. They're going to do more surgery when they get me back to the States."

Dan can hear his mom gasp, she cries, "Why? What's the matter?"

"Mom, I can't move my legs, right now. I'm paralyzed. The doctor said he had to leave a bullet in my back because it is too close to my spine. But keep prayin, because they say when they get the bullet out, I should be fine."

"Oh Danny, I'm so glad your alive. That's all that matters. God will help you heal. Where are they taking you?"

"I'll let you know as soon as I find out. I wanted to call so you and Dad can stop worrying."

"Oh, thank you, God. I'm so glad you called. Your dad has been walking the floor all day. Can you talk to him?"

"Sure, put Dad on." As Dan waits for Jerry to get on the phone, the anticipation of hearing his dad's voice makes that lump even larger in his throat.

Jerry's unmistakable raspy voice comes on the line, "Dan, your mom's burnin so many candles, I have the fire department on stand by."

Struggling to get the words out, Dan says, "Hey Dad, it looks like I'm coming home a little sooner than expected."

"You're coming home, that's the main thing."

"I guess I'll be in the hospital a while."

"They can't keep you down for long, Danny. I can't wait to see you. When you get better, we'll go fishing, just like we used to."

Dan wants to get the circumstances of the attack off of his chest. He says, "Dad, we didn't have a chance. Those Afghan soldiers turned on us, they shot us in the back. I let Paul down, Dad, he was counting on me. They were all counting on me."

"We're so sorry about Paul, but don't blame yourself. I'm sure you did the best you could."

"Dad, I have to call Katie. But I don't know what to say to her."

Even though Jerry is seven thousand miles away, he can tell Dan is on edge. He tries to comfort his son, "We're driving down to Fort

73

Polk tomorrow. Katie needs some help getting through this. She's worried about you too, ya know. Hang in there. We'll all get through this together."

VIII

Dan spends the next 24 hours in the recovery ward. The constant coming and going of medical staff has little effect on him. They are continually giving him shots and changing his bandages. Normally, it would keep one from resting, but in Dan's case, he is not resting anyway. His unsettled mind keeps him wired. He cannot stop reliving the attack on the COP. The voice in his head asks the questions, "Why didn't Captain Craig stop that truck? Even if there were more Taliban out there, you don't allow a vehicle to drive right up to the gate. We could round up the Hajis after stopping the truck. Oh, what are you thinking? There were no Talibs out there, except for Nassir and his ANA traitors. Our intelligence was wrong again. Don't they ever suspect the ANA could be infiltrated? They don't, but you should have. You let your men down and there is no way to make up for it." There are more questions than answers and the unknown is tormenting the restless soldier.

The next morning, Dan is loaded onto a plane that is rigged up like a flying ambulance. It has many of the same machines as the recovery ward, with the same blinking lights and beeping sounds. The workers are wearing the same blue scrubs and they are diligently preparing the patients for the flight. One of the patients making the trip is Pfc. Bailey. Dan blames himself for what happened to Z and all of the others. His body language portrays his guilt and that is without even being able to move. Unable to look Z in the eye, Dan looks away and says, "Hey Z, how are you?

Z is happy to see Dan. He flashes a broad smile and speaks with muted enthusiasm, "Hey Sergeant, am I glad to see you, I didn't know if you were going to make it."

Likewise, Dan manages an uneasy smile, "I made it. I guess, we're the only ones that did."

"Yeah, that's right. Those were some good guys. I'm really gonna miss them."

Dan can only see Z from the shoulders up to his head. There are blankets woven around Z's torso and lower body. It's hard to tell, but it looks like the blankets are thicker around Z's legs. Dan is afraid of the answer, but he has to ask, "Are your legs still there under all those blankets?"

The smile disappears from Z's face and he says, "Yeah, they're still there. I got hit in both of my legs. They tell me my left shin bone is shattered. I guess, once I recover, I'll be able to walk ok, but I'm out of the Army for good."

Dan is saddened that Z is wounded, but relieved the wounds are not worse. "That's too bad. You were planning on a career, weren't you?"

"Yeah, I guess I'll have to make different plans, but we're lucky. I'm still in shock about the others. It's like a bad dream that won't go away."

"It really is. I've been having those nightmares, too. What about your folks? Have you talked to them yet?"

"I called home yesterday. My mom cried. She's happy I'm through with the Army. How 'bout you?"

Dan looks straight up at the ceiling of the aircraft, "I talked to my mom and dad, but I haven't gotten up the nerve to talk to my sister, you know, Paul's wife."

"Don't worry, Sarge, your sister's not going to blame you for what happened to Paul. She knows it not your fault. She'll be glad you're still alive. You're the best sergeant in the whole battalion, hands down. That's why they had to shoot us in the back, they knew they couldn't face up to you."

Dan appreciates the nice words, but they do not make him feel less guilty. He blames himself for not suspecting Nassir could be capable of such an attack. He is heavily sedated and he sleeps most of the time on the trip back to the States, which is exactly what the doctors want. That bullet is dangerously close to doing a lot more damage. The sooner they get the bullet out, the better chances are for a full recovery. The plane is scheduled to make a brief stop in Germany and then it is on to San Antonio, Texas. He faces more surgery at Brooke Army Hospital. Upon arrival in San Antonio, Dan is taken straight into the operating room. According to the doctors, the surgery goes well. After three full days of recovery, Dan is still unable to move his legs. He is frustrated that he needs help to do practically everything.

It is midmorning on the third day of his stay in San Antonio when a nurse with a big smile on her face comes bouncing through the door of his room. She says, "Sergeant Ross we have to get you into a wheelchair. You have visitors."

Dan perks up and asks, "Visitors? Is it my folks?"

The nurse rolls a wheelchair up to the bedside, "It sure is, now let's get you out of that bed." Dan can pry his upper body up with his arms, but the nurse has to grab his legs and swing them off of the bed. She gets underneath Dan's arm with her shoulder. That provides the leverage to lift Dan out of bed. Next, she spins him around and gently sets him down into the wheelchair. She pushes Dan to an outside visiting area. There are neatly manicured beds of flowers soaking up the bright sunshine. Although it is only the first week of May, the temperature is already over 90 degrees in San Antonio. Still, there is a constant breeze that makes it quite comfortable on the terrace. Peggy, Jerry and Katie, his whole family, are there to see him.

"Oh Danny," Peggy says, as she bends down to hug her son. "You look so good to me. Thank God you're safe."

Jerry watches as big tears stream down Peggy's cheeks He reaches out one of his large hands and squeezes Dan on the shoulder and says, "I can't imagine what you've been through, Dan, but I'm sure it's been a rough deal."

Katie bends down and hugs Dan in his wheelchair. She cries as they embrace, but she is too overcome with emotion to speak.

Finally, Dan breaks the silence, "I'm sorry about Paul. I wish it were me that died instead of him."

Katie is not going to tolerate such an impractical desire, "Don't talk like that. It's God's plan and we have to live with it. God saved you because you are going to do great things with your life. Paul died, but he will live through this baby I'm carryin."

"I don't know what great things I'm going to do from a wheelchair. Nobody wants a cripple around."

Jerry tries to ease his son's mind by saying, "Don't get down on yourself. Look at the bright side, you made it out, alive. You're only a cripple, if you consider yourself to be a cripple. If you maximize the abilities you still have, you'll be ahead of 95% of the people in this world."

"I don't need a pep talk, Dad. I need to get out of this chair."

Peggy looks at her husband and says, "Jerry, try not to get him upset. It's going to take some time. Let's be thankful for the time we have together."

There is a brief silence before Dan asks, "What about Paul's funeral? When will it be?"

"There will be a service at Fort Polk the day after tomorrow," Katie says, "Paul's parents are coming down for that. He will be buried in his home town in Montana. That funeral will be next week."

"I hope I can go to the service at the Fort. Dad, are you and Mom going to be there?"

"Oh yeah, we'll be there, But we can't make it to Montana. I have to get back to work."

Dan holds his chin with his hand and says, "I'll talk to the doctor. Maybe I can ride to Fort Polk with you guys. When are you leaving?"

"We have to leave tomorrow morning, early," Katie says, "I have some things to do for the service."

"Is the service for Paul, only?"

"No, it is for all of the men that were killed that day. Some of the wives and relatives are planning to speak."

Dan turns away from his visitors and he stares out toward the horizon west of town. After a little bit of thought, he hangs his head and says, "Maybe I better not show my face over there. Not with all of the relatives of the men I let down."

Again, Jerry chides his son, "Quit blaming yourself, Dan. Nobody else is blaming you."

Dan snaps his head around to look at Jerry. He says, "Nobody else was their squad leader."

Peggy moves over in front of Dan and she kneels in front of the wheelchair. She lays her hands on the top of Dan's thighs and pleads, "Dan, please don't get upset. You have to be calm, if you are going to get better."

Dan reaches out and holds his mom's hands. He says, "Don't worry, Mom. I'm getting better. It hasn't shown up yet, but I can feel it." The little family spends the next hour talking on the terrace, that is when a nurse shows up to take Dan back to his room. When the doctor is making his rounds that evening, Dan asks about going to the memorial service at Fort Polk.

The doctor cocks his head as though he is surprised Dan is not better informed, "Didn't anyone tell you? You're being transferred to Bayne-Jones Hospital at Fort Polk. The remainder of your recovery will be spent there. The Army will transport you in plenty of time to attend the service."

"Doc, I thought when the bullet was removed from my spine, I'd be able to walk, again. It's been a few days and I'm not getting any feeling in my legs, at all."

"Nothing is ever certain. There was more damage than we originally expected."

That statement scares Dan. He says, "Am I going to be paralyzed forever?"

"Not necessarily," The doctor says, "There is plenty of inflamation and swelling, right now, but in time, that should go away. If you follow your doctor's orders and stick to the rehabilitation schedule, I think you may get some feeling back in your legs."

"Get some feeling back? Does that mean I'll be walking?"

The Doctor scribbles on the chart and says, "I think there is a good chance you will be able to walk again."

"But how long is it gonna take, Doc? I've got things to do."

"It's hard to say. The important thing is to be patient and try not to get frustrated. It may be two weeks or two years, but I'm confident you will walk again."

In a frantic voice Dan says, "Two years…two years, it can't be two years, Doc. I can't live in this chair for two years."

The doctor begins to act more like the officer that he is and he sternly says, "Calm down soldier. We don't have any control over it. You were hurt bad, but you're alive. Stop and think about the men that didn't make it home."

"That's the trouble, Sir. That's practically all I do think about."

81

IX

Early the next morning, Dan is transported to the hospital at Fort Polk, Louisiana. He is given a room in the rehabilitation section. The room is more private than the post surgical wards to which he has become accustomed. The room is small and it resembles a hotel room more than that of a hospital. Absent are the monitors and medical supplies. Instead, there are posters adorning the walls. The posters have uplifting messages designed to motivate the patients. His physical wounds are healing nicely, but the paralysis persists. His mental wounds are something else altogether. He does not think he will ever overcome the guilt and anger that consumes him. It is midafternoon. A hospital volunteer is assigned to show Dan around the facility. The candystriper pushes him through the halls, showing him the cafeteria, the workout facilities and all of the pertinent areas of the hospital. The tour winds up in the recreation area and Dan runs into some familiar faces. Pete Lester and Z, both in wheelchairs, are sitting side by side talking to each other near the windows.

The volunteer pushes Dan over to his friends. Dan says, "Pete Lester. How the hell are you? And Z. boy, if you two aren't a sight for sore eyes."

With the help of the candystriper, the three wounded friends maneuver their chairs into a semi-circle, so they can talk. Lester replies to Dan with a chuckle, "You're not exactly ready for "Dancing with the Stars", but hey, it's good to see you, Dan."

Dan looks at the volunteer and asks, "Is it okay if I stay here for a while? I need to get some lessons on how to live the easy life from these two slackers."

The young girl shrugs, "I guess it'll be allright, I'll tell the nurses where you are."

Z tilts his head and watches the volunteer walk away. He stares until she disappears around a corner, then he presses his lips together and shakes his head, indicating how hot he thinks she is. Lester says, "Hey watch it Z, she's not old enough for you."

Dan says, "Yeah, I think you need an older woman. You know the motherly type."

The three soldiers laugh and Z says, "Hey Sarge, are you doing any better since we talked on the plane?"

"I think so. They got the bullet out of my back, but I still can't feel anything from the waist down."

"I'm sorry to hear that. Lester and me, we're both goin home right after the service tomorrow."

Dan asks, "Pete, Are you going to be able to stay in the Army?"

Lester looks down and says, "No Dan, I'm not. They're giving me a medical discharge."

"Me too," Z says, "What about you Sergeant?"

Dan shrugs his shoulders and holds his hands out, "I don't know yet. The doctors keep telling me this is temporary, just until the swelling goes down. I hope they're right, because I want to go back and get even with those SOB's that ambushed us."

Lester and Z glance at each other without speaking. They can tell Dan is being unreasonable. Chances are, he will be discharged and even if he is not, he will never go back to Afghanistan. Lester looks at Dan and says, "We've done our share. There are plenty of others to pick up the ball."

"If they'll let them," Dan says, "You know as well as I do, the Army won't go after those guys. They will only return fire after being shot at first. Those guys that got us are the kind that have to be tracked down. They know the rules as well as we do."

"Oh Dan, It's not the Army. It's the politicians. The Army wants those guys as bad as you do, but their hands are tied."

Dan shakes his head and stares into space. He says, "If the politicians think they can talk those Hajis into becoming boy scouts, they're crazier than I thought. Do you think Battalion might do somethin'? I know Captain Craig won't."

"There's no easy answer over there," Lester says, "The whole deal is all messed up. We're just lucky we're out of it. Z told me about what happened at the COP. Why didn't the Captain fire on that truck and stop it?"

Dan rolls his eyes and says, "He was going by his intel reports. He played right into their hands."

"Makes you wonder," Z says, "Whose side our Intel people are on."

Dan nods his head and gets a blank expression on his face, "It sure does. Captain Craig should have known better, but that's just between us, right guys?"

Lester looks at Dan, "Oh hell, Dan, we're not talking to anyone. We're done with the Army and the Army is done with us. By the way, thanks for helping me with that field tourniquet. I don't think I could have done it by myself and Doc said it saved my life. They say I would have bled out in ten minutes."

"Glad I could help. What about Big Al? Has anybody heard from him?"

Lester says, "Oh yeah, I see him every now and then. He'll be there tomorrow. He's out of the hospital, but he comes in for rehab sometimes."

"I'm glad he's OK," Dan says, "I'm real sorry you guys got hurt so bad. I just can't get over the rest of the squad being dead." The soldiers sit silently thinking about their fallen friends. After more small talk the reunion breaks up they head back to their respective rooms.

Later in the day, Peggy and Jerry show up at Dan's room to take him to supper. Peggy holds the wheelchair steady and Jerry helps Dan slide off the bed and into the chair. Jerry pushes the chair and Peggy walks beside Dan as they try to figure out which hall leads to the cafeteria. Dan asks, "Where's Katie? Did she stay home?"

Peggy replies, "They are getting together at one of the officer's homes. She and some of the other wives are making plans for the service tomorrow. They are eating supper while they plan things."

"Dan you are looking better every time I see you," Jerry says, "I think he's getting his color back, don't you mamma."

Peggy smiles and asks, "Are you in any pain?"

"Not really, Mom. The wounds are healing pretty well. My legs itch a lot, but they are getting better."

"They'll come around. We're just so thankful you're back in the U.S.A." Peggy goes through the cafeteria line and picks out all of Dan's favorites, while Dan and Jerry remain seated and talk. After Peggy sets Dan's meal in front of him, she and Jerry go through the line. Soon they are all eating, but not talking a whole lot. His parents are careful to avoid talking about Afghanistan. They know he is tormented by those events and there is no reason to agitate him any further. They figure, if he wants to talk about it, he will bring it up. Jerry turns up his nose at his plate, "With the money our government spends on the military, you'd think the food would be better around here."

"Dad, you know better than to order the meat loaf. Grandpa always said, to never eat hash in a restaurant, well meatloaf's the new hash."

"I guess you're right. I guess I'm spoiled by your mom's cooking."

"I am too. I would lay awake at night and actually smell Mom's meatloaf. At least I thought I was smelling it. That's how much I missed it."

"The Army never was known for its food. Did you eat MRE's all the time?"

"Not always," Dan says, "Recently, we had a mess tent, with cooks, at our combat outpost. In fact, during the attack, those cooks came out of that tent with rifles in their hands. Yeah, they came out of there with those guns a blazin. They probably saved my life. I'll never complain about their cooking again."

"God bless those young men," Peggy says, "I thank God you're home and I wish all those other young men could come home, right away."

"Thanks so much for coming down. I know it's not easy for Dad to get off work this time of year."

Above the din of the busy cafeteria Jerry says, "Oh it's no problem getting off work. We're just so glad we got to see you."

Peggy takes a drink of her iced tea and says, "Dan, maybe they'll let you out a little sooner. Maybe you won't have to finish your last year in the Army."

"That's right," Jerry says, "You can come back home and get on with your life."

"They might do that, if I make that request," Dan says, "But I've decided to stay in the Army. I have a job to do and the only way to do it is in the Army. I have to get even with those killers. I have to get back with my outfit and go find them."

Peggy drops her fork and her mouth falls open. That is the last thing she wants to hear from her son. She has been on pins and needles for three years, praying for Dan to come home alive. By the grace of God he is finally home and now he is talking about going back. She says, "Oh Dan, you're bein unreasonable. You aren't goin back to Afghanistan. You've done your fair share."

Dan freezes in a steely stare and monotonic voice, almost as though he is possessed, "It just so happens, I owe those Hajis a little more than my fair share. I owe them for Paul and the others."

Jerry is both dismayed and disturbed by his son's words. He says, "That's plain crazy talk. Stay here and follow the doctor's orders, you'll be healed in no time. Get those nutty ideas out of your head, you're finished with combat. You have your whole life ahead of you. Don't look back."

The lines in Peggy's forehead and around her eyes do a better job of illustrating her concern more than any words. She sets her glass down and says, "He's right Dan. You're still so young. Don't worry your life away with things you can't do anything about. What's done is done."

Dan is not able nor is he willing to give up on his twisted ideas. In his mind, it would be like giving up on his men that suffered such unjustified deaths. He is also beginning to realize that no one else feels like he does, not even his own parents.

The next day the parade ground at Fort Polk is prepared for the memorial service. A stage is built facing the grand stands. There are rows of folding chairs set up in front of the raised platform. The deceased soldiers' family members are dressed in their best clothes and sitting in the first few rows of folding chairs. The flags are raised only to half staff and they hang limp against the poles. There are high ranking officers from Division Headquarters at Fort Drum, New York. There is a U.S. senator and a congressman ready to make their speeches. All of the soldiers are wearing their dress uniforms. The sky is overcast and there are threatening clouds overhead. The air is heavy and humid and it is hard to breathe. Dan thinks the weather is appropriate for this solemn occasion. He cannot take his eyes off of the families of the deceased men. There are mothers of slain soldiers outwardly weeping. There are widows stoically trying to comfort others. There are young children and babies in the arms of grandpas. Dan closes his eyes and envisions the faces of his men that died that day. One by one the images pass through his mind like snapshots in a photo album. He pictures them bleeding in the dust at the COP. As he watches the families pour out their emotions, he is consumed by guilt. Although he is sitting in his wheelchair at the end of the row next to Lester, Z and Big Al, he is unable to cope with his feelings and he rolls himself to the rear of the assembly. The ceremony begins with a chaplain citing scriptures that illustrate how the men are in a better place. There are the usual words from politicians about honor and sacrifice. They stress that the nation is indebted to the young men that gave so much. There are the childhood stories from friends and classmates. There are former teachers who tell of the young men's acts of responsibility and how the teachers knew the young men were destined to serve their country. There are family members fighting back tears as they deliver emotional eulogies. Dan would like to cover his ears and close his eyes. His mind is a gurgling cauldron spilling over with raw emotions and frazzled nerves. Tears and smiles and pomp and circumstance punctuate the proceedings that last more than two hours. As the ceremony comes to a conclusion, the rain holds off and a lone bugler hoists his instrument to the microphone. There is not a dry eye as the somber notes of "Taps" billow over the entire fort.

Dan is not asked to speak and that is a good thing. In his current frame of mind, he would be little comfort to the mourners. The guilt and hate that have been simmering within him would come spewing out like an erupting volcano. The brass would frown upon that sort of display. It would show a lack of discipline and no respect for the families in attendance. He would probably say something he would regret. Memorials are all about love and at this point, any love Dan may have is shackled in the farthest reaches of his soul unable to escape from the darkness that has engulfed his spirit. By the time the service ends, Dan is an emotional wreck. Perhaps he should not have attended the service. It has provided a whole new set of images that torment him. Not only do the memories of his squad haunt him, but now, the faces of the grieving families haunt him, as well.

As the service breaks up, Dan remains at the back far from the crowd. Many of the mourners go out of their way to speak to him. They are all very gracious. None of them blame Dan, but he harbors enough blame to go around. He blames the Army for putting the ANA in position to betray his squad. He blames Captain Craig for not recognizing the danger posed by the suicide bomber. Most of all, he blames himself for getting suckered into the Taliban's dastardly devised trap. He is desperately trying to reign in his emotions when Big Al comes over to speak to Dan. Big Al approaches Dan with tight lips and a locked jaw. He shakes his head and says, "It ain't right seein you in that chair, Sergeant. Ain't nobody was ever able to keep up with you."

Dan looks up and says, "Hey don't worry, I'll be back on your case real soon. I'll be puttin you to shame on those twenty mile runs, so you better get ready." They both laugh as they shake hands and Dan says, "So uh, where are you working?"

Al chuckles as he answers, "They got me over at headquarters doin clerical work."

"That's not your thing, man."

"Naw, it's not, I feel like a third wheel over there, but with our company deployed, they haven't found a new home for me."

"Do you think you might be going back to Afghanistan?"

"Oh heyull no. And I'm glad of that. They'll find me a cushy job in the motor pool or somethin."

"Well I'm goin back," Dan says, "I have to or else I'll go insane."

Big Al takes a step back and his face scrunches up showing his surprise at Dan's comment. His eyes scan the wheelchair and he looks at Dan's legs before saying, "You can't even walk, Sergeant. There ain't no way you're goin back. But hey, guess what? Workin over at headquarters, I hear some things."

"Like what things?"

"Like Lieutenant Blake put our whole squad in for silver stars because of what we did at that hill. You know, capturing that Amir and all."

Dan scoffs at the news. He says, "So what? I'm not interested in medals."

Big Al looks both directions to see who may be close enough to overhear their conversation. He steps closer to Dan and leans down. Speaking in hushed tones, he says, "You might be interested to know that Captain Craig denied the medals. He wrote that you took unnecessary risks and that soldiers shouldn't get medals for puttin lives in danger."

Dan blurts out, "What? Are you serious? That's all I ever did was look out for my men, but there are times when you have to fight. That is what war is all about. That's what Captain Craig never understood. I'll tell you, Craig is out of his mind." Some of the mourners' attention is drawn to the commotion Dan is making. They look over at Dan and Big Al, so Dan tones it down until the mourners turn away.

Big Al looks around again and holds his finger to his lips to try to get Dan to speak softer. Just above a whisper, Big Al says, "They like Captain Craig at headquarters. Did you know his uncle is a retired general?"

Dan shakes his head and says, "That explains a lot."

The two men finish talking and Big Al mingles with some of the other attendees. Dan turns his chair away from the thinning crowd. He cannot help but wonder why Captain Craig would make up such lies. Could it be Craig is trying to cover up his own ineptitude? After all, Craig did attack the wrong hill and he never did disengage to help out Fourth Platoon. Not long after he finishes speaking with Al, Katie comes over and gives Dan a hug. She says, "It was a beautiful service. I'm so glad you were here." Dan can tell she had been crying by the eye liner trailing down her face.

Dan looks at the ground and shakes his headback and forth, "This sure isn't the homecoming I pictured for my squad. They were too good of men to come home in bags."

Katie can tell her brother is still roiled in shame. "Come on," She says, "Let's get outta here. Let's find Mom and Dad and go get some lunch or something."

"Allright, but I have an appointment with a therapist this afternoon. I have to be back in my room by three o'clock."

X

After having lunch at Katie's apartment, Dan is back in his room at the hospital. He is excited about the meeting with the physical therapist. He is sure it will lead to his first steps since he was wounded. He has remained in his wheelchair and he is spinning in circles, doing doughnuts in the small space next to his bed, when a woman carrying a black zippered case enters the room. She unzips the case and takes out some forms and other items. She reaches out a hand and introduces herself, "Hello Sergeant. I'm Mary Lowrie. I'm here to help you get around better."

Dan knows most of the staff in the rehab wing is comprised of non military employees, but he asks anyway, "Are you an Army doctor, or civilian?"

She goes about her business and says, "I'm not a doctor nor am I in the Army. I'm an occupational therapist. It's a fancy name for someone that helps you get along in spite of your disability."

Dan's eyes open wide and they light up like a kid on Christmas morning. He asks, "Are you going to show me how to walk?"

Mary laughs under her breath and shakes her head ever so slightly. Her movements imply that Dan is rushing things. In her most upbeat and perky manner, she responds, "I'd like to Sergeant. I'd like to walk right out of this hospital with you, but I'm afraid that's not realistic. At least not right now. Actually, you know how to walk. You're just unable because of the paralysis. I can show you how to get dressed and other everyday things you may be having trouble with, all without being able to walk. That sounds good, right?"

Her cheery disposition grates on Dan's nerves. He is deflated, again. He slumps down in his chair and cocoons himself, displaying his most uncooperative posture. He is not getting well and he is beginning to wonder if he ever will. As far as he is concerned, they can send all of these people with the positive attitudes and helpful hints elsewhere. He needs results. Dan lets out a long sigh and says, "I need to start walking. There are things I have to do that can't be done from a wheelchair."

Unfazed by his obstinance, Mary remains positive. She continues, "I'll show you some exercises that will help you. You'd be surprised what all you can do from that chair."

With a steely stare and serious demeanor, Dan asks, "Can I hump through the mountains and track down killers in Afghanistan?"

Mary is taken aback by the question. She has worked with a lot of wounded soldiers and that is a question she has never had to deal with before. She is uncomfortable and stammering for words, "Oh uh, well uh, no you can't, but you don't have to worry about that anymore. It's unlikely the Army will ever send you back over there."

Without a change in expression, Dan says, "That's exactly what I do worry about. I'm afraid they may not send me back. I have some unfinished business over there and I'll be damned if I don't get it done."

Mary is still reeling from his comments, "That's insane. I admire your determination, Sergeant, but you need to face reality. You have a disability. You need to use that determination to get well and to get adjusted to a new lifestyle."

"I don't want a new lifestyle," Dan says, "If I don't get out of this chair, my life is over."

Mary begins to realize that Dan is not just physically wounded. She can see he is mentally damaged, as well. Her perky disposition gives way to that of a serious counselor offering up some tough love, "You're feeling pretty sorry for yourself, aren't you? Perhaps it's time you stopped wallowing in self pity and started being thankful you came home alive."

Dan clinches his fists and hammers the arm of his chair. He screams, "I wish I hadn't come home. Not like this and not without the rest of my squad."

Mary takes a step back and shifts her weight to her back foot. She places one hand on her hip and stares at Dan. She does not speak out loud, but her body language says what she is thinking. Which is, "Really? So now you're screaming at me?" After a few more moments of silence, Mary tries a second time to reason with Dan. She says, "Look, I've worked with a lot soldiers, some in a lot worse shape than you. The ones that can put their experiences behind them and can concentrate on their futures are the ones that accomplish the most."

Dan is still staring into space with a glazed expression. He asks, "What about the others, the ones that can't forget?"

"I'm not saying any of them forget," Mary says, "I'm sure none of them do. What I've seen is that some tend to dwell on their problems more than others. The soldiers I've worked with that cannot turn the page are extremely self destructive."

Dan finally breaks his stare and he looks into Mary's eyes. He pleads for her understanding, "But my situation is different. We got ambushed by men we thought were on our side."

Mary knows not to give any creedence to the justifications offered by his sick mind. It will only prolong his mental healing. She says, "Does it really matter how you got here? Everybody in here has a story. Yours is nothing special. Nobody sees it coming."

Dan is miffed at her lack of understanding. She is supposed to be supportive and helpful, but he can see it is not working out like he had hoped it would. He hangs his head and says, "Look, I have to get out of this hospital and I have to walk out. If you can help me with that, I'm all ears. Otherwise, fill out your forms and go away."

Mary packs her things. It is hard for her to be so cold. Especially, since she got into her line of work to help people, but she knows she cannot let Dan continue with his victimous atttitude. He has to turn the corner, or he will never get well. She takes a few steps toward the door and says, "Obviously, you're in no mood today. I'll come back tomorrow. Perhaps you'll be more receptive then. Good day, Sergeant."

Dan rolls forward crashing into the door as it closes in her wake. He pushes it back open and yells down the hall, "Thanks for coming by, but I'm never going to be receptive to being a cripple." The defiant soldier is upset the meeting with the physical therapist yields only more frustration. He had such high hopes, but it looks like another dead end. He wants to bury his head beneath a pillow and make this nightmare go away.

Dan struggles to get from the wheelchair into his bed, but he is so flustered he cannot do anything right and he falls to the floor. A nurse comes in to check on him. She finds Dan sprawled on the floor face down. His wheelchair is turned on its side with the big wheel still spinning in the air. She shakes her head back and forth and says, "Sergeant Ross, it looks like you're stuck."

Dan looks over his shoulder and says, "I am stuck. I wish they'd just cut these legs off. They're not doing me any good. They're useless."

The nurse drags the wheelchair out of the way and helps Dan get up from the floor. He is sitting on the edge of the bed with his legs dangling over the side. The next thing the nurse does is bend down and set the wheelchair back upright. With her back facing Dan, she says, "Oh now Sergeant, God's giving those legs a rest, that's all. When he thinks they've rested enough, He'll put them back to work. I'm sure of it."

Dan sits with his shoulders slumping. His demeanor and weak voice are clear signs of his disappointment. He says, "Everybody keeps telling me what God is doing for me. First it was my sister, then it was my Mom, and now you. I might be better off if God would stop being so good to me."

The nurse parks the chair in a spot that Dan can reach from the bed, "Oh don't say that. You're never better off without God, no matter who you are or what you're doing. He knows you're going through some trials, so he won't hold those words against you."

Dan lies down and stares at the ceiling. He ponders the nurse's words for a few moments. In his current state, he tries to rationalize why everything is against him. He is not even above questioning God. He silently asks God in a desperate prayer, "Why are you doing this to me?" Before the nurse leaves his room, he asks, "Is the doctor coming by today? I need to see him."

"I think he is. He usually makes his rounds after supper, around seven o'clock. Let me know if you need help getting in that chair."

"Getting down is no problem, I can fall into the chair. It's getting back up that's hard."

The nurse presses her hand against the door and she pushes the door partially open before turning back to Dan and saying, "A lot of people have trouble picking themselves up, lean on God and it gets much easier."

It's only three thirty and Dan won't go down for supper for quite a while. He closes his eyes and tries to sleep. Of course, he has trouble sleeping. He thinks about all the things people have told him. Such as, his life was spared because he is destined to do great things, or God has some unknown purpose for his life. From his perspective, there are two big problems with the God theory. One is he believes that not being killed with the rest of his squad is more of a curse than a blessing. He is confined to a wheelchair, useless to the Army or anyone else and he is living with survivor's guilt. The second problem he has with the God theory is any one of the guys that were killed were more suited to do great things than he is, especially Paul. Paul was the most generous and thoughtful man Dan ever knew. All of those guys were working to make the world a better place. Dan has never been that benevolent, he is much more selfish. He lies there and wrestles with his thoughts until he dozes off. He does not sleep well. He continually wakes up to the sights and sounds of his last battle, tossing and turning all the way through the dinner hour. He has not been working hard enough to build up an appetite and all he has been doing is eating. If he keeps this up, he is afraid he will get fat. He looks at the clock and learns it is almost seven o'clock. Dan is anticipating his next meeting with the doctor. Sure enough, not long after seven, there is a knock on the door and the doctor enters. He takes a clipboard from the wall and makes a little small talk before giving Dan some news, "We have ordered an MRI for you. We want to see if there is any progress around the damaged spinal region."

A puzzled Dan asks, "Shouldn't it be healed by now?"

Picking up on Dan's anxiety, the doctor tries not to alarm the already agitated soldier, "Not necessarily. We just want to make sure there are no impediments to the healing process. We want to make sure we have done everything possible."

"And if you did everything possible?"

The doctor sighs and says, "Then it's out of our hands."

Dan rolls his eyes, "Please don't tell me it's in God's hands. Everybody's been telling me that."

As the doctor flips through pages on the clipboard, he says, "He has taken pretty good care of you so far. In my years of practicing medicine, I've seen some miraculous recoveries, some that have no scientific explanation. Why not trust God? I do."

Dan snaps his head around toward the doctor, "I thought doctors believe in science, not God."

Without hesitation the doctor looks up and responds, "And I thought there are no atheists in fox holes."

Dan concedes the point, "There really aren't, I'm no atheist. I'm just having a hard time coping with the hand he dealt me. If these legs don't come around, I'm afraid I'll be a burden on everybody."

"Be patient, I know that's easy for me to say, but it may take some time. Try reading some books to take your mind off things."

Dan thinks the doctor does not fully understand his plight. In Dan's twisted, self absorbed mind, he perceives a lack of urgency among his care givers. Dan gets the notion that they are satisfied he is alive and they may not care when or if he ever walks again. He says, "How am I supposed to take my mind off things? If I can't walk, I'm no good to anybody. No books will ever change that."

The doctor tries to calm Dan down, "Perhaps, I misspoke. Of course, you are unable to stop thinking about your paralysis, that's normal. But maybe, a little distraction can help ease the tension. There is one book in particular I believe will help, the Bible. Have you ever read it?"

"No, I haven't, but my mind's too cluttered for that right now. I'm not interested in easing the tension. To me, that sounds like giving up and I'm not giving up. I can't."

The doctor places the clipboard back on the wall and says, "It's not giving up. It's more like putting your trust in something. There is only so much you can do on your own. I believe that worry and stress are debilitating in their own right. I can't think of a better time for a little spiritual healing."

XI

That night, Dan lies awake in his bed wrestling with his thoughts, just like every other night since the attack. The memorial service is still fresh in his mind and there is something that just started nagging at him regarding the service. It is the fact that none of the officers spoke to him and it really has him worried. Some of those officers came from as far away as New York, but none of them even acknowledged him. He wonders why and he tries to rationalize their behavior. Perhaps they realize, as he does, the idea of mixing ANA units with Americans never was a good idea. The Afghan government is such a fractured mess, even they have no idea who the ANA soldiers are or where they come from. Those ANA should have never been anywhere near the COP in the first place. Maybe our top command is ashamed of their policies that make it unnecessarily dangerous for the front line soldiers. It is not yet daylight and hospital workers are coming in to prepare him for the MRI. Dan is surprised they have come by so early, but it does not matter, it is not like he was getting any sleep, anyway. In fact, it is a welcome relief from his constant anguish. He says, "I didn't know you were coming this early. How long will this take?"

Dan's hospital bed converts into a gurney. One of the men uses his foot to unlock the wheels and says, "Not long, only about an hour or so."

"That's good. My folks are going back home this morning and I'd like to meet them for breakfast before they leave."

The hospital worker carefully shoves the bed through the door held open by another orderly. Without much emotion, he answers, "That shouldn't be a problem."

The MRI is finished and Dan rolls down to the cafeteria to have breakfast with his folks. He scans the room and sees his folks are already seated. Dan wheels over to join them. He looks around and asks, "Where's Katie?"

Jerry says, "She already left for Montana. After Paul's funeral, she'll get things wrapped up here and she's moving back to Quincy."

Dan looks straight ahead without focusing on anything in particular. He is thinking about how much Paul was in love with Katie. There was seldom a day that Paul did not mention her name. He marvels how Katie has exhibited such strength through the grief and he fears she will eventually break down. He would like to be with her when she needs some support. With heavy eyes, he says, "I wish I could have gone with her."

"We do too," Peggy says, "She reaches across the table and places her hand on top of Dan's. Peggy is worried about Katie, but she knows Katie has always been so stable, at least outwardly. Dan has always been more flighty, like his dad. Peggy worries more about Dan, especially with the haunting dreams and inability to sleep. She is upset that they cannot stay longer. She is afraid Dan is going through a dangerous stage in his mental recovery. The whole time they are eating breakfast, Peggy reassures Dan that God is with him. She stresses there is never a need to do anything drastic. Prayer will get him through the darkest moments. Dan realizes his mother is afraid he may take his own life, like many tormented soldiers do, but that is not an option for Dan. He is more concerned with taking the lives of those killers in Afghanistan. After they have finished breakfast, Jerry looks at his watch and stands up signaling it is time to go. Peggy looks at Dan and says, "Danny, let us know how things are going. If you need anything, just call." They all hug each other and say their goodbyes.

Dan watches his parents until they have disappeared into the hallways of the hospital. He is scheduled for physical therapy in thirty minutes, so he wheels his way over to the rehabilitation area. At this stage, he is mainly getting consultation from the therapists. His back is still too tender to be subjected to a lot of stress, although they tell him those days will come. After therapy he returns to his room to decompress. Shortly after that the doctor comes in for a surprise visit. He says, "Hello Sergeant, how are you feeling today?"

Dan is still in his chair. He is getting tired of lying in that bed. In fact, he is beginning to get repulsed by the bed, by his room, by the hospital and by his life in general. He responds, "You got a couple hours, Doc? I could tell you some stories."

"Oh, I'll bet you could." The doctor laughs, but soon realizes Dan is not in a jovial mood. In fact, Dan is staring as if to question the doctor's sanity. "But uh, the reason I came up here this morning is that we have been studying the images from the MRI."

Dan cocks his head and opens his eyes much wider. He says, "That was quick, I thought it took a few days to get results from those things"

"Not in this day of digital imaging. The pictures are ready immediately, but it normally takes a doctor a few days to get around to looking at them. In this case, headquarters has asked us to expedite our prognosis."

Dan is even more perplexed to hear Headquarters is making demands with regard to his health. "Why are they in such a hurry to find out about my back? Haven't they got a war to run?"

The doctor smiles and laughs under his breath. He says, "Of course they have a war to run. I'm not sure why they made the request, but it is highly unusual. I've never had this sort of request before."

Dan's eyes roll as he ponders the thought, He says, "I guess there is extra special interest because it was a green on blue attack."

Sensing some uneasiness on the part of his patient, the doctor gets back to the reason for his visit. He flips through a clipboard holding images of Dan's back and says, "Maybe, but let's get back to the MRI. Unfortunately, there is a little more damage to the nerve endings than we had hoped."

After hearing that news, Dan first slumps in his chair. Then he thrusts his upper body upward. He is not moving any real distance. He is simply deflating and inflating his posture in correlation with the ebb and flow of his emotions. He asks, "Does that make this permanent?"

"No no no no, don't get excited," The doctors says, "It means it may take longer than we originally hoped. There is still a reasonable chance for a full recovery. It's going to take more time and more effort on your part."

"Can you do more surgery to speed it up?"

The doctor tucks the clipboard under his arm and says, "No, we have done everything possible from a surgical standpoint. Time and therapy are the only things that can make a difference. Oh, and don't forget about prayer, that will help the most."

Skepticism exudes from Dan's voice, as he asks, "Are you telling me the whole story, Doc? You're not trying to give me false hope, are you?"

The doctor stiffens his upper lip and says, "We don't give false hope in this business. We tell it like it is. It is up to you as to whether you want to keep trying or just give up."

After a brief contemplation of the latest bad news, Dan is more determined than ever. He grits his teeth and scowls, as he says, "I'm not giving up. I can't. I've got too much to do. Somebody has to hold those killers accountable. I'm afraid there is nobody to do it but me."

"Revenge is one of the most effective forms of motivation, but the side effects are devastating."

Later that same afternoon, Dan is returning to his room after another session in the workout room. He finds it strange the door to his room is open. He finds it even stranger that two officers are waiting for him inside. Dan rolls in the room and extends an arm to greet the officers. The officers find it awkward to shake hands rather than salute, but things are a little different in a hospital. One of the officers says, "Good afternoon Sergeant. I'm Major Jenkins and this is Major Landry. I hope they're treating you well in here."

Dan's curiosity is evident by his facial expression. He is wary of officers, especially when they come in pairs, but he is polite to the two men. "Everyone is very nice, thank you. Did you guys come all the way down from Fort Drum?"

"That's right," Jenkins says, "We've been enjoying the Louisiana culture. We had something called gumbo last night and my mouth is still burning. Whew, that stuff is hot. I mean like spicy hot."

Dan laughs and says, "Yeah, I guess nobody warned you, but Cajun cooking takes a little getting used to."

The officers are cordial, but serious. There is a coolness to their demeanor. They trade looks at each other and search for a starting point to conduct their business. Jenkins looks at Landry and then at the floor, He finally lifts his head and looks Dan in the face. He says, "Sergeant, we would like to express the gratitude of the entire 10th Mountain Division for your contributions to our efforts in Afghanistan. We are grateful we have devoted men, like you, to carry on the proud tradition of our division. This division is indebted to you for the sacrifices you have made as a result of those contributions. You have given a lot for the Army and for our country. However, in light of your injuries, the Army is discharging you from any further service commitments."

Dan is blindsided by the well rehearsed statement. He slumps down in his chair and buries his face in one hand. He begins to rub his forehead so hard, it looks like he is trying to remove a stubborn smudge of grease.

He shakes his head back and forth and says, "No, no, you can't. I'm going to be fine. I'll be walking soon. I still have almost a year left and I plan on reenlisting after that. You have to give me the rest of the year to get well. You have to."

The second of the two officers, Major Landry, rubs the underside of his chin with the back of his hand. He clears his throat and speaks sternly, "You are as well as you are going to get, for the foreseeable future. The Army has decided it would be best for you to go home and get started on the next phase of your life. The Army is grateful to you, but it is unable to utilize you any longer."

Dam slams the arm of his chair with his fist. He ignores military decorum and expresses his true feelings, "So that's it? You're throwing me on the scrap heap like a burned up truck or something?"

Major Jenkins steps closer to Dan and attempts to show some compassion for the young soldier's plight. "Not exactly, Sergeant. We understand your frustration, but you have to be realistic. This is for your own good."

Dan leans his head back on his shoulders and stares at the ceiling. That is the last thing he needed to hear. "What do you mean for my own good? You guys use me up and when I have a temporary problem, you want to toss me out like yesterday's garbage." Pointing at the wall, Dan says, "You see that poster the Army put in this room. It says don't give up. It looks to me like the Army is giving up on me. Maybe they ought to take these posters down."

Major Landry is adamant, "Calm down, soldier, you are out of line. The Army is not abandoning you. The Army is committed to your health and well being for the rest of your life."

Dan appeals to the two bearers of the devastating news, "Is there an appeal process? Do I have right to fight this?"

"That is not recommended," Landry says, "In this case, you are actually getting off easy by accepting the medical discharge."

At this point Dan is not only demoralized, he is also bewildered. He asks, "What are you talking about?"

Landry looks down at the floor and clears his throat. He says, "Your CO, Captain Craig, has petitioned for court martial proceedings against you. His official report on the incident at COP Geronimo cites your failure to follow standard procedures. By ignoring those procedures, you failed to insure the well being of the soldiers in your squad."

Now Dan is mad. He feels like all of his insides are gone and a chill consumes him. He turns his head sideways and says, "That's crazy. If anyone was at fault, it was Captain Craig."

Jenkins appeals to Dan's common sense, "Look Sergeant, you've been through hell. The Army recognizes that. That is why the Army is offering the medical discharge with full benefits. In all probability you'll never be able to return to full duty, anyway. This way, you are taken care of."

Common sense is lost in Dan's mind. It is overwhelmed by emotions of anger and betrayal. He argues, "But what about the record of the incident? The official record is all wrong. It has to be set right. Craig is making a scapegoat out of me to cover his failure to act. He doesn't want the blood of those dead soldiers on his hands."

Jenkins must disregard any comments from Dan and stick to the cold business he has been assigned. Without emotion, he states, "The Army is looking out for your best interests."

On the other hand, Dan is overcome with emotions. He continues his obstinate tirade, "My best interests, that's a laugh. It looks like the Army is trying to cover up the actions of an inept officer. The Army doesn't give a damn about me. The Army only cares about the Army. Well I have news for you, plenty of guys that were there that day will agree with me. The radio transmissions alone will exonerate me. Not to mention the deployment orders Captain Craig issued prior to the incident. Ask the other men in the company."

In a brief departure from his machine like persona, Jenkins says, "I know a lieutenant in Bravo Company. He has expressed some concerns to me, off the record of course. You may have a case, in fact you probably do, but those young officers may say one thing off the record and something else when it's official. Besides, a court martial would take years. Bravo Company would have to get back home and there are lengthy legal proceedings before the trial can even start."

Dan does not waver from his stubborn stance, "I don't care how long it takes. This is not right. I know I'd be proven innocent of any charges made by Captain Craig."

Landry says, "You have to realize that a court martial is not like a trial you see on TV. There is no jury of your peers. In fact, the decision is handed down by men that have much more in common with Captain Craig. And those witnesses you would rely upon, they're still in the Army. They're trying to make careers for themselves. When push comes to shove, it is hard to predict what they will say. Do you really want to spend the next two years fighting a system that knows how to take care of its own? Or do you want to move on with your life?"

Although he feels like he just got kicked in the teeth and he feels a pit in his stomach the size of a watermelon, reality begins to set in. Dan slumps down a little lower in his chair and says, "I want a lot of things, but, lately, nothing seems to work out." He really has no bargaining power. This is not negotiable. The Army has made their decision and Dan knows it. These two officers are only trying to provide a personal touch to the official notification.

Sensing a good opportunity to wrap things up, Landry says, "As soon as you are cleared by the medical staff, you will be released to go home. You can continue your rehabilitation there. Quincy, Illinois, isn't it?"

"Yes sir," Dan says, "That's where I'm from."

Landry smiles and says, "No kidding. I'm from Davenport, Iowa, just up the river from you, small world, right?" After that comment solicits only one of Dan's cold stares, the smile disappears from Landry's face. He says, "Thank you for your service and good luck."

The officers shake Dan's hand, pat him on the back and leave. Just like that, his military career is over, almost as quickly as his squad was wiped out and with almost as much betrayal. It is a non violent betrayal, but it hurts even worse. There is no ceremony. There is no proclamation. There are no friends or family to share the moment. There is only an official record that includes a bogus account of his last combat action. Dan places his face in the palms of his hands and wonders how things could get any worse.

XII

Two weeks later the former sergeant finds himself back home, living with his parents and still confined to the wheelchair. He is no longer Staff Sergeant Dan Ross. He is simply Dan Ross, civilian. He does have full strength in his upper body, which enables him to get around with the ever present wheelchair. Peggy is thrilled to have him back home. He has moved back into his old room and Peggy waits on him hand and foot. Dan is unhappy with the arrangement. He would like a little more independence, but that is impractical, for now. It is the first Sunday since he came home. Dan's parents want him to go to Mass with them. At first, Dan is unwilling, but after Peggy implores him, he sees how much it means to her and he decides to go along. Dan wheels up near the front door of the church with his parents walking behind him. Father Donovan is the pastor at St Anne Catholic Church and he has known Dan since the young man was a baby. He is a small little man with a ruddy complexion and a thick Irish brogue. The old priest rushes over to greet the young man. He reaches out both arms and places one hand on Dan's shoulder. He says, "Oh Dan, it's good to see ya, boy. Praise God your home."

To say the least, Dan is embarrassed at the attention. He can feel his face turning red as he speaks, "Thanks Father, It's good to see you too. I've thought about this old church a lot the last three years. I wasn't sure I'd ever see it again."

Father Donovan laughs heartily from deep inside his diaphragm and pats Dan on the back. He says, "We prayed a lot for ya, boy. Your mom made sure of that. You know, while you were gone, there was many a day that I saw your mom kneelin in the day chapel. She'd be holdin her rosary and prayin all alone. Well, God brought you back home and we're not through yet. We're prayin that He lifts ya out of that chair, real soon. I'm sure He will, too, because in the thirty years I've been at this church, no kid ever squirmed around the pew more than you. On many occasions, I had to stop in the middle of my sermon to ask your mom to do something about your squirmin."

Jerry laughs and asks, "Were you afraid somebody might miss part of those riveting messages?"

The old priest turns to Jerry and deadpans, "And just what would you be knowin about my sermons, Jerry? Unless ya can hear with your eyes closed."

In a mock defensive tone, Jerry counters, "I concentrate better with my eyes closed."

Accenting his Irish brogue, the old priest comes back with, "Oh, and I suppose ya concentrate better while you're snorin, too?"

Score one for the Padre.

Peggy shakes her head and tells Dan, "You see what I have to put up with? These two never let up."

After a good laugh, Father Donovan composes himself and says, "Seriously Dan, if ya need to talk about anything, come by and see me. I was an Army chaplain in Vietnam. I saw some things in those rice patties that nobody should have to see. Stop by and talk if ya feel like it. You're welcome, anytime."

Many of the parishioners come over to express their gratitude to Dan. Parents of guys Dan grew up with, friends of Dan's parents and some people he didn't know at all. They all came over to wish him well. It is exactly the reason Dan did not want to attend Mass this morning. His shame is on display for the entire parish. During Mass, Dan feels like he is in a fish bowl. He feels like everybody's eyes are on him. It is an uncomfortable feeling, like being in a freak show at the carnival. Dan thinks the Mass is geared especially for him. There are readings from the book of Job, talking about enduring pain and suffering without giving up on God. There are more readings about Joseph, who was betrayed by his brothers, yet he rose to become a powerful prince of Egypt. Even though he hears the words, they do not displace the dark emotions that consume his soul. His feelings of guilt and hate are too strong to alter his disposition. After Mass, Dan quickly wheels himself to the car without speaking to anyone.

Outside the church, Peggy speaks to all of her friends as they approach her and Jerry after Mass, but she cannot help but notice Dan brooding in the parking lot. Peggy excuses herself from the wellwishers and goes over to the car. She asks, "What's the hurry Dan? Is something wrong?"

"Can we just get out of here?" Dan says, "I can't stand this, anymore. I'm tired of the sympathy. I'm tired of the encouragement. Don't these people see me for what I am? I'm a cripple. I'm useless. Why are they so happy about that? I know everybody means well, but it's not helping. I'm not ready to see people. Can we go home, now?"

Peggy and Jerry are surprised at Dan's reaction. Peggy says, "Those people are glad you're home. They've been thinking about you for three years. They're happy that you're alive. They know you'll walk again, someday. Can't you see that?"

It is not only that Dan is wrapped up in his inability to walk that has him so ungracious. That is only part of it. He is beginning to bow at the weight of the whole situation and there are many components. It is true, he cannot walk and that bothers him. But it is also true that he cannot stop thinking about his squad members and those snakes that are responsible for their deaths. Dan feels like Captain Craig laid all the blame on him for the botched defense of the COP. Adding to his frustrations, Dan feels like everybody is satisfied to have him home alone, whether he can walk or not. They do not understand how helpless he is in the wheelchair. Nor do they understand how afraid he is that he may never be able to retaliate against the Taliban on behalf of his dead friends. Perhaps he has seen so much inequity that he cannot recognize anything good, anymore.

Jerry wraps his arms around Dan to help him get in the car. As he grabs hold of Dan's dangling legs to swing them inside, Jerry says, "Your mom and I are going to look around for a place for Katie to rent. She'll be moving back next week. She got her old job back at the elementary school. Don't you want to go with us?"

"No I don't. It's too much trouble getting in and out of the car. Drop me off at home."

"Come on Danny," Jerry says, "You can see how much the town has changed, since you've been gone."

"Nothing changes, Dad. Nothing changes in Quincy or anywhere else in the world. Most people wake up every morning trying to figure out how to screw over the next guy and the few who are trying to make a difference end up spinning their wheels and getting nowhere."

Undeterred by his son's negative outlook, Jerry says, "But we have to keep trying. Imagine what the world would be like, if we all stopped trying to help each other."

"I don't have to imagine, I've seen it in Afghanistan."

"Wait a minute. Now hold on there. You guys were trying to help those people out, weren't you?"

"Some were," Dan says, "And I still have some unfinished business myself. I'm never going to be normal until it's done."

Jerry perceives that Dan is getting a little too agitated and he decides to change the subject. "OK, we'll take you home and tomorrow I'll show you around the plant. Mr. Gherig said he has a job for you, wheelchair or not. You'll feel better when you get back into a routine."

The next morning, Jerry takes Dan to work with him. It is a short drive down to the plant. Jerry talks constantly, mostly about his favotite baseball team, the St. Louis Cardinals. During the trip, Dan does not even hear his father's running commentary.

Dan is consumed by the sounds in his own head. It is the ever present furor that keeps him from sleeping at nights or concentrating on much of anything. He relives the attack on the COP over and over again. He rehashes the events leading up to the attack and the aftermath, as well. There is nothing that can drive those images from the forefront of his mind and the longer they are in the car, the more apprehensive Dan becomes.

Dan is sure his dad is rushing things and he is afraid this whole job thing will end badly. In his current state, he is worried he may not do well and that may be a poor reflection on Jerry. Mr. Gherig started the business thirty years ago and Jerry has been with him from the beginning. Jerry is the plant manager. They make rubber inserts for air conditioning compressors and air turbines. There are about twenty workers in the plant and Mr.Gherig and his secretary are in the office. As Jerry shows Dan around the plant, Dan begins to get the same feeling he had at church. It is the freak show effect all over again and there is a swelling lump of anxiety developing in his throat. One by one, Jerry introduces Dan to the workers in the plant, Each one shakes Dan's hand and offers words of gratitude and encouragement. To Dan, it is simply a steady stream of colorless, expressionless chatter jarbling through his mind. He smiles and pretends to be attentive, but he is not. His torment has robbed him of any social skills and he is incapable of retrieving them for this occasion. Jerry walks up a newly built wheelchair ramp to open the office door and Dan wheels his way inside. Mr. Gherig is not there, but his secretary, Mrs.Grant, greets Dan and the three of them make some small talk. Soon, Jerry goes back out to the plant and Mrs. Grant leads Dan down a wood panelled hall to a freshly cleaned office with a desk, a phone and a computer. There are no windows. In fact, it looks like a storage closet that was converted to an office just for Dan. There is residue from greasy parts that has permanently stained the floor and walls. There are cobwebs in the corners of the ceiling that were missed by whoever cleaned out the place. The lighting is muted, but sufficient. Mrs. Grant smiles and says, "This is where you'll be working, this is your office."

Dan attempts to show some enthusiasm. He chooses adequate words, but he is involuntarily void of emotion when he speaks, "An office for me, wow, it's nice." Dan has no interest in the business, but Mr. Gherig has been good to Jerry and Dan is trying to be gracious.

Mrs. Grant detects a lack of focus on the part of her new trainee, but she writes it off as first day jitters and proceeds into the office. She makes sure Dan has rolled into position behind the desk before she starts her training spiel. "I'll show you how to do everything on this computer. You can do shipping, purchasing, payroll and accounting all right here."

Dan summons one of his sarcastic replies, "If I do all of that, what are you guys going to do?"

Mrs. Grant laughs, "It'll take some time to learn it all. We'll train you a little at a time. I understand your mom will take you to physical therapy in the afternoons."

"That's right," Dan says, "Every day at three o'clock."

Mrs. Grant sits down and begins to show Dan some small tasks on the computer, but Dan's mind is far away. Dan wants to build things. He has no desire to stare at a computer screen and print reports all day. But it doesn't matter, in his frame of mind he has trouble concentrating on anything. He is completely preoccupied with the images of Afghanistan that will not stop flashing through his mind. He stares into the screen, but sees nothing. Mrs. Grant asks check questions after demonstrating each step, but Dan is unresponsive.

She pushes his shoulder to get his attention and asks, "Dan, have you heard a word I've said? Do you understand the production reports?"

Dan snaps out of his trance, "I'm sorry Mrs. Grant. Can you show me that again?"

Mrs. Grant is now convinced that Dan's heart is not in this. She says, "Please, just call me Linda. Are you sure you are ready for this?"

Dan slams his palms on the desk and pushes himself backwards until the big wheels on his chair crash into the wall behind him. He rubs his forehead and answers, "No, I'm not ready. I'll never be ready. I'm not cut out for an office job. I know Dad will be disappointed, but this is making my skin crawl. The very thought of being tied to this desk is like being in jail. Mr. Gherig has been so nice to me and I don't want to let him down, but this would kill me."

Mrs Grant takes hold of one of Dan's hands and asks, "Have you told your dad?"

"No. Not yet. He was so excited and hopeful that this will help me, I thought I'd give it a try, but I can see it's not for me."

She leans back against the desk and says, "I'll speak to him for you?"

"No thanks," Dan says, "I'll tell him tonight. I need to think of the right words. He's a great guy. I don't want to hurt him, but this isn't going to work."

When Peggy arrives at the factory to give Dan a ride to his physical therapy appointment, she is surprised to find him waiting outside in the parking lot. Just by the look on his face, she can tell something is not right, but she ignores her intuition and greets him with the standard, "How was your first day?"

Dan does not speak, nor does he make eye contact with his mother. He wheels up to the passenger side of the car and grabs the door handle. Dan has learned to lift himself into the car without any help. All Peggy has to do is fold up the wheelchair and stow it in the trunk. After she returns to the car, Dan stares at the factory and says, "It's not for me, Mom. I tried. I really did try for Dad's sake, but I can't be tied to a desk that way. It's probably going to break his heart. I guess I'm just an ungrateful, spoiled brat, but my working there wouldn't be good for anybody."

Peggy starts the car and asks, "What did your dad say?"

Dan runs his hand over his head down to the back of his neck and says, "I haven't told him, yet."

Peggy can sense that Dan is uneasy about telling his father. She says, "Don't worry. He'll understand. He only wants the best for you. He may pout a little, but if this job's not going to make you happy, there's no sense draggin out the inevitable. It's best to move on to something else. You'll be back in school soon and I'm sure you'll find your calling." Peggy hits the gas and heads for the physical therapy center.

The only part of the day that Dan gets some relief from the noises in his head is when he is doing his exercises. He is so determined to walk, he blocks out every external distraction. However, the internal turmoil persists. He knows he cannot do anything about that until he is back on his feet and walking. He really puts everything he has into the workouts and he gets the full benefit from these sessions. Peggy waits patiently in the lobby while Dan runs through his daily routine. Sometimes she leaves to do a quick errand, but most of the time she will pass the time by reading. On the way home, Peggy turns into the grocery store parking lot and finds a spot near the door. Dan is upset about the detour, because he knows she will ask him to go inside. Peggy says, "We need a couple of things for supper tonight. I'll get your chair."

"Don't do that Mom. I don't feel like going in, right now."

"A lot of our neighbors are in there. They've all been asking about you. Don't you want to say hi?"

Dan cannot understand why his mom is so oblivious to his suffering. She insists on acting like everything is normal when it is not. He thinks that is how her generation deals with these kinds of things. They ignore them in hopes they will go away. He tries to be emphatic without hurting her feelings. "No Mom, I don't want to say hi to anyone. Maybe later, okay?"

After a few minutes, Dan sees his mom coming out of the store with another woman. The two of them are talking and laughing as they approach the car.

Peggy crouches down and speaks through the open driver's side window. "Danny, look who I found." It's Carrie Hight, a girl Dan knew in school. He took her to a couple of dances, but they didn't stay in touch after he left for the Army. She is obviously working at the store because she is wearing her uniform smock. Dan is embarrassed that he has to face her in his condition.

Carrie walks around to the passenger side of the car and she leans through the window to give Dan a hug. She says, "Hey Dan, I'm glad you're back. Your mom told me what happened. I'm so sorry. "

Dan is both ashamed and upset his mom brought Carrie out to see him. He tries to hide his displeasure and says, "Thanks, you look great, Carrie. How have you been?

"O K, I guess. I'm going to the community college and working here. I'm sorry about your legs, but at least you're still in one piece."

Seeing his old girlfriend adds embarrassment to the shame and displeasure he is already feeling. Although his face feels like it is on fire and is as red as a beet, Dan tries to act nonchalant. He says, "This is only temporary. The doctors say I have a good chance to be walk, real soon."

Carrie lifts her hand above her forehead to block the afternoon sun from her eyes and says, "Yeah, that's what your mom said. I always wondered what became of you. I knew you were in the Army, but I didn't know where you were or what you were doing. I'm ashamed of myself for not asking your mom about you. I see her in the store all the time."

"No, no, don't worry. It's my fault we didn't stay in touch. I could have written you. I just never was too good about that. Do you still live at home?"

"No, I share an apartment over by the college. You remember Brooke, don't you? We're splitting the rent."

"Brooke Evans? Sure, I remember, how is she doing?"

Carrie rolls her eyes and sighs, "She's engaged. They are getting married in a few months."

Even though Dan has been self absorbed since he came home, he can detect some apprehension in Carrie's voice, "What's the matter? You don't like the guy or something?"

"I don't know. I don't think he's right for Brooke. He doesn't work. She plans on supporting him while he finishes school. I think he's playin her, but what do I know?"

"Well. I hope it works out for them, but what about you? Are you going to find a new roommate?"

"I guess I'll have to. It's hard making ends meet when you're goin to school and workin for minimum wage"

"I'll bet. I've been taking classes in Louisiana, when I get the chance."

Still squinting from the sun, she nods her head and says, "Oh, that's good." Carrie continues to nod, but they have reached that awkward point of the conversation where they have run out of things to say. She waits, hoping Dan will say something, but he just stares through the windshield. After a brief silence, she says, "Maybe we can go see a movie sometime?"

Dan always liked Carrie, but he was always shy around her and now he is totally humiliated. In his mind, her offer to go to a movie is only a blow off line designed to help her get away gracefully. He hangs his head and says, "You'll have to drive."

"No problem, give me a call. Your mom has my number." Carrie gives Dan another quick hug and says, "I better get back inside before old Mister Whipple misses me. It really is good to see you. Goodbye."

Peggy smiles and waves to Carrie while fumbling to get the key in the ignition. She starts the car and says, "I always liked her and I know you did too."

Agitated by his mom's intervention, Dan says, "Yeah Mom, I like her, but we'll never go see a movie. She doesn't want to go around with a guy in a wheelchair. She only said that to be polite, because you put her on the spot."

Peggy gets defensive and replies, "I didn't put her on the spot, I mentioned you were waiting in the car and she wanted to see you."

In his most sarcastic way, Dan says, "Sure Mom, I'm sure that's just how it happened." Then Dan holds both hands out toward Peggy and makes another plea for privacy, "Look Mom, would you please quit bringing people to see me? I don't want to see anybody right now."

In rare moment of assertiveness, Peggy says, "Well, I can't control people. You have to accept the fact that there are people who care about you, whether you are in a wheelchair or not."

XIII

That evening, at the supper table, Dan breaks the news to his dad. He says, "Dad, I appreciate what you and Mr. Gherig are doing for me. Giving me a job and showing me the business, but honestly, it's not for me. I can't be cooped up in an office all day. I believe it would drive me nuts."

Jerry was waiting for Dan's revelation and he is not happy. Jerry does not buy into all of the psychological aspect of Dan's situation, maybe it is the generational thing again. He does not understand that Dan is incapable of working. He thinks Dan is unwilling to work. He says, "Yeah, I know. Linda Grant told me all about it this afternoon. You didn't give it much of chance, did you?"

Peggy has seen this attitude from Jerry many times before, it is a lot like when Dan told his dad he was putting off school and joining the Army. Jerry was beside himself then and he is getting that way now. She jumps in on behalf of her son, "Now Jerry, take it easy. It's only been a few days. You have to give him more time to get adjusted."

Dan quietly worries about his parents getting into an argument, but he remains silent. Jerry has a temper that cools down just about as quickly as it heats up and Peggy knows how to handle him when he is in one of those moods. After stewing for a few more seconds, Jerry says, "Oh hell. Do what you think is best. Hell, I'm sick and tired of that old factory myself. I'm thinking about retiring, in fact, I'm going to retire." He turns to Peggy and says, "What do you say, Honey?"

Peggy's jaw drops, as Dan says, "Hold on, Dad. I didn't mean to get you all riled up."

"No, no, I've been thinking about this for a long time. You're mom and I have talked about it, too"

Peggy looks at Dan and holds up her index finger and she silently mouths the word, "Once."

Jerry continues his tirade, "I only hung around to keep a door open for you. But there's no reason for you to slave your life away in that dirty, stinkin hole. Hell, my brothers aren't doin anything with the farm. Maybe your mom and I will move back into the old farmhouse. I can fix it up a little and add on another room. It'd be perfect for you, too…." Jerry's voice trails off. He knows he has said too much. He is upset at himself for inadvertently sending the message that he is considering long term accommodations for Dan's disability. It is an unintended message that did not go unnoticed by his hypersensitive son.

Dan looks at his dad with a hurt in his eyes that shames Jerry. He feels like Jerry has lost hope that the he will ever walk again. Dan shakes his head and says, "You don't think I'm gonna get well, do you? My own dad is givin up on me. You think I'm goin to live with you guys forever, don't you? Look, I'm gonna show you just like I'm gonna show the Army. I'm getting out of this chair and it's gonna be sooner than you think. And then I'm gonna do somethin about those guys that got killed. You may not believe it, hell, why should you be different than anybody else? But it's sure as hell gonna happen. You can count on it." Dan pushes himself away from the table and starts for the hallway to his room. Jerry just hangs his head without saying another word. He knows he hurt Dan and he is sorry he did.

Peggy stands and chases a few steps after her embattled son. She pleads, "Danny, please don't go. Finish your supper. Your dad didn't mean anything. Of course he knows you'll get well. He's not givin up. None of us are. Come back and finish eating." Her words fall on deaf ears, as Dan wheels down the hall.

Deep down, Dan knows his dad is pulling for him, but in his fragile state of mind, it does not take much to send him into a rant fueled by self pity. He remains in his room while his folks do the dishes. When the kitchen is clean, Peggy and Jerry go into the den to watch TV. Just like when he was a kid, Dan waits an arbitrary amount of time until he thinks he has punished his parents enough. Once that time has passed, he rolls into the den and without uttering a word, he joins them. His parents do not speak, but there is an understanding among all three that the latest turbulence is forgotten. As always, Dan has trouble concentrating and he becomes disinterested in watching television. He finds the morning paper folded on the coffee table. He scans the front page and then thumbs through the first section. Buried back on page 9, he finds an item that gets his attention. The caption reads, "Taliban kill 6 Afghan villagers". The dateline is Zabul Province,

Afghanistan, only four days ago. Now Dan is really curious. The story reports of Taliban insurgents killing civilians in a small village named "Murzani", that's the town in the valley, close to COP Geronimo. It's the exact area that Dan was most recently deployed. As he continues to read, the article explains that the civilians were killed when the Taliban raided a party that featured music and women dancing. Two things strictly prohibited in the Taliban controlled areas of the country. The slain civilians were mostly young people, but two old women attempted to intercede. Those women were shot and killed along with those they attempted to help. The Taliban enforcers proceeded to behead their victims. The last line of the article states that the atrocities are believed to have been ordered by the prominent cleric Amir Sadiq Nurzai.

Dan slams his hand on the paper and shouts, "That's him. That's the guy we captured."

The outburst alarms both Peggy and Jerry. They turn from the program they are watching and Peggy asks, "Are you allright?"

With paper lying on the coffee table, Dan points at the story and repeatedly taps his finger against the paper. He asks, "Didn't you see today's paper? Didn't you see the story about Afghanistan?"

Jerry says, "Yeah, I read the paper, but I didn't see anything about the war."

His discovery substantiates his long held suspicions and Dan is fuming. He picks up the newspaper, fans it in the air and says, "That's because they bury these things back on page 9. They're either hiding it, or they think nobody cares. Well I care. That's the guy we captured.

That's the same bunch that killed Paul and the others, he's still killing. Somebody's got to stop that guy."

Jerry reaches for the paper, and says, "Let me see that. I read the paper this morning. I guess I missed that item."

With a demented grin, Dan says, "Of course you missed it. They don't want you to see it, because our government is trying to suppress bad news relating to the war. It's the only explanation."

"Oh Danny," Peggy says, "The paper is full of bad news. There is no conspiracy."

"Don't be so sure, Mom. Anyway, that dude in the article, Amir Sadiq......whatever, he's the guy we captured at that hill. He's the reason they attacked our post. That creep is still killing people by the boat load and we're not doing anything about it."

Peggy kneels in front of Dan's wheelchair and she grasps his arms to try to calm the young man down. She gently holds his hand and says, "What do you mean, we? You're not in the Army anymore. There's no we. Let the Army do what they think is best."

Dan's mouth falls open, he says, "I can't believe you said that, Mom. You're just like everybody else in America. They don't care about the war. There's no homefront like there should be. I know I'm not in the Army anymore, but I'm still an American. I still care about what's going on over there and every person in this country should too."

The next morning Dan gets up before anyone else in the house. He wrestles with the front door, as he forces his wheelchair onto the porch. He is looking for the morning paper, but it is lying in the front yard. Unable to get down the steps, he has to squeeze his chair back inside the house, wheel out the back door and go around to the front yard to get the paper. He is anxious to see if there is more news about Afghanistan. After all of that, there is no follow up to the report of the massacre at Murzani in the paper. Undeterred, Dan turns on the old desktop computer he once used when he needed help with homework assignments. He searches the internet for more news about the band of killers in Murzani. However, he is unable to find any more details than those he learned in the newspaper account. Meanwhile, Jerry has stumbled into the kitchen and started a pot of coffee. The aroma of the brewing coffee persuades Dan to abandon his internet search and have a cup with his dad. Dan wheels into the kitchen to find Jerry sitting at the kitchen table. Jerry is engulfed in the sports page, scrutinizing the box score from yesterday's Cardinals game. During baseball season, it is an every day ritual that Jerry goes through prior to leaving for work. After a few minutes of drinking coffee and talking baseball with his dad, Dan hears his mom coming down the hall. Dan is eager to get to the gym. He asks, "Mom, can you take me to therapy a little early this morning?"

Peggy jockeys a jug of milk and some other things around in the refrigerator until she finds the carton of eggs. She says, "Sure Honey, did they change your appointment?"

"No, I just want to go in early and do some things on my own. I can do a lot of stuff without my trainer standing over me." The newspaper story has rekindled some of Dan's worst memories. He didn't sleep well last night, because thoughts of the Amir and the whole scene played in his mind over and over. Even with very little sleep, Dan is energized. He decides to rededicate himself to get even more out of his therapy. He is hypermotivated to do anything and everything he can to bring attention to the guys that doublecrossed his squad. The therapy sessions seem to be the only thing that makes him feel like he is accomplishing anything. Peggy scrambles some eggs and fries some bacon while Dan and Jerry talk at the table. She sets a plate in front of each of them. Dan's mind is racing with thoughts of Afghanistan. He is trying to imagine what is really going on over there. He has no faith that the news accounts are either accurate or complete. The last thing he is thinking about is eating, "Oh, none for me Mom, coffee's all I want."

"You'll need your strength, if you're going to do all that extra exercising," Jerry says, "Go ahead. You never ate this well in the Army."

Dan reigns in his emotions and tries to calm himself. He takes a deep breath and slowly exhales, "You're right about that." He takes a bite of bacon and says, "Thanks Mom."

Jerry eats quickly and leaves for work. Dan gives the paper one last glance as he finishes his plate. He spins his wheelchair out from under the table and his legs dangle around in pursuit of the chair. Like many times before, Dan knocks his knee against the table leg, but unlike all of those other times, he feels something. He feels a faint pain shooting from his knee and travelling up his leg. In his overagitated frame of mind, it may as well have been a sledge hammer banging against his kneecap. He shouts, "Mom, hey Mom, I felt something. I felt my knee hit the table leg."

Peggy is standing at the kitchen sink and peering out the window. She is watching the morning rays of sun filter through the oak trees that surround the house. She turns and runs over to Dan. She is trembling with joy, "You felt your knee? That's wonderful. Oh thank God."

Dan grasps the big wheels of his chair and he pushes back and forth. Using his wheelchair for propulsion, Dan swings his legs into the table again and again, trying to recreate the sensation. He asks, "What do you think it means, Mom?"

Peggy is standing beside her son with her hand on his back, "It means God hasn't forgotten about us. It means he is listening to our prayers."

Dan gets Peggy to drop him off at the physical therapy site with the agreement that she will pick him up for lunch in a couple of hours. Dan is working out with renewed vigor and determination. Although he is unable to replicate the sensation he felt at breakfast, he is ecstatic that that there is progress. He now has tangible evidence that there is light at the end of the tunnel. Upon returning for his regular afternoon session, Dan meets with his trainer, Brad Simpkins. Brad is a workout guru that sticks to a strict gluten free, vegan diet. Brad is thirty years old and has built a good business in Quincy. He studied kinesiology in college and had a promising football career curtailed by knee injuries. Brad really knows rehabilitation and Dan has a lot of respect for his opinion.

Brad is amused at Dan's exuberance. He says, "It looks like you've already put in a full day's work. Are you tryin to put everybody to shame around here?"

It is hard for Dan to suppress his excitement. With a broad smile that he has not shown since he got hurt, Dan says, "I've got good news. For the first time since my injury, there was feeling in my leg this morning."

Brad nods with approval, "Wow, that's exciting. What did you mean by feeling?"

"Well, I was sitting at the kitchen table and when I spun around to move, my knee knocked against the table leg. I felt a tingling pain run up my thigh and it went all the way to my back. My leg has hit that table before, lots of times, but this morning was the first time I could feel it. That was the best pain I ever felt."

The look on Brad's face indicates that the wheels are turning in his brain. He begins to analyze the situation, "Can you still feel it? Is the sensation still there?"

"No, I haven't been able to recreate the pain. My knee is turning black and blue from the beating I'm giving it, but I can't get that feeling back."

Brad puts his hands on Dan's legs and he squeezes and pushes in a few places. He does the same thing to a few places on Dan's back. After each probe, he asks, "Do you feel anything now?"

"No, I can't feel anything. What do you think?"

Brad sits down on a bench next to Dan's wheelchair. He rests his chin in his hand and considers the information he has gathered. He says, "It could be a sign of good things to come or it could be psychosomatic."

The highs and lows inside Dan's head are as volatile as ever. On one hand, he is buoyed that this may lead to his recovery, but on the other hand, he is still fearful that this is another in a long line of dead ends. He asks, "What do you mean by that?"

Brad is not one to mince words. He has been through seven knee surgeries and the ensuing rehabilitation that goes along with those operations. He knows a body can play tricks, especially when the patient has the internal pressure that Dan exhibits. He asks more questions, "Have you been overly emotional lately? Did something get you abnormally excited? If so, the extreme rush of emotion can trigger a false signal to your brain. Your brain may think the pain is real, even though it may not have existed."

Even though negative thoughts are swirling in his head, Dan fights the temptation to get deflated. He replies, "I've been pretty emotional since this happened, but last night, I read a newspaper article that got me real upset. It was about things in Afghanistan. But that didn't have anything to do with it. The pain was real. I know it was real."

Brad can sense that Dan is struggling to suppress his fears. He tries to put his client at ease by saying, "I think it may be progress. Stay positive because this is encouraging. Now, let's get to work."

By the end of the week, Dan is getting more and more feeling in his legs. He can feel everything that touches them, but he still can't move a muscle. Obviously, his nerves are coming back to life, even if his muscles are not. When he wakes up Sunday morning, he swings his legs over the edge of the bed like every morning. For some reason, his wheelchair is slightly beyond his reach. Without giving it a thought, he instinctively slides off the bed and takes a step toward the chair. He is walking. He has to stop in his tracks and look around to make sure he is not leaning against anything. When it sinks in, Dan is overcome with elation. He drops to his knees and throws his head backward to rest on his back. His eyes are closed, but they are aimed toward the heavens. He silently thanks God, before standing and flexing his knees to make sure he is not dreaming. His parents are still asleep, so Dan decides to surprise them. He walks up and down the hall, using his hands against the wall for balance while he gets used to walking again. He rolls his wheelchair into the kitchen and makes a pot of coffee. When he hears someone stirring down the hall, he quickly jumps back into his wheelchair. Peggy walks into the kitchen rubbing her eyes to get the sleep out. She lets out a big yawn, as she squints to get adjusted to the bright kitchen light. Feeling around the counter top for her glasses, Peggy gives Dan a smile then she sits at the kitchen table. She looks at Dan sitting near the table and says, "You're up early for a Sunday. Are you goin to Mass with us this mornin?"

Dan is having a hard time masking his absolute joy, but he wants to make this surprise dramatic. He ignores the question about church and says, "How about a cup of coffee?"

Peggy stretches her arms in the air and yawns. She says, "Yeah, I think I'll fix a cup." She begins to stand and says, "How about you, would you like some?"

"No, no, no, sit back down. I'll get it for you." Dan stands up out of the wheelchair and walks over to the cupboard. He looks back over his shoulder to see his mom's reaction.

Peggy's mouth opens at the sight of her son walking across the kitchen. She covers her face with both hands and cries. Her tears are streaming between her fingers and down her arms. She removes her glasses and wipes her eyes with the back of her hands. Even when she tries to compose herself, her wide eyes and gaping mouth show she is in shock. She springs from her chair to give Dan a hug. Unable to control her sobs, she has a hard time speaking, "Oh Danny, you're walking. Thank God." She takes a step over to the hall and yells, "Jerry! Jerry! Come in here, you gotta see this."

Jerry comes into the kitchen to find Dan standing next to Peggy. He says, "What's all the commotion about? I'm trying to brush my teeth."

Peggy runs over and grabs Jerry by the arm. She says, "Look at Dan, he's walking."

Jerry laughs and slaps Dan on the back and says, "Hey Danny, you're walkin." Jerry is smiling from ear to ear and tears fill his eyes. He says, "What do you say we go fishing to celebrate?"

"Nobody's going fishing until after Mass," Peggy says, "We have so much to be thankful for."

"Mom, I don't think I'm ready for Mass. It was a freak show before. If I go walking up there today, it could be chaos. I'll give thanks on my own, for now."

Peggy tears off some paper towels and wipes her face, "That's okay. But Father Donovan is going to be so happy. He'll want to see you real soon."

"I'll stop in and see him sometime during the week, when there are no big crowds around."

Peggy smiles and nods her head, "Yeah, he'd like that. I can't tell you how many times he's asked about you."

Dan hands his mom the cup of coffee and says, "I think I'll take a walk around the block. I need to give these legs a little more practice."

"Good idea," Peggy says, "I'm calling Katie. Jerry, you get ready for Mass."

Jerry shakes his head back and forth, "Oh no. If you call Katie now, you'll talk all morning. You get ready first then call Katie."

Dan takes his coffee with him on his walk. It is early Sunday morning and there is nobody outside. Dan walks down the street of the old neighborhood. He knows who lives in almost every house. He mowed the grass and did odd jobs for many of them when he was growing up. Almost all of his buddies are away at college or have moved away. There are lots of memories of riding bikes and playing football in those front yards. Even on this joyous occasion, his childhood memories are crowded out of his mind by the constant torment of the events in Afghanistan. He cannot shake them out of his head. His wounds are healed and he is walking again, so there are no more excuses. He has to find a way to avenge the deaths of Paul and the others who were killed that day at Geronimo.

While his folks are at church, Dan reads the Sunday paper from cover to cover. He's looking for more information about the war, but there is nothing there. There is half a page about the Chicago Bears' quarterback. Apparently, he has a sore pinkie and it would be catastrophic for the whole state of Illinois if he were required to have surgery.

There is half a page about a pro football team that does not play a game for another three months, but not a single word about the one hundred thousand men and women risking their lives to rid the world of some of the worst killers in Afghanistan. Perhaps, after ten years of war with no real progress, the American public has grown weary of the whole thing. Perhaps, the Army is at fault for not being aggressive and ending the war, like they should. Most likely, it is the politicians' fault, for imposing the ridiculous rules of engagement that hamper the Army's ability to defeat the insurgency. Who knows the reason, but the war is hidden from everyday life in America. Dan speculates about whether the American people would put pressure on the politicians to change their policies if they were more informed about the situation. He thinks to himself, "That's it. It's not that people don't care. They just don't know what's going on. Nobody really cares what some semi-famous tv personality eats for breakfast, but it's hammered into their heads morning, noon and night. It's on television and in magazines. You can't get away from it. If people were exposed to news about the war one-tenth as much as they are to celebrity gossip, they may see things like me." That might be his best way to help bring the Amir to justice.

When his folks get home from Mass, Peggy makes a picnic lunch. Katie comes over and the whole family loads up in the car for a little fishing trip to celebrate. Jerry knows a creek near the old farm house where he says the catfish practically jump onto the banks. He jokes, "We don't need any poles or bait. All we're gonna need is a catcher's mitt."

Ideas are running through Dan's head and he would like to run some of them by his folks, but he is not going to bring them up today. Katie lost her husband to the war and Dan knows she can use a break from his rants. His parents are so thrilled with his recovery he wants to avoid anything that will take the luster off of their day. Any mention of the plans he has would suck the joy out of the celebration. He feels like his family deserves a day to relax. After all, this whole ordeal has been hard on them, too. He is making a conscious effort to keep any wet blankets under wraps. Still, it is hard for Dan to let go, because he is anxious to get started on getting even.

It is one of those hot, humid summer days, but there is plenty of shade on the banks of the little creek. They all have a good time catching fish and enjoying the picnic lunch. Dan is more quiet than normal and his distant demeanor is cause for both Peggy and Katie to worry that Dan is a long way from well.

XIV

Monday morning Dan gets dressed in his only suit, he borrows his mom's car and drives downtown. He pulls into a parking lot and walks over to the newspaper building. It is a granite and glass structure that stands seven stories high. Engraved in the granite wall by the door is a sign that reads, "The Quincy Daily Monitor, Established in 1847, Edward Scott Greenbiar, Editor". Dan enters the building through one of the glass revolving doors. As busy people dressed in office attire rush to their appointed destinations, the marble floor sends sounds of shoe heels echoing throughout the cavernous lobby. There are small groups of people holding styrofoam coffee cups and briefcases huddled near the elevators, waiting for the next car. Others crisscross the lobby with determined expressions, paying no attention to Dan, whatsoever. These same people take these same steps every work day and yet, they seldom speak to one another. They are like ants with their heads down going about their business with robotic precision. Not knowing anyone, Dan is uneasy as he approaches the front desk. His throat is dry, so he covers his mouth with his hand and conducts a quick test of his vocal chords. He wants to make sure he sounds confident when he speaks to the receptionist. He stands at the desk and waits for the woman to get off of the phone. She presses a button and transfers a call, before looking up and saying, "May I help you, Sir?"

A cold chill descends upon Dan and he almost forgets what to say. He remembers the name on the sign by the door and he blurts out. "My name is Dan Greenbriar. I'd like to see Mr. Ross, please." The receptionist makes a funny face and Dan slaps his forehead with the palm of his hand. Realizing his mistake, he closes his eyes and looks upward, "No, wait, I'm sorry. Let me try again. I'm Dan Ross and I'd like to see Mr. Greenbriar."

The woman at the desk can tell Dan is nervous. She laughs and says, "Do you have an appointment, Sir?"

Dan shakes his head, "No, no appointment."

"May I ask who you are with? Do you have a card?"

Dan was not expecting these questions. He thinks for a moment then answers, "I used to be in the United States Army, but I'm not anymore. I'm here to help Mr. Greenbriar sell newspapers."

The woman is very adept at keeping people from bothering Mr. Greenbriar. She says, "If you have suggestions, you may go online to our 'Letters to the Editor' page. It's on our website."

Dan is not put off by her attempt to dissuade him. He explains, "Well, it's not really a suggestion. I'm more of a consultant."

The phone on her desk rings again. She holds up a finger to interrupt. After transferring another call, the receptionist says, "I'm sorry, Sir, but Mr. Greenbriar has a very busy schedule this morning."

Dan lifts his hand to his head and rests his forehead in his palm. He presses his thumb into one temple and he uses his fingers to caress the other. He says, "I really need to see him. Shall I make an appointment?"

The woman begins to feel sorry for him. She knows Mr. Greenbriar is not that busy. She says, "Hold on a moment, Sir. Let me ring that office. You may sit over in the waiting area, while I try to get a hold of someone."

Dan walks over to the waiting area, but he doesn't sit down. He paces back and forth, rehearsing his pitch beneath his breath. After a short time, another woman appears.

"Mr. Ross?" She says, "I'm Melanie Simms, Mr. Greenbriar's secretary, please come with me. Mr. Greenbriar will see you now."

Ms Simms leads Dan to the elevator. It is a quick ride to the seventh floor. She takes Dan right in to Greenbriar's office. Greenbriar is a tall thin man with a thick shock of white hair. He is around seventy years old and is quite distinguished looking. There are plaques hanging neatly on every wall, evidence of an illustrious career in journalism. The small area of wall space that is not dedicated to awards is adorned with colorful pieces of modern art. The office is not overly spacious, but there is room for a large desk and a sitting area with a couch and coffee table. Behind the desk is a big window overlooking downtown Quincy.

Greenbriar extends his hand toward Dan. He flashes a toothy smile and in a boisterous voice, he says, "Hi, I'm Ed Greenbriar. It's nice to meet you."

Dan clasps the tall man's hand and holds on for the ride as Greenbriar gives it a vigorous shake. Dan says, "I'm Dan Ross I'm pleased to meet you. Thank you so much for taking the time to see me, Mr. Greenbriar."

"Call me Ed. Now, how can I help you?"

Dan stands with his hands tightly clinched in fists and sweat is accumulating on his brow. He takes a deep breath and exhales all at once. He thinks he has come this far, so he may as well go for it, "I'm here to see about writing for your paper."

Greenbriar tilts his head to one side. It is obvious he is caught off guard by Dan's objective. His head sways back and forth, his shoulders lift and his palms open toward Dan, "The receptionist said something about helping us sell papers. I have no need for a new columnist, at least, not right now."

Dan knows that this is his only shot. He does not want to blow it. He counters, "Well, I'm not exactly a columnist. I just got back from Afghanistan and I believe your paper is doing a disservice to your readers by almost entirely ignoring the war."

"I thank you for your service, Dan. May I call you Dan?" Dan nods and Greenbriar pulls out a chair so Dan can take a seat in front of the big desk. Greenbriar walks around and sits in a brown leather chair. He says, "Like I said, I thank you for your service, but there is very little interest in the war among my readers."

Dan finds that hard to believe, he cocks his head and asks, "How do you know that?

Greenbriar spreads his arms apart and chuckles as he speaks, "Public opinion polls of course. Have you seen them? I can show you that the American people, by and large, are indifferent about the war and they certainly don't want to read about it."

Those facts are not as obvious to Dan, "I'm proof of the contrary. I was in a wheelchair for six weeks and people would go out of their way to express their gratitude. People may be tired of the reports of body counts and political policy, but they will never tire of the human aspect of war. You know, the soldiers' stories. If they are exposed to real stories of the men on the front lines, the men that don't know from one minute to the next whether or not they are going to be alive. That will awaken their emotions and they'll buy more papers."

The old editor leans back in his chair and silently ponders Dan's words. Dan can see Greenbriar's demeanor begin to change. The editor's instinctive doubt is overwhelmed by his curiosity. His eyes brighten and his creative juices, those that earned him a wall full of hardware, begin to flow. His initial aloofness gives way to his unlimited imagination. His buttoned down facade is replaced by an energized animation. He leans forward and rests his forearms on the desk. He is so excited that his butt is lifting out of his chair, and he says, "You might be on to something. Are you from Quincy?"

"I was born and raised here," Dan says, "I have a huge following at St. Anne's Catholic Church."

Greenbriar gets a captivated look in his eyes. He asks, "Hometown boy huh, how long were you in the Army?"

"Three years. I did two combat tours, but my second one was cut short. I was wounded and ended up with a medical discharge."

Greenbriar has always been more P.T. Barnum than Horace Greeley, so he starts thinking more like the huckster he is at heart and he begins to piece an angle together. He thinks to himself, "A hometown boy who happens to be a war hero, this could work." Greenbriar looks at Dan and says, "Where'd you go to school? Have you done any writing?"

Dan shakes his head, as he mulls the question. His eyes brighten and he replies, "I've taken my basic engineering classes at the community college near Ft. Polk and I took a speech class in high school. Writing newspaper articles can't be that much different than writing speeches."

The editor's roller coaster of emotions takes another drop. From his perspective he knows this guy has a compelling story, but he probably cannot write a lick. He says, "But the paper can't afford to take on another writer, especially a green cub."

Dan knows he has no credibilty as a writer, but Greenbriar is also a businessman. He makes a proposition, "You agreed to see me because I mentioned selling papers. I know your circulation is down. I walked around my neighborhood yesterday morning. Only about one house in eight had a paper out front. Maybe it's content that's costing you sales. I'll work for nothing. Just put my story on the front page, that's all I ask."

Greenbriar slumps down in his chair and throws a hand outward in disgust, "The front page? You've never written anything more than letters home and you want the front page?" The old editor straightens up in his chair and regains his stuffy façade. He says, "I'd have to bump one of my best writers for that space. That's not reasonable. I'd be a laughing stock. The whole town would think I'd gone crazy."

"Your best writers are running you out of business. Give me that space and you'll sell more papers. Just give me a try. I'll write an article for Sunday's paper. You'll have it by Thursday. If you like it, print it. If not, I'll go away, deal?"

Greenbriar's curiosity is clouding his better judgement. He can envision an entire promotion centered on Dan's war stories, but he refuses to allow his hopes to get too high. He really does not expect much and agreeing to this deal will get Dan out of his office. He stands up, extends his right hand and says, "It's a deal. Get me the story by Thursday morning and I'll let you know something by Thursday night."

After supper that night, Dan sits at the kitchen table with a pencil and a notebook. He feels a little bit ashamed that he did not tell Greenbriar his real motive, but he is afraid that would nix the whole deal. He knows his article has to be different. It has to show a new perspective. It needs to be an article that will stir the emotions of the readers and hopefully, compel them to action. He writes something and immediately scribbles through it. He stares into space for minutes at a time. He writes something else and quickly rips the page from the notebook. He crumples it into a ball and throws it in the direction of the kitchen waste basket. There are a dozen of the crumpled balls of paper scattered near the base of the waste basket, not to mention the heaping pile of those that made it inside. Peggy has been watching her son from the other room. She goes into the kitchen and asks, "Dan, are you having trouble getting started? Maybe if I show you some of the letters you sent home, maybe that will give you some ideas."

Although Dan is physically healed, his emotions are no less volatile than when he was confined to the wheelchair. He sits with his elbows on the table cradling his head in his hands. He stews in quiet anguish with his palms covering his ears. His palms slide down his cheeks and his contorted expression appears to be a byproduct of his inability to find a starting point. He says, "Problem is, I have too many ideas. Everytime I start writing, my mind keeps taking me back to the attack on the COP. I can't write about that. That's too much bitterness for this article. That's just gonna turn people off."

Peggy pours a glass of water and says, "I heard a writer say that he just starts writing anything that comes into his head and in no particular order. Then he goes back through it and picks out the things he likes and arranges them into a story."

That absurd notion draws a chuckle from Dan, "I guess that's one way to do it, but my mind's not right for this story. I think I need to put myself in Paul's shoes or Cuz' or Hambone's. Those guys were over there for all the right reasons. I never had any love for the Afghan people, but Paul and the others did. I was just putting in my time in order to get the GI Bill benefits. Paul and them were trying to make a difference. I need to write this from their point of view."

Peggy is glad to hear Dan speak in positive terms for a change. Finally, he is remembering he friends for what they were, not for how they died. She reasons that it is a sign that he can get beyond the hate. She smiles and says, "I think writing about your friends could be good for you. It could be therapeutic. It might be good for your soul."

Dan tries to explain his reasons for writing this article, "This isn't about my soul. This is about getting the public to realize what we're up against in Afghanistan. It's a call to action to get people fired up enough to demand a change in our policies."

"That's awfully ambitious for one kid from Quincy."

Jerry quits watching TV and he bolts into the kitchen. He says, "You know, Dan's right. This Country needs to get fired up. We've forgotten how to win a war. Ever since Harry Truman fired General MacArthur, we've become the whipping posts for the whole world. Politicians don't know how to run a war, they never did. We need to get back to good old fashioned hardball with these mickey mouse terrorists. This country used to lead. We used to stand for freedom and morality in the world. Now, instead of setting the bar high, we've lowered ourselves to the level of most third world countries. How is the world going to get better if we don't show them? You tell 'em that in your article."

Peggy grabs Jerry by the waist and pulls him back toward the den. She says, "Oh, now you got your dad going. He said the same thing about the Catholic Church when they quit saying the Mass in Latin."

Jerry momentarily retreats to the den. After hearing Peggy refer to the Church, he does an about face and returns for one last thing. He says, "Hey now that's really true. You've got to admit, there's nothing worse than a bunch of Catholics acting like holy rollers."

Peggy gives Jerry a playful shove, "Settle down, Jerry," Peggy says, "The world's changed. It's never going to be like that again. Just sit down and watch TV. Leave Dan alone so he can concentrate."

Dan works on the article until the wee hours of the morning. The subject matter is painful for him, but he knows he has to get it done. It is the only way to get back into the fight, for now. He spends the next two days fighting with that old computer until his article is typed to his satisfaction. He e-mails the article over to Greenbriar on

Thursday morning. He is on edge the whole day, wondering if Greenbriar will even bother to read it. He fears the old editor might write him off with all of the other crackpots who want to use newspapers for their bully pulpits. Dan is pacing back and forth. Peggy cannot help but notice that Dan walks the floor just like Jerry. She says, "Why don't you do something to take your mind off things?" Dan agrees that he needs to do something to pass the time. So he drives over to the gym for a workout. He returns home for lunch and the phone rings. The caller ID reads, "Quincy Monitor." He fumbles for the phone and almost drops the receiver, before composing himself enough to say, "Hello."

"Dan, this is Ed Greenbriar. I've decided to run your article in Sunday's paper."

Dan is both shocked and relieved. He leans his head back and looking toward the ceiling, he lets out a sigh, "No kidding, that's fabulous, thanks a lot."

"Everything in the story is true, right?"

"Oh, you bet it is."

"The writing is a little raw," Greenbriar says, "But that's how a soldier's story should be. We'll give it a try this week and go from there."

"You mean it's not permanent? You've been in the newspaper business for almost 50 years, can't you tell if a story is any good?"

"Sure, I know the story's good," the old editor says, "But, like you said, good stories are running me out of business. Let's see how the public reacts, that's all that matters. I'm going to have Melanie get your background information. We're going to run the story with you as a guest columnist. We'll print a little bio and really play up the hometown boy angle." Before hanging up, Greenbrair says, "I can't wait for Sunday's paper."

Dan concurs, "Neither can I."

XV

Sleeping Saturday night was an especially futile endeavor for Dan. His normal torment is supplemented by the anticipation of seeing his article printed on the front page of the paper. He gets up way before daylight and goes out on the front porch. Sitting in a wicker chair beneath a faint overhead light, Dan props his elbows on his knees and clutches the sides of his head with his hands. He stares down at the wooden porch planks. The paint is peeling from the edges of each plank and Dan is ashamed he has not been more help with things around the house. Dan thinks about Paul and the others getting cut down at the COP and he remembers those ANA soldiers bowing their heads to the Amir near the stockade. The visions make him shake and he is stricken with fear. He wonders if this whole thing is a waste of time. Dan realizes nothing can help his fallen squad members, but he needs to make those traitors pay. His only chance for a normal life is to make sure the Amir is dead. For Dan, there is much riding on this far fetched plan and doubt is creeping into his mind. What if the opinion polls are right? What if nobody reads the article? What if it does not work? Drops of sweat bead on his forehead and his fingers tremble. His moment of doubt is ended when he hears a car barreling around the corner. The headlight beams slice through the darkness and music is blaring from the car radio. A newspaper is hurled out of the car and it splats onto the yard. The paper is wrapped in a plastic bag and it slides over the grass, lifting a spray of morning dew into the air. Dan watches the paper come to rest near the foot of the steps and he springs to his feet and runs down to pick it up. Bolting through the front door, Dan cannot wait to unfold the paper and reassure himself that the article is actually there. When he spreads the paper out on the kitchen table, that lump reappears in his throat. Everything is just like Greenbriar promised. The article is front and center on page 1. There is a head shot photo and a brief biography that Dan thinks makes too much out of his military service. Before reading the article to make sure nothing was edited, Dan leans back in the kitchen chair and takes a deep breath. It's been a long two months for Dan, but this is a huge step and he hopes it works.

As the morning progresses, the phone will not stop ringing. Friends of Dan and his parents, some they have not heard from in years, are calling about the article in the paper. Jerry and Peggy spend a big part of the day fielding the calls and catching up with old friends. Dan is excited, but unsure what to think until he hears from Greenbriar. Finally, Monday morning arrives and Greenbriar calls Dan down to his office.

When Dan enters, Greenbriar jumps up from his desk and boxes Dan's shoulders with his large hands, he says, "You're a hit! Our e-mail account is overloaded with responses. Hell, there is so much, the damn thing shut down on us."

Dan is embarrassed by the attention from Greenbriar. He does not know how to act. With a thin smile, he asks, "Are the responses positive?"

The old editor slaps Dan on the back and laughs, "You got a lot to learn, son. Who cares if they're positive or not? The important thing is that they're responding. We ran an extra edition late yesterday and sold every copy. We're going to run the article again Wednesday, too."

"Does this mean I get the job?"

"I can do better than that, boy," Greenbriar says, "Before hard times hit the newspaper business, I worked at the Chicago Tribune for forty years. I still have a lot of connections. I think I can get your article syndicated into papers from coast to coast. We'll tear their hearts out. Not to mention, it will bring in money for you and the paper."

Money is the least of Dan's motives. He is not interested in profiting from the memories of the men he left behind. Still, he is excited that the article has piqued the public's interest and he is beginning to believe his strategy will work. He says, "That's better than I ever dreamed."

Greenbriar begins to treat his young protégé like a hired hand. He says, "Start writing another story for next Sunday. We'll let the readers know that it's coming."

True to his word, the old editor gets Dan's stories in some of the biggest papers in the Country. There are many businesses in Quincy that were so unhappy with results from their newspaper advertising they swore to never again buy space in the Monitor. However, seeing papers flying off of the racks has them lining up to get into the Sunday editions. Greenbriar is thrilled at the turn of events and Dan is developing a nation wide following of loyal readers. But after only a few short weeks, Dan is becoming discouraged. Sure, papers are selling and people are enjoying Dans's articles, but that is where it stops. The political pressure Dan had hoped to incite has not materialized. Dan makes another trip down to the newspaper office to express his frustrations to Greenbriar.

"I'm not writing to entertain people," Dan says, "I want to get them fired up. I want them to call their congressmen and demand more aggressive tactics against the Taliban in Afghanistan."

Greenbriar is taken aback by this new objective Dan has revealed. He spreads his arms displaying a wingspan stretches from one end of the desk to the other. He says, "I thought you wanted to sell newspapers."

"I want to inform people, I want to wake them up. I'd like to see a real homefront develop in support of our efforts to win the war. Where am I going wrong?"

The old editor leans back in his chair and he studies Dan face as though he is seeing it for the first time. After a long pause, he finally speaks, "It's your expectations, that's what's wrong. How do you know our Congress wants to win the war?"

Dan is floored by the notion that our own government does not want to win the war. He asks, "Why would they send 100,000 men and women into harm's way, not to mention the billions of dollars worth of aid and equipment, if they aren't committed to winning?"

Greenbriar explains, "Winning a war is a brutal and ugly process, some might even call it primitive. In order to win a war you can't contain the enemy, you have to kill them. You have to beat them into submission. Did you ever see the pictures of Germany or Japan at the end of World War II? Entire cities and I mean big cities were leveled by the relentless bombing. Civilians died by the tens of thousands. That's what winning a war looks like. In today's World, people are too sensitive for that. A politician gets a lot more flak for brutality than incompetence. If we unleashed the entire might of our military on a backward place like Afghanistan, our world image would take a beating. And image is all that matters to our politicians. Why do we get involved in wars we have no intention of winning? That's a good question. One reason is that the military industrial complex is a large part of our economy. If we don't use those weapons once in while, our economy will suffer. When the economy suffers, politicians lose their jobs."

Dan thinks back to what Paul said when asked about the motivation for the war. Paul said it was economic, too. Dan is beginning to believe Paul was right. All of that is enlightening, but the war is still raging and Dan clings to his hopes that the public can make a difference. He says, "Even if our government doesn't want to win, the American people do. We have to get a grass roots movement started. The public has to be tired of throwing away our young people's lives for nothing."

The old editor chooses his words carefully in an effort to show Dan the futility of his plan. He says, "You're touching these people, we know that from the feedback we've been getting. We have a mail room full of reaction to your articles. But if you do rally them to action, it will likely be to demand an end to our involvement in Afghanistan rather than an escalation."

Dan leans forward and slams his fist on the desk. He says, "That's the exact opposite of my intentions."

Greenbriar stares through the window behind his desk, he asks, "Did you ever read about the protests to the Vietnam War?" Without waiting for a reply, he spins back to face Dan, and says, "Those protests did eventually have an effect on our government's policies, but those were peace protests. People were burning city blocks in the name of peace. There was a draft back then. Guys were required by law to fight and in many cases, die for this Country. If there were a draft in effect today, you'd see the same things happening now, only I think it would be ten times worse. The American people have become used to an anything goes attitude. In other words, 'Do what you want as long as it doesn't bother me. You want to kill bad guys on the other side of the earth, go ahead, but don't force me into it. And don't smoke a cigarette within a five mile radius of me, because the second hand smoke can kill me.' Do you understand where they are coming from?"

Dan is starting to get the picture, "You mean that, since we have an all volunteer Army, the American people say 'To hell with those guys, they signed up for it'."

Greenbriar nods, "Unfortunately, that's pretty much right. In fact, we send these young men over to do a job. It's a lousy, ugly, dirty job that nobody else will do. We send them over there so we can work in our high rise towers and still sleep at night, even though these young men can't. When they return, we berate them as mentally ill and we use psychological tests to deny them opportunities for careers in fields like law enforcement. Jobs for which the veterans are infinitely more qualified than many who are currently working in that field."

"So, not only do they hate the war, but they also hate the warriors."

Greenbriar rubs his chin and says, "Hate's too strong of a word. Most Americans appreciate what our servicemen do. They'll buy them a drink at a bar or give them a big ovation at a ball game, but that's about the extent of their involvement. When it comes to their everyday lives, I would say most people tend to ignore the war and the warriors."

"Then I'll write about that."

"No, don't do that," Greenbriar says, "If you do, I won't print it. The American people embrace certain ideas, some of which they are not particularly proud. They would be very uncomfortable to be called out for those self centered attitudes. That's not your style anyway. You need to stick to the soldiers' stories."

Dan leaves the meeting even more discouraged than before. After talking with Greenbriar, Dan is convinced the American public is part of the problem rather than the key to his solution. He has been writing for about six weeks and he is running out of patience. Dan is still not sleeping well. The lingering torment from the events in Afghanistan continues to disrupt his every thought. He knows that the Amir and his band of cutthroats are still thriving. He is beginning to formulate a new plan and he is eager to give it a try.

A few days later, Dan makes another appointment with Greenbriar. Late one afternoon, he takes a seat across the desk from his boss. Dan does his writing from home, so Greenbriar is always glad to see his young protégé. The old editor is as effervescent as ever, as he crows, "How's my best guest columnist? Is there something on your mind?"

Dan refuses to abandon his climb to get back in the fight and this is the next rung on the ladder. As the two men take their usual seats on opposite sides of the desk, Dan fidgets in the chair before saying, "Yeah there is Ed, I have an idea and I'm wondering if you can help me out."

Greenbriar feigns as though he is in pain, he says, "I'm almost afraid to ask, but what is it?"

"You said you worked at the Chicago Tribune for forty years, right? You must have known all of the politicians in Chicago?"

"Yeah, I knew 'em. I knew 'em all." A light goes off in his head and Greenbriar is way ahead of Dan. He leaps to his feet and asks, "You're not thinkin of runnin for office, are you?" Without waiting for an answer, Greenbriar starts pacing in front of the window, "I can get you with the best people in the business. I know 'em all. You'd be a shoe in with your war record and all. We'll start with city council and work our way up. Why we can make you governor someday."

Dan stops listening to the old editor when he hears the words "war record". Those words echo in his head. Those two little words conjure up the circumstances of his discharge. His mind is instantly cluttered with painful images of the attack. He can picture Captain Craig pointing at the map with the unlit cigar. He can hear Craig's slow southern drawl saying, "Nobody shoots until I give the order." He remembers the two officers who visited him in the hospital. He gets the same hollow feeling in his stomach that he got when they informed him of the court martial. Dan shakes his head to clear his thoughts and get back on track. He says, "No, no Ed. I'm not running for anything. I couldn't be a politician. I'm just asking if you knew some of them."

Greenbriar slumps back down in his chair and says, "I'm sorry. I guess I got carried away for a second. Like I said, I knew 'em all. Some were good guys, some not so good. I thought it was the end of the world when I lost my job at the Trib, but I really don't miss some of the people in that town. Now, I got you and you're the hottest damn columnist in America."

Dan tilts his head to one side and asks, "So you must know some of the people in Washington now? Most members of the current administration are from Chicago."

"Sure, I know a lot of people at the White House including the President. What are you driving at?"

Dan leans forward and rests his arms on the desk. He looks straight into the old editor's eyes and says, "I want to go to Afghanistan as a war correspondent." Offering a false explanation that he hopes is convincing, Dan continues, "Everything I am writing about happened months ago. I want to get a fresh perspective."

Greenbriar leans back and places his finger tips against his temples. He says, "What are you talking about? You said yourself that those battlefield reports of body counts turn people off. What's changed your mind?"

Dan came prepared to sell the old editor on the idea. Borrowing some of Greenbriar's exuberance, Dan goes into his pitch, "I'll still write from the soldier's point of view. I'll still write the soldier's story. I just want to get closer to the action. I want to see if anything is changing."

Greenbriar stands and paces back and forth in front of the window and the panoramic view of downtown Quincy. He stops to take a look out over the city. With his back to Dan, the old editor gets introspective, "Dan, you've helped this paper a lot and you've helped me a lot. Not just by boosting our circulation and ad sales. Sure, you've done that, but you've done more. I was caught up in the decline of the newspaper industry. I was so worried about operating costs and dwindling revenues that I forgot what I loved about this business. I forgot about the excitement of putting out a good product, but you reminded me of that. All of my other writers are doing better because of you. We have all been revived by the honesty and simplicity of your stories. It's funny, I've been in this business for a long time and so has most of my staff. But it took a green cub for us to realize we needed to get back to basics." Greenbriar spins back toward Dan and says, "If you want to go to Afghanistan, I'll see what I can do."

Dan is pleased that Greenbriar has agreed to help. However, Dan feels guilty, once again, for misleading the old editor. He failed to reveal his true motive for going back to Afghanistan, and it weighs on him. Dan has lost interest in writing because it is not working. His new plan to return to Afghanistan as a war correspondent is only a cover for his ultimate objective. Once he gets over there with some freedom of movement, he plans to find the Amir, Nassir and the others.

Unencumbered by rules of engagement and other military parameters, he plans to carry out his revenge all by himself.

XVI

At home that evening, Peggy and Katie are returning from a shopping trip. Being seven months pregnant and carrying overloaded shopping bags makes a tight squeeze for Katie, as she enters through the kitchen door. Likewise, Peggy is right behind Katie and struggling with more bags. Jerry and Dan both jump up and run into the kitchen to help. They set all of the bags on the table and start peeking at the trappings. The whole family is getting excited about the impending birth. Peggy is converting Katie's old room into a nursery, because she will be babysitting when Katie is working.

Peggy wipes her brow with the back of her hand and says, "Jerry, did you and Dan eat anything? We were both starving, so we had to stop and eat."

"I can see why Katie couldn't wait," Jerry says, "She's eating for two, but what's your excuse?"

Before Peggy throws something at Jerry, Dan says, "Don't worry Mom, we ate. I made grilled cheese sandwiches and soup."

Peggy slouches and says, "Eating like that will give you flashbacks. Can I fix you something else?"

"No Mom, we're full."

Jerry pipes up, "Speak for yourself, son. Hey, what's in the box?"

Katie hands the box to Jerry and says, "Oh Dad, I forgot, this is for you. We got samples of cake for the baby shower. I brought them home for you to try out."

Jerry looks for a fork in a kitchen drawer and says, "Well, I'm glad somebody's looking out for the old man. Anybody else want some?" Nobody responds, so Jerry tears the top off of the box and he carries it over to the table. He sits down and takes a bite, "Hey, this is good. I hope you chose this one for the shower."

As Katie unloads some of the bags, she says, "We did, but you're not coming to the shower."

After another bite, Jerry says, "There's always the leftovers."

Dan sits down at the table next to Jerry and the girls show them what they bought. It was mostly baby stuff, but there were some groceries too. Peggy opens a cupboard to stash some of the canned goods and says, "Dan, we saw Carrie at the grocery store. She said to tell you hi."

"She seems like a nice girl, Dan," Katie says, "Why don't you ask her out?"

"I don't have time for girls. I have plans to take care of, first."

"You mean like finishing school," Jerry says, "The new semester starts in a couple of weeks. Did you get registered?"

"No Dad, I didn't."

Jerry wipes some frosting from his chin and says, "You can't work at that paper forever. There's no future in it. You have to finish school and get your engineering degree."

"I know, and I will," Dan says, "But there is one thing I have to do first."

"Before finishing school," Katie asks, "What's more important than that?"

"I have to get even with those butchers that killed my squad," Dan says, "It's the only way I'll ever have any peace. I haven't slept through the night in four months. If I don't do something, I'll go crazy."

Katie is disappointed to hear that her brother is still dwelling on the past. She tries to convince him to let it go, "Paul wouldn't be asking for revenge nor would any of the others. Let God punish those men his way. You have to move on. Besides, what can one man do? You're not in the Army anymore."

Dan leans back in the kitchen chair and spreads his arms apart, "That's the beauty of my plan. The Army's rules no longer apply to me. Now, I'm on the same playing field as the Taliban."

Jerry is not overly concerned because he cannot envision a scenario in which Dan would go back overseas. He says, "Except, they're half way around the world from here."

Dan looks at his dad and drops the bombshell, "If things work out, I'll be back in Afghanistan very soon. I'm going to be a war correspondent."

Peggy's mouth falls open. She drops a jar of pickles and it shatters on the floor. She says, "Oh Danny no, you can't, you almost died over there. Let someone else do it. You've done your part. I can't go through that again."

Dan leaps to his feet and starts cleaning up the mess, he says, "Oh Mom, you're stronger than all of us put together. I have a job to do and I'm going to do it."

Jerry leans back in his chair and stares at Dan, "You've been through a lot and we've been walking on egg shells trying not to upset you. Well, I'm through handling you with kid gloves. This is insane. What makes you think you can get those guys when the entire Army hasn't been able to. Now you go down tomorrow and get back in school. Get those crazy ideas out of your head and get down to business."

Dan drops some broken glass in the waste basket, he says, "That's just it, Dad, I can't get those ideas out of my mind. Don't you understand, they're haunting me, they won't go away."

Peggy clears off the table and takes a seat across from Jerry. She pleads, "Go see Father Donovan, Dan, he can help you. I know he can."

Katie chimes in, "Dan, you're my brother and I love you. This baby's already growing up without a dad. Please don't let him grow up without his uncle, too."

Dan smiles and says, "Don't worry Sis. I plan on playing baseball with that kid everyday, just as soon as he's big enough to swing a bat."

"What if it's a girl?"

Dan laughs, "Well, in that case, sis, you're on your own."

Katie is getting upset, "It's not funny, Dan, you can get killed over there and for what? Nothing, that's what. You seem to care more about the dead than the living. Don't you care about your family? Don't you know that you can't change the world."

"It'll change my world. This thing is eating me up inside. I'm at the end of my rope."

Katie lays her hand on Dan's back and says, "You're already crazy if you think killing a handful of men on the other side of the planet will make a difference. It won't. Can't you see? Nobody cares."

Dan turns away from his sister and replies, "Katie, you're just like everybody else in this country. You don't get it, do you? Those are the worst predators on earth. Killing a handful or even one, will save innocent lives."

"You're the one that doesn't get it," Katie says, "You're not doing this for Paul or anybody else. You're doing this for yourself. You're consumed with self pity and hate. Go ahead, go back over there and get yourself killed. It won't help the other guys, they've found their peace."

With no emotion in his voice, Dan says, "I'll get some of them."

"And die doing it. Don't you realize it will crush Mom and Dad?"

"I'm no good to anyone right now. I'm damaged goods."

Katie leans with her back against the counter, "You know, Paul always said you went in first in every fight. You were the first one through any doors or up any hills. Why is that? Do you have a screw loose, or somethin?"

"I did it because I didn't want this to happen. If anyone in my squad was gonna get it, it was gonna be me. I didn't want to come home alive and leave dead men behind."

Peggy sits at the table with her face buried in her hands. The tears dripping from her face are soaking into the table cloth. She is crying and speaking at the same time, "Give it some more time, Danny. You need more time. It's only been four months. Your legs healed, your mind will heal, too. You have to be patient. You're not an executioner. The Army didn't turn you into a killing machine. You're just a sensitive young man"

"Every day that Amir and his gang are on the loose, somebody dies. You may not know them, but they are dying and I have to help."

Jerry stands and begins pacing back and forth, silently taking in the conversation. Finally, he lets loose, "Dammit Dan, stop fooling yourself. You're not fooling any of us. This whole thing is about revenge, pure and simple. You don't care about how many people die over there. You never did until it was someone close to you. You can tell us that it's about stopping the killers, but we know it's all about getting even. I agree that you're damaged goods. You're eaten up with hate and that hate's gonna destroy you, if you don't shake it loose."

"That's right, Dad, and I'm gonna to shake it loose or die trying."

A few days later, after Dan and his folks have finished supper, Dan is at the kitchen table working on his next piece for the paper. Peggy and Jerry are in the front room watching TV when the doorbell rings. Peggy opens the door to find Father Donovan standing on the front porch. Peggy grabs the old priest's arm and leads him inside. She says, "Oh Father, thanks so much for coming over. Come in, come in. Hey Jerry, look who's here."

Jerry leaps out of his easy chair to greet the old priest, "Hello Father, how's the golf game? You still hittin em straight down the middle?"

The old priest takes jabs at Jerry whenever the opportunity arises, so he can't let this one go. His voice gets a little higher and his Irish brogue gets a little thicker, he says, "Well Jerry I tell ya, I haven't had too much time for golf lately. I've been too busy tryin to keep fellas like you on the straight and narrow."

The two men laugh as they shake hands. Peggy tilts her head toward the kitchen and gestures that direction, she whispers, "Dan's in the kitchen, he'd love to see you."

The three of them walk into the kitchen. "What would you like to drink, Father?" Jerry asks, "I've got your favorite, Old Bushmills."

Father Donovan holds up his hands and says, "No thanks, Jerry. Not right now. Coffee's fine, if ya got it. I'm kind of on duty." He walks over to the table and puts his hand on Dan's shoulder. He asks, "What are ya workin on, Danny?"

Dan knows the old priest did not drop by for a random social call and he knows his mom has everything to do with the visit. She has brought in a heavy hitter in a dire attempt to reason with Dan. Without looking up, Dan says, "My next story for the paper."

Father Donovan nods, "Ah yes, the paper, I've been readin your articles. They're terrific, but somethin doesn't add up."

"What is there to add up, they're just newspaper articles?"

The old priest pulls out a chair and sits down at the table. Peggy sets a cup of hot coffee in front of him and then she and Jerry return to the front room, leaving Dan alone with the old priest. "Well, I'll tell ya, Danny, those articles appear to written by a well adjusted, even tempered fella sharin his inner most thoughts with his readers. And now, your mother tells me you're thinkin about goin after the men that betrayed you. So which is it? The well adjusted veteran movin on with his life or the vengeful victim hell bent on gettin even?"

There is an awkward silence as the old priest leans back and takes a sip of hot coffee. Nobody ever accused Father Donovan of being tactful, but even Dan is startled by the full frontal attack. With his eyes fixed on Dan, the old priest waits for a response. His stare is one that Dan has seen before. It's been a few years, but when Father Donovan used to catch Dan and his friends skipping Sunday school to play basketball, Dan got that look then and it is as provocative as ever. It is a look that depicts disappointment, betrayal and anger, all emanating from deep inside the old priest's soul. It causes one to examine his own essence and immediately come clean. It is one of Father Donovan's most effective weapons and it is what makes him good at what he does. Dan has not forgotten the futility of lying to the old priest, so he figures to relate to him in biblical terms.

"It says in the Bible, an eye for an eye, a tooth for a tooth, doesn't it, Father?"

"It does indeed." The old priest counters, "That's in the Old Testament. It is part of the Mosaic Law. Those of us that follow Jesus Christ know that his teachins supersede some of the Mosaic laws. Jesus knew a little bit about betrayal, yet he taught us to turn the other cheek. I know in reality that is a very difficult thing to do. But to be completely out of the fray, as you are, and to travel half way around the world to exact your revenge, that is certainly goin out of your way to reject Christ's teachins. Don't attempt to use religion to justify revenge. That's what your enemy does. Revenge is just another name for justifiable hate. Justified in your mind, perhaps, but nobody else looks at it that way."

Without making eye contact, Dan says, "I know my mom asked you to do this, but it's not gonna help. All I want from you, Father, is to pray for my mom."

The old priest takes another sip of coffee, a little longer drink this time as he continues his appeal to the stubborn young man. "Sure Dan. I'll pray for your mom, but I'll be prayin for your soul, as well. It's your soul that needs the most help. What a man has to do in war is one thing, but to pursue this pigheaded plan is somethin else altogether. If you are successful in your quest, dependin on how it's accomplished, you may damage your own soul in the process."

Looking down at his notebook, Dan says, "I'm still young there is plenty of time to repent."

"Repentance does not eliminate the consequences. The road to salvation has many twists and turns, it's true. But if I were tryin to get there, I wouldn't start from where you are. Your head's in the wrong place. A man can be saved, but he still has to pay for his sins. If you are truly contrite, you may receive an indulgence, but I'm not sure that applies to willful transgressions. I'd hate to think of you wanderin the afterlife in Purgatory. It's a dreadful fate. I hope you think about what I've said and I hope you think about what you're puttin you're mom through." Father Donovan stands up and pats Dan on the back and yells into the front room, "Hey Jerry, I'll take you up on that Bushmills now."

Jerry and Peggy come running into the kitchen, Peggy asks, "Did you talk him out of it, Father?"

"No, not yet, but maybe I gave him a guilty conscience. I'm afraid he has a wee bit of Jerry's stubborn steak in him."

Jerry pours two glasses of the famous whiskey and hands one to the old priest. He smiles and says, "At least he gets it honest."

Father Donovan chuckles under his breath and nods in agreement, "Indeed he does." The two men walk into the front room talking and laughing. Peggy sits down at the table next to Dan. She lays her hand atop Dan's forearm. She gently squeezes his arm and sobs.

Dan has talked to Greenbriar a few times concerning the status of his request to go overseas. Greenbriar has assured Dan that the application is on track, but it takes time. About a week after the visit from Father Donovan, Dan gets a call from Greenbriar. The old editor requests a meeting with Dan at ten o'clock that same morning. Dan rushes down to the newspaper building and straight into Greenbriar's office.

"Come in, come in," The old editor says, "We've got good news."

Dan stands in front of the desk and asks, "You mean about my application. Did you hear from the White House?"

"You bet I did. Those guys are some of your biggest fans. They've been reading your stories in the Washington Post."

With his arms spread apart, Dan asks, "What did they say?"

"These things normally take a long time, but with your Army background and notoriety, it sailed right on through. I have your credentials and itinerary right here."

Dan falls back in a chair and says, "Wow, it has happened so fast."

"That's what you wanted, isn't it? You're not having second thoughts, are you?"

Dan shakes his head, "No, no, nothing like that. It just reminds me of the first time I was deployed. I always get a little nervous."

"That's adrenaline, boy. That's excitement," Greenbriar says, "Your about to do something few journalists ever get to do. Now, we have a laptop computer, digital camera, expense money and a credit card for you. If you need to buy something, put it on the card. That way we won't have to reimburse you. Oh how I envy you, boy. I wish I were forty years younger, I'd go with you."

"I'll bet you were something forty years ago."

"Yeah, back then we were hell on wheels. We were going after government corruption like crazy. But newspapers have changed. Do you know the government threw a guy in jail the other day, just because he made a video they didn't like. If that's not a political prisoner, I've never seen one. Oh, they said the video stirred up hard feelings in the Middle East, as if that legitimizes the subversion of our First Amendment. The sad thing is that nobody got mad. Not the press, not the movie industry not even the ACLU."

"I guess he didn't have many friends."

The old editor points his index finger straight at Dan and says, "That's where we come in. We are the friends of the friendless. We're the watchdogs. We should be exposing oppression and injustice, not sugar coating it. We have the power to make these people accountable. Go after 'em boy. I know your forte is the soldiers' stories, but keep your eyes open. If you see something they're hiding from us, let me know. I'll write the stories and I'll print 'em, too. I started out exposing government corruption and I want to go out that way. I guess I got lazy, but we have to get back to hard hitting journalism. No more of this cheerleading for the government. Let's print the facts and let the chips fall where they may."

XVII

Saturday morning, Dan stuffs everything he'll need into his sea bag. He mainly packs underwear and toiletries, although he has not been using his razor much. He has been letting his beard grow for a couple of weeks. The Army will supply uniforms for him to wear. Jerry and Peggy drive Dan down to Fort Polk, Louisiana. It's a long quiet drive. Nobody talks much. Each one feels they have said enough and there is no sense rehashing their arguments any further. It would add a bitter mood to the already melancholy parting. His parents are dead set against the trip, but they have made their peace and they are leaving it in God's hands, like they did when Dan was on his combat tours. The mood in the car is surreal. Any conversation purposefully omits Afghanistan. It is as though there is a seven hundred pound gorilla in the back seat and they all pretend it is not there. Jerry pulls up at the headquaters building and they say their goodbyes. Jerry helps his sobbing wife get back to the car. Peggy has lost all of her strength and she would collapse if not for Jerry holding her up. Once inside the car, they immediately start back for Quincy. Dan reports as scheduled. He sails through processing and briefings.

Ten days later, Dan is gazing at the Afghan countryside from a helicopter making its approach to FOB Apache. There is a soldier sitting across from Dan on the helicopter. The soldier stares at the mountains on the horizon and he motions toward them with his thumb. He looks at Dan and says, "This ought to be a real eye opener for a newspaper reporter. Why do want to do this anyway? You writing a book or somethin?"

Dan smiles but does not reply, instead he closes his eyes and his mind drifts back to the last time he was making this same approach. It was one of many stops on their journey to COP Geronimo. He pictures each of his friends, fully fettered by combat gear, anticipating their first taste of action. Their expressions exuded a poise and confidence that belied their ultimate vulnerability. They had a job to do and they were ready to do it. The pictures in his mind fast forward to the green on blue attack at Geronimo. He sees those same men falling amid the muzzle flashes. Dan winces and presses his fingers into his forehead. He slides his fingertips across his brow, hoping to wipe the disturbing images from his psyche. It is not a good thing for his mental state to retrace the footsteps he and his dead friends took together, but that is what is required and that is what he will do. In order to make the ruse look even better, he has submitted two articles chronicling his trip. He figures he owes Ed Greenbier something for all of the strings the old editor pulled and the readers might be interested in the sights and sounds one encounters when travelling into a war zone.

Forward Operating Base (FOB) Apache is like a small town. It is the hub of all military operations in Zabul, Province. There are metal buildings in all shapes and sizes. There are rows and rows of tents neatly assembled for living quarters. There are trucks, humvees and other vehicles lumbering through the FOB on a well planned grid of streets. There is an air field with a steady stream of incoming and outgoing helicopters. There are Afghan citizens walking along the road between the FOB and an adjacent city. Upon arrival at the FOB, Dan finds most of the officers are accomodating, but not overly friendly. He gets the feeling they would rather not have to wet nurse a civilian when they already have plenty on their plates. On the other hand, the enlisted men are more than happy to talk with Dan when the opportunities arise. Shortly after getting moved into the quarters the Army has designated for him, Dan is summoned to the Colonel's office. Dan is standing at the desk outside of the office when the Colonel hollers at Dan from behind his desk, "Come in Ross. It's good to see you again." Colonel Willis is about forty five years old. He is a big burly man. Commanding a battalion in a war zone requires an officer to wear many different hats and Willis handles it with apparent ease. He stands and reaches across his desk to shake hands. He says, "Please sit down. You're looking great. I'm glad you healed up so well."

Dan is a little surprised Colonel Willis is acting like a long lost friend. He asks, "Do you remember me, Colonel?"

The Colonel and Dan both take their seats. Colonel Willis leans back in his chair and says, "Well, honestly, there are a lot of sergeants in this battalion, but your face is familiar."

"You have a good memory, because, I think I only saw you three or four times and we never spoke."

Willis nods his head, "I do have a good memory." The Colonel sits upright and he scoots his chair closer to the desk. He says, "I'm going to cut to the chase, Ross. It's ironic the Army decided to send you back here, but that was their decision, not mine. Apparently, your work as a journalist made quite an impression on some people in high places. It must be very colorful. Unfortunately, I'm not familiar with that work. I am however, most familiar with your record as a soldier. It is quite colorful, also. Obviously, Captain Craig has substantially influenced your record. He has inserted quite a bit of his own commentary."

Dan speaks before the Colonel is finished, "Colonel, I can explain…"

Colonel Willis cuts Dan off in mid sentence, "There is no need to explain. I don't know what happened between you and Captain Craig and I don't care. I'm aware of the shortcomings of most of the officers in this battalion. I know Captain Craig has his deficiencies and for now, I am obliged to live with them. The one piece of advice I have for you, while you're embedded in this battalion, is to follow the rules. Don't be a cowboy. I don't see what trouble you can get into with a pencil and paper, but do your job and don't stir up any trouble. If you do that, we'll get along fine. Understood?"

Dan shrugs, "Sure Colonel, I understand."

Colonel Willis stands to signal the end of the meeting and Dan does the same. Before Dan leaves, Colonel Willis takes a step back and looks at Dan as though he is trying to size him up. After making an assessment, he discards the stuffy military protocol and says, "You know, it's funny, but you don't look like one of those soldier of fortune types. I can't understand why a guy like you would want to come back to this cluster. You should be back home chasin women and havin fun." The Colonel shakes his head, but does not expect an answer. He regains his military decorum and continues, "You're welcome to interview anybody here, as long as you don't interfere with their work. We'll send you out to COP Cochise in a couple of days. It's only about forty miles north of here. You'll get a little closer to the action. Good luck."

Dan stands up and reaches out to shake the Colonel's hand. He says, "Thank you, Sir."

Dan is given access to the entire FOB. He spends a lot of time talking with soldiers while they are eating. That's when they have time to talk and are relaxed enough to open up. Dan is really only going through the motions. This whole newspaper reporter thing did exactly what it was supposed to do. It got him within striking distance of the Taliban gang that includes Nassir and the Amir. Colonel Willis is right about one thing. Dan can't do too much damage with a pencil and paper. He has to get a hold of something a little more lethal. There is a company of Marines currently stationed at Apache for some rest and relaxation. That night after supper, Dan came upon a handful of the Marines playing poker. He noses around for a few minutes, before approaching a lance corporal holding the cards. Dan says, "Do you guys have room for another player?"

The Marines are sitting on the ground and the lance corporal is shuffling the deck getting ready to deal. He looks around at the other guys and they look uncomfortable. He says, "We aren't supposed to fraternize with Army personnel. Sometimes Devil Dogs don't get along too well with you guys, ya know? There could be too many fights and stuff."

Dan takes a seat between two of the young servicemen and says, "I'm not Army, I'm a newspaper reporter."

One of the other players' eyes light up, "Really? What paper are you from?"

Dan turns to the Marine and answers, "The Quincy Daily Monitor."

The soldier wrinkles his nose and asks, "Where's Quincy?"

"It's in Illinois right on the Mississippi River. Where are you guys from?"

The same Marine says, "We're all from Texas, except for Jason. He's from Oregon."

Dan looks at Jason and asks, "How'd a guy from Oregon get hooked up with all these Texans?"

Jason shoves the guy next to him and says, "I was looking for an easy game and I found these pigeons from Texas. After all, we're supposed to be relaxing and I don't want to tax my superior intellect any more than I have to."

The other Marines hiss and return the taunting. The lance corporal asks, "If we let you play, will we be in your paper?"

"You can, but only if you want to be. Have you guys been anywhere near Murzani. It's about 90 miles south of here."

The last of the Marines in the game answers, "We know where it is, but that's all Army down there. We've been patrolling along the border with Pakistan. mainly in those mountains east of here."

"Have you seen many insurgents around there?"

The Marines exchange glances with one another and one says, "We've seen some."

Fishing for any information he can get, Dan asks, "Have any of them said anything about Murzani?" The Marines all shake their heads, but none offers a reply. Dan gets the idea that any insurgents these guys come across do not get the opportunity to talk. These guys are not out there to take prisoners. The lance corporal deals Dan in and over the next hour, Dan proceeds to win about two hundred dollars from the four Leathernecks. Dan gathers his winnings. He stands up to leave and says, "I can see why you don't play cards with Army guys, because you'd be broke all the time."

The four losers stand up and the lance corporal says, "You're not going anywhere, buddy. Not until we have a chance to get our money back." The Marines encircle Dan and each one steps in to tighten the noose.

Dan raises his hands, "Hold on there guys, I don't want your money. In fact, I have a deal for you. I'll give you back the two hundred dollars I won, plus I'll throw in another forty, if you can get me a K-bar."

The Marines look at each other and nod in agreement. One of the Devil Dogs reaches into his combat boot and pulls out a knife. Holding the K-bar by the handle, he menacingly extends his hand toward Dan. The blade is only inches away from his chest. Dan swallows hard and thinks about taking a step back, but he holds his ground and the Marine flips the knife into the air and catches it by the blade. He hands the knife, handle first, to Dan, "Do you need the sheath, too?

Dan says, "Why not?" He hands over the money and slips the K-bar in the sheath. He says, "It was nice doing business with you." He takes a few steps toward his quarters.

The Marine that was excited that Dan was a reporter asks, "Is this going to be in the papers?"

Dan looks back and says, "I don't think so. Good luck to you guys."

The next morning at breakfast, Dan sees some recognizable faces among his old battalion. However, he is unable to recall any of their names. While they are in the mess line, Dan strikes up a conversation with a staff sergeant from the company that is stationed at the FOB. The soldier is behind Dan in the line and Dan turns and says, "You look familiar, but I can't remember your name."

"It's Cody Bruce, I think I remember you, too. You were a staff sergeant, weren't you?"

"That's right. I'm Dan Ross. I was in Bravo Company."

The soldier shoves his tray toward a server. "Now you're a newspaper man. How'd you get out so quickly?"

It would not serve his purpose to rehash the whole ordeal, so Dan says, "It's a long story, but I'm here to write about you guys. I try to give the readers a look at this war through your eyes."

Bruce looks down at his tray, purses his lips and wrinkles his nose. He says, "Be sure and write about this slop they're feeding us. I'm not even sure what some of this is." The server gives him a glare.

Dan wags his head back and forth, "Some things never change." He remembers the cooks that came out of the mess tents firing at the ANA during the attack at Geronimo. He realizes the cooks do not deliberately make the food so unappetizing. He says, "But they do the best they can with what they have to work with." The two men sit down at a vacant table and talk while they eat. Dan asks, "Do you hear anything from Bravo Company?"

Above the clamor of soldiers talking and dishes clanging, Bruce answers, "Sure, we relieved them about a month ago. They got a two week break for R&R here at Apache and we went down to Geronimo to fill in."

"Did they ever finish that place?"

Bruce nods his head and swallows, "Oh yeah, Geronimo is like a fortress. They had a bad attack back in the spring. Some guys got killed, so they built that place up solid. There's still sniper fire once in a while. But that's everywhere you go around here."

Dan takes a sip of coffee and asks, "Did you go out on any patrols when you were at Geronimo?"

Bruce wipes his mouth with a napkin and says, "That's all we did. That's gotta be the most desolate place on Earth. It's pretty dangerous down there, too. Those Hajis are getting bolder than ever. One night, they got close enough to launch rockets at us. It only lasted a couple of minutes and they missed us by a hundred yards, but they're thick out there."

"What about that town in the valley, Murzani?"

Bruce shrugs, "What about it?"

"Did you go there? Did you see any Taliban near there?"

"Oh, I don't know," Bruce says, "We didn't even go into the valley. The valley was off limits and that included the town, too. We got as far as the pass, but that was the end of the line for us. We didn't encounter any Talibs that we know of, just some farmers and some children."

Dan wraps both hands around his coffee cup and stares into the distance for a moment. He says, "I have a feeling the town is where most of the Talibs hide out in the whole sector. Why wouldn't they go check it out?"

Sergeant Bruce takes a bite of the mystery entrée and says, "They told us there are too many civilians living in the valley. They don't want us in there unless there's confirmation of a build up of insurgents."

Dan is soaking up as much as he can about Geronimo and Murzani.He fires off another question, "Are they still trucking supplies to Geronimo from here?"

Bruce pauses and looks at Dan, "You sure know a lot about Geronimo."

"I'm a newspaper man. It's my business to know."

Bruce pushes his plate forward and throws his paper napkin on top. He leans back in his chair and grins, "Oh that's right. I almost forgot you're a reporter. Yeah they're still making runs down there. The National Guard units are running the trucks. I'm not sure, but I think they are making two or three runs a week to Geronimo."

Dan scarfs down the rest of his breakfast and stands to leave. He reaches out to shake hands with Bruce and says, "It was nice seeing you again."

"Are you done? You're leaving already? But you didn't ask anything about me?"

Dan tosses his napkin on his tray and begins looking for a trash can. He says, "Oh that's right. Where are you from?"

Bruce crows, "I'm from Richmond... Richmond, Virginia." Next he stands up and hollers toward the fleeting reporter, "Are you going to put me in the newspaper?"

"You bet I will," Dan says. Looking back at the soldier and tapping on his own head, Dan says, "I got it all right here. See you around."

From his chat with Sergeant Bruce, Dan learned there are still trucks going back and forth to Geronimo. Further, he has learned Bravo Company is still stationed there. Dan steps out of the mess hall to search for the Quartermaster's area. That is where he can get information on the supply trucks going to Geronimo. As he is looking around, six large helicopters fly over his head. Their engines emit a deafening noise and their rotors make the ground shake. Dans's teeth are vibrating as the choppers make their approach. Thinking they are bringing supplies to the FOB, Dan is puzzled to see about thirty fully equipped soldiers getting out of each helicopter. He wonders if they are reinforcements or if they are just getting some R&R like the Marines he ran into last night. He sees a large metal building with some trucks parked nearby. Upon entering the building, Dan realizes it is a warehouse.

Soldiers are zipping around on forklifts loading pallets of supplies onto trucks. There are groups of men and women sorting supplies and allocating the proper amount for each truck. There are large roll up doors on opposite sides of the building. It looks as though they bring in pallets from one side, sort the supplies onto other pallets and load the sorted supplies onto the outgoing trucks. At first glance the operation appears chaotic, but upon further examination, the system works like a well oiled machine. Over in the corner near the back of the warehouse, there is a desk with large dry erase boards hanging on the walls. Schedules and other pertinent shipping information are listed on the boards. Sitting behind the desk with her head propped up by one arm, a female soldier is manning the shipping desk. Her cheek is cradled by her palm and she stares at the operations as though she is in a trance. Since she doesn't look overly busy, Dan figures he will start with her. He flashes his credentials and says, "Hello Corporal. I'm Dan Ross. I write for the Quincy Daily Monitor and you are?"

The Corporal quickly snaps out of her trance and she stands to greet the visitor. She says, "I'm Alexis Ponder, but everybody calls me Lexie."

She looks to be in her mid twenties. She has short blonde hair flowing from beneath her hat, but it is cropped well short of her shoulders. She is blessed with an attractive full figure that is apparent despite the unflattering fatigues she is wearing.

Dan says, "Do you have time to help me with my newspaper article?"

"Why would a newspaper man want to talk to supply personnel? Won't that be kind of boring for your readers? What's the matter, did all of the infantry guys give you the cold shoulder?"

Dan walks behind the desk and scans the information written on the dry erase boards. While closely examining the shipping boards, Dan stands with his back to Lexie and says, "A famous general once said that an army moves on its stomach. I thought I'd get a first hand look at the logistics involved in keeping an army in the field."

She gives Dan the once over and likes what she sees, "I'm not sure how I can help you, but I guess I'll do what I can."

Dan turns to face Lexie. He says, "How big of an area do you supply from this FOB?"

At first, she is unsure that she should be sharing her knowledge with Dan. In a tentative voice, she says, "We supply four COPs. COP stands for combat outpost. They are all to the south and east of us." She walks over to a map that is posted to the wall. She slides her finger over the map and says, "You see how they are all spread out in the foothills bordering this mountain range. Most of the enemy is holed up in those mountains."

Dan takes special note of the word enemy. He asks, "When you say enemy, do you mean Taliban?"

She smirks, "I guess they're Taliban. They all look the same to me."

Dan smiles and asks, "Do you supply COP Geronimo?"

Still a little wary, Lexie asks, "Are you sure this is for a newspaper?" She shakes her head with disbelief and decides to answer,

"Geronimo is the farthest we go to the south. It's about ninety miles and it's not an easy trip."

"It sounds like you've made that run before. Are you a truck driver?"

"I fill in when needed," Lexie says, "But I don't like that trip to Geronimo."

"Why not?"

"The roads are bad and we almost always get shot at," she says, "It's pretty rough down there."

Dan leans against the desk and asks, "You must have security escorts on that run?"

"We do. We also stagger the times, so we won't be too predictable. And we started making some of the runs at night."

Dan tilts his head and says, "At night? What about IEDs? You can't see those at night."

Lexie sits back down in her chair. She props one of her boots against the edge of the desk and pushes with her foot to rock back and forth in her chair. She lets her guard down and speaks freely, "Oh hell, we can't see IEDs in the daytime, so that doesn't matter. It's really only the last four miles that are bad. After we turn off of the main road, those last four miles really suck. There are so many holes from rockets and mortars, it gets real bumpy. We have to go real slow to keep from blowing tires. It makes us an easy target."

Dan gets close to the map and points. He asks, "If you stay on this main road and don't turn off those last four miles, it will take you up to the town of Murzani, right?"

"That's right. I think it's about five miles to the mountain pass and a few more through the valley to get to Murzani," the corporal says, "But we only go to Geronimo."

Dan turns from the map and asks, "When is the next convoy to Geronimo?"

Lexie fumbles through some clipboards on the desk and picks one up. She reads a little while and says, "Let's see here…Geronimo….Geronimo…, here it is. There is one going out tomorrow night at nineteen hundred. That's seven o'clock. It won't get into Geronimo until well after dark."

"Are you loading those trucks now?"

She looks out over the warehouse and says, "Yeah, I think we are." The corporal points across the warehouse. "You see those trucks over there? That's the Geronimo convoy. There are four trucks plus security."

Dan has found out exactly what he needs. He takes a step toward the exit and says, "Hey Lexie, where are you from?"

"Warrensburg, Missouri.

"That's not far from Kansas City, is it?"

"Not far. I know where Quincy is, too. My mom's from there."

"No kiddin? Hey, thanks for your time, Lexie. You've been a big help. Good luck the rest of your deployment."

Lexie stands up and walks alongside Dan toward the door. She asks, "Don't you have a note pad or somethin? You haven't written anything down." Dan ignores the question. Lexie keeps walking and says, "You're kind of young to be a newspaper man. Hey, if you're not doing anything later on, I get off at six. Maybe we could hang out. I have some wine stashed in my bunk."

Dan says, "Are you always this timid?"

Lexie doesn't get the sarcasm at first, but then it hits her. She says, "Oh you mean I talk a lot. Yeah, everybody tells me that."

Dan stops just short of the door and says, "It's not how much you talk, it's that you are so plain spoken."

Lexie looks down, rubs the back of her neck and looks at Dan through the tops of her eyes, "Well, I've always figured that if you want something, it never hurts to ask."

Dan reaches for the doorknob and nods, "Maybe, I'll see you tonight. It depends on how things go today. It's been a pleasure meeting you. I'll talk to you later." Dan has found transportation going close to Murzani. All he has to do now is figure out how to get on one of those trucks.

After talking with Lexie, Dan steps out of the warehouse to find an entire company of soldiers filing by him. Upon closer inspection, Dan can tell these guys are not part of the 10th Mountain Division. The patches on their sleeves indicate they are air cavalry. They are the guys that came in on the helicopters earlier in the day. He wonders what an air cavalry troop is doing at FOB Apache. He watches intently as the troopers make their way to some tents that will be their temporary living quarters. As Dan walks near the main entrance, he is drawn to the activity outside the PX. Apparently, the Afghan population is allowed to shop at the store. Quite a few of the townspeople are hanging around and visiting with each other. Dan sees this as an opportunity to get his hands on some native clothing. His beard has been growing for nearly a month and with some authentic attire, Dan thinks he may be able to pass for an Afghan from a distance. There is an older looking man with a little boy coming out of the store. Dan nods his head in the direction of the older man and says, "Hello."

The Afghan man smiles and says, "Hello."

The man seems friendly enough, so Dan gets in front of them to get their attention. He says, "I wonder if you can help me out?"

The man shakes his head and says, "No, no English."

The boy appears to be about eleven years old. He says, "My grandfather does not speak English, but I do."

Dan shrugs his shoulders and holds his hand out toward the old man, "But he said hello?"

The boy says, "That is the only word he knows. He speaks to all of the soldiers, he is a friend to them."

Dan nods and smiles, "I'm a news reporter and I need some help. Do you live near here?"

The boy points down the road and says, "Yes, we live in the town. You are a soldier, no?"

Dan explains, "I wear the same uniform, but I am a newspaperman." He turns his shoulder to the girl and lifts his collar, "See, no stripes. I am writing about the war. Do you think you're grandfather might have some old clothes that he doesn't wear anymore. I will buy them. If he has some old things, I will pay for them."

The boy and the older man talk among themselves. After some back and forth banter that sounds like jibberish to Dan, he asks, "American money?"

"Sure, that's all I have."
The boy asks, "What clothes do you want?"

Dan looks around at the men standing nearby and says, "I guess, one of those onesie outfits. Kind of like your grandfather is wearing, now. And maybe one of those caps, like all of the men are wearing."

He tilts her head and asks, "What is cap?"

Dan pats the top of his head and says, "Like a hat, you know?" He nods, "Yes, hat. I understand."

There is more banter between the boy and the old man. The old man smiles and bows his head to Dan. The boy looks at Dan and says, "Thirty American dollars."

Dan reaches into his pocket and pulls out the money. As soon as the old man sees the money, he quickly removes his hat and outer garment and hands them to Dan. He is wearing tighter fitting clothes beneath the onesie. Dan hands the old man the money. The old man's eyes light up and he laughs as though he got the better end of the deal. He walks toward the gate with an added spring in his step. Dan hollers at the boy as she walks beside his grandfather, "Hey." He turns and looks back, wondering if Dan is upset. Dan motions for him to come back. He turns away from the old man and takes a few steps toward Dan. Once again, Dan reaches into his pocket. This time he pulls out a five dollar bill and he puts it in the boy's hand. "This is for you." The boy smiles and runs to catch up with the old man.

XVIII

Dan returns to his quarters to stash the clothes. He figures he may need to blend in with the locals at some point. He has grown a scruffy beard and now he has some native clothing. Dan keeps thinking about that outfit of air calvary that came in today. He would like to find out why they are here. It's almost lunch time. He decides to hang around near the mess tent and strike up a conversation with some members of the air calvary unit. On his way over to the mess hall, a runner from Colonel Willis catches up with Dan.

"Mr. Ross," The soldier says, "I've been looking all over for you. The Colonel would like to see you right away."

Dan really wants to talk with some of the air cavalry, but he better not get on the bad side of the Colonel. He answers, "Oh, uh sure thing. I'll go right over."

Dan goes into headquarters and once again, Colonel Willis hollers for him go right on in.

"How's the newspaper business?"

Dan figures he better act like a reporter. He says, "Everyone is very nice. I'm getting lots of material," Dan says.

Willis chuckles and says, "Nothing top secret, I hope." The Colonel laughs a little more and says, "Just kidding. That's good you're getting some stories. I'm always glad to give the folks back home an idea of what's going on over here. Look Ross, there is a convoy of trucks running up to COP Cochise the day after tomorrow. You're welcome to go along. It'll give you a chance to get some front line stories. You can go out on patrols or whatever you want. We'll get you back in a couple of weeks. That will be in plenty of time to catch your flight back home."

Again, Dan acts excited, "Thanks Colonel. I appreciate your accommodating me this way." Without missing a beat, Dan asks, "May I ask what the company of air cavalry is doing here?"

The Colonel who had been looking at a schedule on his desk, looks up and glares at Dan. He snaps, "You may ask, but I'm not answering. That information is classified. Don't ask any of the troopers, either. They have been ordered to keep their mission secret. Is that clear enough for you?"

Dan acts like it was nothing, "Oh yeah, I was just curious. I'm looking forward to getting up to Cochise."

Willis is not convinced by Dan's indifference, but he lets it go, for now. He says, "That's all I have for you, Ross. Good luck on your trip."

Dan says, "Thank you Colonel."

Dan leaves the headquarters building and heads back toward his quarters. As he walks across the FOB, he cannot help trying to put the pieces together. One thing is certain, he knows he cannot go out to COP Cochise. That is forty miles to the north and it is also the opposite direction of where he needs to go. Dan gets the feeling that Colonel Willis is trying to keep him away from any real action. The way Colonel Willis got so defensive about the Air Cavalry really has Dan thinking. He is sure that something is up and he needs to find out what it is. He knows Colonel Willis has people watching him and he cannot be seen talking to any of the air cav guys. After hanging out in his room and going through the motions of writing an article, Dan gets an idea. He can probably manage to run into one of those guys over by the latrines. Nobody pays too much attention to the comings and goings over there. He might even be able to get a trooper singled out, so he'd be more apt to talk. His plan works out. Dan is washing his hands outside the latrines, when a young trooper begins doing the same thing next to him. Dan asks, "You're air cavalry aren't you?"

The trooper says, "Yeah, we just got in today. We'll be doing some training out of this base for a few days. You infantry?"

Dan shakes his head, "No, I'm with the Quincy Daily Monitor. My name is Ross, Dan Ross."

The trooper dries his hands. He examines Dan's sleeves and realizes there is no indication of a rank. He asks, "You're with the press?"

"That's right. I write for a newspaper in Illinois. My readers would be really like to know how things are going for you guys."

"Man, you could have fooled me, I thought sure you were a soldier, for sure. But, I can't say anything about our training, especially to the press."

195

Dan is not giving up. He knows he will have to build some rapport, if he is ever going to get anything out of the trooper. He asks, "What's your name and where are you from?"

The two men walk a few steps away from the latrine area. The young trooper says, "I'm Ryan Phillips and I'm from Akron, Ohio. Hey what do you guys do for fun around here?"

"I've seen some guys playing cards, but other than that I don't really know."

The young trooper gets an annoyed look on his face, his shoulders slouch and he hangs his head. He says, "I'm too broke to play cards. I should have known they'd send us to a swingin' place like this before our mission."

"What were you expecting, a Caribbean resort?" Dan remembers Lexie over at the quartermaster corps, maybe she has a friend. "I might be able to help you out, that is, if you help me out. How long has it been since you spent an evening with a beautiful and talkative young lady?" Dan may be over selling a little, but he needs to get the trooper's attention.

The trooper rolls his eyes and says, "Too long."

Dan grabs the trooper by the sleeve and pulls him off the beaten path. He says, "Well, I happen to know a girl who is free tonight."

The trooper takes a step back and turns his face to one side, while continuing to make eye contact with Dan. He questions the thought, "Girls, out here? You mean female soldiers, don't you?"

"I mean a lonely girl a long way from home. What about it, Ryan? All I need to know is a few details about your mission."

The trooper cradles his chin with his hand and says, "I got a buddy. Can you fix him up too?"

"No problem. Just give me somethin, anything you can think of. I'm not puttin this in the paper. This is for me, personally." Ryan turns back toward the latrine area and his voice gets softer, he says, "You sure it's not going in the paper?"

"I'm sure." Dan nods.

"Well, all I know is we're participating in a joint operation with some infantry. We're supposed to be raiding a Taliban camp. It goes down in four days."

"Do you know where?"

Ryan shakes his head and says, "Some valley near a town named Murzani."

Dan's head snaps toward the trooper. He whispers, "Murzani, are you sure?"

"Yeah, I'm sure. There's supposed to be a mountain stronghold with two or three hundred insurgents down there."

"What else do you know?"

"That's all I know. I swear, now what about the girls?"

Dan is satisfied with the details. He says, "Meet me outside the quartermaster's warehouse at six o'clock."

The trooper gets loud and complains, "Don't tell me they're truck drivers?"

"Shhh,shhh,shhh." Dan holds his finger to his lips, trying to quiet the young trooper down. Dan pats Ryan on the back and says, "Remember, this isn't the Bahamas." Dan starts walking away. He turns back to Ryan and says, "And if you don't treat them right, they'll kick your ass."

Dan gets over to the warehouse a few minutes before six. When he sees the two troopers approaching, Dan goes inside to find Lexie.

Lexie sees Dan enter the building, she steps around the desk and hollers, "Hey newspaper man, I didn't expect you to show up." Dan looks over in her direction and says, "You didn't make other plans, did you?"

Lexie laughs, "No, no other plans."

Dan walks over to the desk and lowers his voice, "Hey uh, Lexie, uh I got this buddy with me uh, you wouldn't happen to have a friend for him, would you?"

She holds three fingers over her lips and thinks for a moment, before answering, "Maybe, yeah, I guess I can get Amber to come along."

Dan's conscience gets the best of him. He decides to come clean. He rubs the back of his neck and looks down at the floor, he says, "Lexie, the guy is not my buddy and I'm not planning on going with you. I promised these two troopers, I'd fix them up with dates. They are waiting outside."

Lexie starts laughing and says, "Damn, and you're the best looking civilian I've seen in nine months."

With a deadpan expression, Dan counters, "I'm probably the only civilian you've seen in nine months."

"That's true," Lexie says, "But you're still hot and I was hoping to get in your pants tonight." Under different circumstances, Dan would not be opposed to such an encounter, but he has to stick to the deal. Besides he knows she is just kidding. Lexie continues, "Well, maybe those guys will be OK. We'll go eat with em and check em out. I'll let you off the hook this time, but you owe me one."

Dan drops his hand on her shoulder and says, "Thanks a lot. I do owe you one."

XIX

The puzzle is beginning to come together in Dan's mind. They must have found the Taliban camp in the valley. The Air Cavalry is going to support Bravo Company in the raid and it happens in four days. That means Dan has to get to Murzani ahead of the raid. Otherwise, the Taliban may be so scattered out, it will be impossible for Dan to find the Amir and Nassir.

The next evening, as seven o'clock is rapidly approaching, Dan packs a shoulder bag with his Afghan clothes and two filled canteens. He slips his K-bar in his boot and he leaves everything else behind. He leaves his laptop, his cell phone, everything. He can't risk being traced by his cell phone signal and all of those other things won't help him on his quest. He heads over to the warehouse. He notices the Geronimo convoy trucks have been lined up outside. He lurks around the edge of a building waiting for the right time to make his move. He observes the guardsmen pulling down the roll up doors. Immediately after the doors are secured, he watches a stream of warehouse workers file out of the building. Lexie is among the soldiers exiting the building. She is easy to spot, because she is talking the leg off of a soldier as they fan out across the post. After the soldiers have dispersed, Dan ducks behind the lead truck in the Geronimo convoy. He proceeds to sneak around to the back of the last truck in line. He takes a quick glance to see if anyone is watching, then he jumps into the back of the truck. He crawls over the top of the supplies and restacks the boxes until he has created enough space to ride without being seen. All he can do now is wait and hope he is on the right truck. If it leaves at seven o'clock it should be going to Geronimo. Everything is falling in place, so far. He cannot help but think about his family and everyone else back home. He smiles at the thought of his mom in the kitchen preparing one of her signature meals. He can picture his dad watching the news and then getting on his soapbox about some government program that is failing miserably. He prays that Katie and her unborn baby are doing well. Of course, he thinks about Paul and the others who were ambushed at Geronimo. He relives the memorial service and he sees the suffering relatives of the slain soldiers. As always, the images in his mind progress to the faces of the Amir, Nassir and those ANA soldiers. His only relief is that now, finally, he is poised to make those butchers pay. His thoughts are mercifully interrupted by loud engines roaring. He can feel the truck rumble and some of the boxes he restacked shift around because of the vibration. He peeks around the boxes to find a Humvee has pulled up behind the truck. Obviously, part of the security detail assigned to the convoy. A few minutes later, the convoy starts rolling. The roads are good coming out of FOB Apache, or at least well travelled. The ride is smooth even in the back of a truck. It is difficult for Dan to determine their speed, but they are making good time. The humvee is following closely and it's about the only thing Dan can see outside. He does a little figuring and determines that if they are going thirty five miles per hour, it will take less than three hours to get there. After what seems to be a lot longer than three hours, the truck comes to a complete stop. It is now dark outside and the humvee headlights shine like a spotlight into the back of the truck. For some reason, the humvee pulls around one side of the truck and continues to the front of the column. Dan looks out of the truck and sees only darkness. He decides it is now or never. He quickly climbs over the supplies, holds his shoulder bag like a football and jumps out of the truck. As he hits the ground near the edge of the road, he immediately twists his body and builds up enough momentum to roll off of the edge. He comes to rest face down in a dry swale and can only hope nobody from the convoy saw him jump. Dan remains motionless trying to remain undetected. The convoy has stopped because it has arrived at the crossroads. The lead vehicles slowly turn off of the main road onto the pock marked path that takes them to the COP. Geronimo is four miles to the east and the mountain pass leading to Murzani is five miles farther south. There is very little moonlight, but Dan can't help noticing the hill. It's the place where they captured the Amir. Dan is struck by its unique silhouette. It is really just like a thousand other hills around there, but it sticks out in his memory. The shape is not the only thing he remembers. He remembers the way his squad stormed up that hill. That battle seems like a long time ago, but it has been less than six months. In his mind, the hill is a monument to the eagerness and passion that his men displayed that day. The last truck is turning off of the main road. Dan watches the trucks maneuver around big holes. He sits on his knees as the last vehicle fades out of sight. He looks ahead but sees only darkness. He can only guess at what is out there. All he knows is that it is five miles uphill to the pass and a few more miles to Murzani. Other than that, he will have to learn and react the best he can. He throws his head back and gazes at the starry sky. It reminds him of those fishing trips with his Dad. Dan would lie on the bank and stare at the stars, while his Dad fumbled with the lantern and rummaged through the tackle box. Jerry would rig up the poles and bait the hooks and Dan would wish he was at home in bed. He decides that first thing he will do when he gets back home is take his Dad fishing. He shakes his head to clear out the memories of home and his plans for reuniting with his dad. He needs to focus on the here and now. Dan sits upright and thinks about his predicament. He is sitting beside a road in the middle of nowhere. He is on the opposite side of the planet from home, all alone and he cannot go for help. His only weapons are a steel bladed knife and an iron will.

Dan gets up and starts walking toward the mountain pass. The temperature always drops dramatically at night, especially in the higher elevations. Dan is glad his fatigues are heavy enough to keep him warm. He turns his collar against the cold night breeze and fastens the top button to stay warm. During the night Dan makes it all the way through the pass and into the valley. He begins to second guess his plan. What if those guys are not in the valley? What if they have moved on? What if they are dead? He reassures himself. No, they have to be here. That joint operation the trooper detailed is proof. Plus, the newspaper report of the massacre in Murzani was only a few weeks ago. The Amir was here then. He must still be here. His thoughts alternate from those of confidence he is on the right track, to those of doubt he will accomplish anything. There is only one way to find out the answers to all of his questions and that is to keep plugging along toward Murzani.

It is almost midnight, so Dan decides to get some rest. He retreats a little way up the side of a mountain to find some cover. He lies down on the ground and falls asleep. The next thing he knows, he is awakened by vehicles moving on the road below him. He glances at his watch. It's six thirty. He looks down at the road and sees two of the trademark Toyota trucks the Taliban use all over Afghanistan. They are the typical beat up little trucks and they are travelling north toward the crossroads. Dan turns to look out over the valley. It is like another world from the parts of the Afghanistan Dan has seen before. The land is flat, but surrounded by massive mountains on both the north and south ends of the valley. For as far as he can see, there are lush green fields of corn intertwined with golden wheat gently blowing in the breeze. The morning sun illuminates the dew on the crops causing the water droplets to gleam brightly and throw multi colored prisms of light into the sky. It reminds him of the farmland back home in southern Illinois. He can see the roofs of small farm houses dotted randomly throughout the countryside. Then he sees a faint outline of small buildings about five miles farther down the road. He thinks to himself that must be Murzani.

The day is getting brighter as the sun climbs higher in the sky. Dan decides to stay about thirty yards off the road and use the tall late summer crops for cover on the final leg of his trip to Murzani. He is moving parallel to the road so he will not get lost in the fields. It is a good thing he has yet to don the native clothing he brought, because the loose fitting clothes would get torn and soiled in the heavy brush. As he makes his approach to the town, Dan hunches down below the tops of the crops, always keeping an eye on the road for navigation. His fatigues are soaking up the dew that has not yet dried from the foliage. He plods through the tall stalks, but every so often, he finds himself among plants that are much closer to the ground. The shorter plants are blossoming with white flowers. Dan reasons that they must be the notorious poppy plants he has heard so much about. The poppy is carefully hidden by the taller crops. Dan hears a vehicle on the road. He freezes in his tracks to avoid being detected. He peers through the stalks to see a farmer puttering toward the town on a tractor. Before the farmer has passed by, a couple more of those mini pickups speed past him going the opposite direction. Dan always thought all Afghans were the same, but he can discern a noticeable difference between the farmer and the men in the trucks. He should have seen it before, but for some reason he did not. Maybe it is because he is more observant now that he is on his own. He will need to use all of his senses and wits to stay alive, even more so now than when he was part of a large group of soldiers. The Afghan men dress the same, but the difference is in their eyes. The farmer is more calm and peaceful, but the Taliban have a wild look in their eyes. They seem to be tormented and tired. Dan thinks that if he were to look at himself in a mirror, his eyes would resemble those of the Taliban more than those of the farmer. Dan continues his walk toward Murzani when he sees a small figure on the adjacent road. It is a child walking toward the mountain pass. Dan studies the child's face and he realizes it is Jahen, the boy who hung around the COP. Dan knows he can trust Jahen. He hurries through the corn field to get to the edge of the road. He is almost out of the field when he hollers, "Jahen, Jahen, hey Jahen."

The young boy turns back toward Dan. He squints to try to determine who is yelling his name. He asks, "Who is there. Who is speaking English. Are you American?"

Dan steps out into the open and gets closer to Jahen. He asks, "Do you remember me, Sergeant Ross?"

Jahen remembers Dan as a gruff soldier who never liked him much. Except for the last time he saw Dan. That was when Dan ordered him out of the COP just before the explosion. Dan probably saved Jahen's life that day. Jahen runs toward Dan and says, "Sergeant Ross, yes, I remember, but you look different."

Dan removes his hat and asks, "Can you tell it's me, now?" Jahen wraps his arm around Dan's waist. He says, "Yes Sergeant Ross, I can see it. They told me you got hurt real bad. I thought you might be dead. I am glad you are back, but where are the other soldiers?"

Dan glances down the road in each direction, keeping a constant watch for any people or any vehicles. He says, "I'm alone and I need some help." He reaches into his shoulder bag and pulls out the clothes he has packed. He puts the Afghan garb on over his fatigues. His GI hat is replaced by the native cap the farmers wear.

Jahen asks, "What are you doing? Why are you dressing that way?"

Dan ignores the questions as he adjusts the clothes to cover his fatigues. He hands his discarded Army hat to Jahen. Finally, he answers, "I'm not in the Army anymore. I have to look like your people."

"Did you run away from the Army? Why are you here?" Dan begins to walk toward the town and says, "The Army kicked me out. They don't want me anymore. I came all the way from America to find some of those men that ambushed us."

Jahen walks beside Dan and asks, "You are alone? You are here with no others?"

It is as though Dan's head is on a swivel, as he constantly keeps a lookout for any trucks. He nods and says, "That's right. I'm all alone."

Jahen throws his arms in the air and points toward the pass, "But there are many of them. Some went by in a truck. Did you see them?"

Dan stares into the distance and says, "I know there are lots of them. I don't have to get them all." He turns back to Jahen and asks, "Do you live around here?"

"I live with my Grandfather. We have a farm," Jahen says, as he points toward the town. "It is on the other side of Murzani, it is only three kilometers from the town. Come with me. We will go to my home."

"Do we have to go through town?"

Jahen points to the east, "There is a closer way. We do not have to go through Murzani." Jahen places the Army hat on his head and says, "Look at me. I'm in the American Army."

The young boy leads the way to his Grandfather's farm. The two talk as they walk. Jahen says, "You are a good soldier, Sergeant Ross. My grandfather will like you very much. He hates the Taliban."

"What about your brother?" Dan asks, "Will he like me?"

Jahen tilts his head to one side and asks, "My brother? Oh…yes, my brother. He will like you, too."

"Don't you ever go to school?"

Jahen gets a little defensive, "Yes I go to school, but we are on holiday, right now."

Dan smiles, "It seems like you're always on holiday. What do you hear from the Army post? How are they doing over there at Geronimo?"

"I do not know. They do not let me inside the fort anymore. After the time that you got hurt and the others died, Lieutenant Blake told me not to come back. I have seen Lieutenant Blake on the road and he is nice to me, but I cannot go inside the fort."

"I guess they've changed the rules. They're probably tightening security."

A light goes off in Jahen's head and his eyes widen, "Are you a spy, Sergeant Ross? Is that why you are alone and have no weapons?"

Dan laughs a little and says, "No, I'm not a spy. I'm playing this by ear."

"What is playing by ear? What does it mean?"
"It means I'm not sure how I'm going to do it," Dan says, "But I'm going to get the men that killed my squad."

After walking for a little less than an hour, Dan and Jahen arrive at Grandfather's farm. The farm house is small. It is surrounded by fields of bright green corn, blowing in the wind. Dan scans the grounds near the house. There is a barn with an attached pen containing goats and lambs. There is another smaller building with a tractor parked inside. There are a few chickens scratching at the ground and clothes hanging on a line. There is a large garden with plump vegetables thriving in neatly tilled rows and a pile of wood stacked near the back steps. Dan follows Jahen up the steps to the porch.

"Please come in Sergeant Ross," Jahen says. He opens the front door and yells for his grandfather.

Entering the farm house is like taking a step back in time. The house has a wood burning stove, a brick oven and a pump at the sink. There is no electricity and they have kerosene lamps for light. There are only three doors off of the main body of the house. The main part of the home features a dining table in the front of the room and the kitchen sink and cupboards at the back. There is a window over the sink that lets the morning sunlight flood into the little home. There is a back door off of the kitchen and the stove is in the middle of the room that provides heat for the whole house. An old white haired man emerges from a bedroom.

"Salaam, Salaam," the old man says, "Sob bakhir."

Obviously, Grandfather does not speak English. Jahen falls back into his familiar role of interpreter. Jahen says, "He said hello, good morning."

Grandfather is a short stout man with a bushy white beard. The exposed portion of his face is leathery and wrinkled. Although he is probably only a few years older than Dan's father, he has aged much quicker than Jerry. He has clear eyes that disappear when he smiles. Instead of walking, the old man always trots. He trots around the table to greet Dan. He extends both of his hands out to grab Dan's hand. The little man embraces Dan like an old friend. He asks, "Nametar chist?"

That's a question Dan understands. He has heard it many times before. He answers, "Dan, my name is Dan."

Grandfather smiles and says, "Dan...Dan"

In their native Dari language, Jahen proceeds to explain who Dan is and why is in the valley. After listening intently, Grandfather's eyes droop and he shakes his head. He says, "Ne, ne." He trots around the room doubling over and grimacing, as though he is pain. Then he stops next to Dan and says, "Ne, ne." He puts his hand on Dan's shoulder and looks into Dan's eyes. He hopes his eye contact will send a nonverbal warning to Dan. Next, the old man simply hangs his head and slowly shakes it back and forth. Finally, Grandfather trots to the back door and he goes outside, leaving Jahen and Dan standing by the table.

Dan watches the old man exit, before turning to Jahen and saying, "I take it your Grandfather is not in favor of my plan." Before Jahen can answer, Dan's attention is drawn to the other bedroom door. A young woman appears holding an empty basket. She has long black hair with curly locks that bounce far below her shoulder blades. Her thin face is dominated by almond shaped eyes. In spite of their dark brown hue, her eyes shimmer in the morning light. Her sculpted cheeks are perfectly accentuated by full lips and a chin that disappears into her slender neck. Her skin is a light caramel color and her arms are thin and willowy. She has a slight, yet shapely figure. With just one look, Dan is mesmerized by her beauty.

She takes one hand off of the basket to wave into the air. She yells at Jahen, "Why did you bring this man here? Do you want to get us all killed. I heard what you said to Grandfather. This man is a fool."

Ignoring the young woman's anger, Dan asks, "Jahen, who is this?"

"She is my bossy sister. Her name is Pari."

Dan bows his head in her direction and says, "How do you do. My name is Dan."

Pari stares at Dan and she labors to breath. She lets out a big sigh before looking away and saying, "I know who you are. I have seen you on the road."

Mocking his sister in a high pitched voice, Jahen says, "She likes you, Sergeant Ross. She told me that a long time ago."

Pari throws the empty basket at Jahen and says, "Be quiet. That is not right. You talk all the time too much." She looks at Dan and says, "That was before I found out that you are foolish. I used to watch you on the road. You were forceful, but you were also compassionate. I could see you wished to be in another place and that you were bothered by the farmers, but you were not mean to them. I dreamed that I could know a man such as you. "

Jahen turns to Dan and says, "She made the candy for you, remember."

"Pari made the candy?" Dan asks, "I thought your brother made the candy."

211

Jahen acts disappointed. He lifts his head toward Pari and says, "I have no brother, only this."

Dan turns back to Jahen and asks, "Who is that kid that rides around in the wagon with you?"

Before Jahen can answer Pari says, "My grandfather makes me dress like a boy when I am away from home. He tries to keep me safe."

Dan picks up the basket and hands it back to Pari. He asks, "How does dressing like a boy keep you safe?"

That is a question that Pari does not like to think about. She takes the basket from Dan. She opens the back door and goes outside to the clothes line. Dan follows hoping to continue the conversation. Pari begins taking clothes off of the line and folding each garment before placing each one in the basket. She finally begins to open up with Dan. She says, "My mother was murdered by the Taliban. They like to attack women more frequently than men." She continues folding clothes and telling the story. "It was ten years ago. I was only nine years old and Jahen was too young to remember. It broke Grandfather's heart. He never talks about how it happened, but it must have been bad. He wants strangers to think I am a young boy who does not speak. He thinks the Taliban will leave me alone."

"That might work for the blind ones," Dan says, "But even they would have a hard time thinking you are anything but female. I think you need a better disguise."

"You saw me on the road. Did you think I was a girl?"

"No, but you were pretty far away from me. I thought you were just another farm boy in a wagon."

"You see, Grandfather's plan works. The people that know me keep my secret. I am not the only one. I have friends that do the same thing."

Dan begins to help with the laundry. He steps back and takes a long look at Pari. His eyes scan from her head to her toes and back up to her head again. The clothes she wears at home are inadequate to conceal her hourglass figure. He shakes his head and says, "I know one thing, for sure. You're not anybody's brother."

Pari blushes, but she enjoys the compliment. She smiles and snatches the basket out of Dan's hands. They both laugh as they enjoy each other's company. Jahen is watching them from the house. He shakes his head back and forth and smirks at their curious behavior. After getting all of the clothes from the line, Pari picks up the basket and says, "Get a piece of wood from the stack and come inside. I am sure you are hungry."

"Yeah, okay. I could eat. I've been too busy to think about eating."

They go back in the house and Dan looks at Jahen. He says, "Pari is going to make lunch for us."

Jahen is jealous of the attention Pari is getting from Dan. He says, "I am not hungry. I will go to help Grandfather in the barn."

Dan sits at the table and watches Pari prepare his lunch. He is enthralled by her every move, as she makes her way around the kitchen. First, she tosses the wood into the stove and she stokes the fire with a poker. Next, she places a pot of water on a burner and she adds some rice to the water. Finally, she pulls a loaf of bread from a cupboard and she cuts a few slices. Pari takes the bread over to Dan and says, "Naan. That is how we say bread. The chalow will take a few minutes." She sits at the table across from Dan.

Dan smiles and says, "Thank you." He takes a bite of bread and says, "I thought I saw lights coming from the town last night. It looked to me like they have electricity, over there."

"They do have electricity in Murzani," Pari says, "They built the generator building more than ten years ago. They burn coal and there is a big pipe where the smoke goes into the sky."

Dan says, "I saw the smoke stack. I figured it was an IED factory or somethin."

"What is IED?"

"Oh, it's a name we have for bombs the Taliban use against us."

"There are no bomb factories in Murzani. The people there work very hard at their shops. They have no interest in making bombs."

"Okay, okay, I get it. There are no bomb factories that you know about, but if they have a generator plant, why don't you have electricity?"

"The whole valley was supposed to have electricity by now, every farm. But the Taliban will not allow the workers to put in the poles and wires. Grandfather says the whole valley could be wired in a year, but the workers are too afraid. Someday, we will all have electricity."

"What's the town like?

Pari walks over to the stove and stirs the pot. She says, "There are many shops. There is a grain exchange, a farm tools store, a food store and other shops for clothes. There is everything we need. There is an old widow in town that owns a restaurant. I think Grandfather likes the old woman, because her food is not so good and he still eats there many times. My favorite store is the book store. Well, it is also a newspaper office. We have a school and a mosque. Oh, and there is an inn, but the man there cannot be trusted."

"Is he Taliban?"

Pari nods, "He tells the Taliban everything. They get rooms from him."

"Are there police in Murzani?"

Pari scoffs at the idea, she says, "You can say it, but the police are afraid, too. They do nothing to anger the Taliban."

Dan asks, "Do you go to town often?"

"Grandfather and Jahen go almost every day," Pari says, "But Grandfather says it is not safe for me. He must go to trade our vegetables for things we need, but I do not go always. I do have to go sometimes to trade for books."

"You and Jahen speak English well. Did you learn it in school?"

Pari shakes her head, "No, it is forbidden for girls to go to school in this valley. If girls were caught attending school, it would be bad for everyone. Jahen is supposed to go to school, but he wanders around the valley instead. They start teaching English to the boys when they are young. They teach English and the Koran."

"So, how did you learn English?"

"Walid at the newspaper taught me. He has many books in his shop. When I was younger, I would stay at the book shop while Grandfather did his trading. Walid showed me much English and I read his books to learn more."

"What about Grandfather? He does not know English, does he?"

Grandfather did not go to school. He knows very little English, but he knows how to read our language. There were Catholic missionaries in this valley when he was a young man. They gave him a Bible written in the Dari language and they taught him how to read it. He read many stories from the Bible to me and to Jahen. There was a church in Murzani, but the Taliban burned it down many years ago." Pari takes the pot from the stove and makes a plate of chalow for Dan. She says. "Grandfather still reads his Bible all of the days."

Dan digs into the rice and asks, "Are there Christians in this valley?"

"Only some of the old farmers, like Grandfather," Pari says, "We are required to be Muslims, or we can be killed."

Dan takes bites in rapid succession, "This rice is good." He is eating so fast, he barely takes time to breathe. He says, "I guess I was hungrier than I thought, or maybe, it's like my Grandfather used to say, hunger's good sauce."

"What does that mean?"

"It means when you are hungry, everything tastes better."

Pari's shoulders slump and she says, "Do you not think I cook good?"

"No no no, this is very good. I guess I was just thinkin about home." After taking a few more bites to convince Pari he likes the food, Dan asks, "What about your father? Where is he?"

Pari prepares another plate of chalow and she sits down to eat. She says, "My father ran away with the Taliban before my mother was murdered. He never returned, Grandfather thinks he is dead."

"Are there many Taliban in Murzani?"

Pari stands up and goes to the sink. She says, "The Taliban are every place in the valley. They do not live in Murzani, but they pass through all the time. They get the poppy from the farmers and they take what they want from the shops. Sometimes they pay, but usually, they do not. Everyone is too afraid to fight them. Would you like some tea?"

"No, water's fine," Dan says, "I saw a lot of wheat and corn and I saw poppy growing, too."

Pari refills Dan's glass of water and she resumes eating her chalow. She says, "Each farmer must grow poppy and sell it to the Taliban. If they do not, they take a big chance. I think you do not know the chance you are taking."

"Tell me about the incident that happened a few weeks ago," Dan says, "I read about it in the paper, back home. It said a lot of young people were murdered in Murzani."

"Oh, it was so sad. Some that were killed were my friends. I was supposed to be at that party. I was invited, but Grandfather was ill that day and I stayed home to care for him. After it happened, Grandfather did not let me go to Murzani for weeks. He would not tell me anything, except that my friends were dead, but I learned some things from Walid at the newspaper. My friends were not doing anything wrong. It was only a birthday party. The Taliban men went crazy. They killed my friends and two women. Nobody is certain why they did that, but since it happened, things keep getting worse in Murzani."

XX

Jahen comes back inside through the back door. He asks, "Dan, can you help Grandfather? He is repairing the tractor. I am not strong like you. He needs you to help."

Dan says, "Sure, I'll be right there." He takes his plates over to the sink and thanks Pari for the lunch. Out in the barn, Dan is a little amazed that the tractor will run at all. It is a relic more suited for a museum than a working farm. Dan estimates the tractor is at least forty years old. Grandfather has a workbench that stretches the entire length of one wall. There are lots of tools hanging on the walls. There are also metal cans filled with nuts and bolts. The cans are stacked on shelves in no particular order, but Grandfather can go straight to what he needs. It looks as though he has never thrown anything away. In fact, it looks like there are enough spare parts lying around to build another tractor. Dan can see the front end of the tractor is attached to a hoist, but neither Jahen nor Grandfather have the strenghth to lift it off of the ground. Dan grabs the chain and without too much exertion, he is able to get the front end high enough for Grandfather to get underneath. Dan secures the chain and asks, "What's wrong with it?"

Grandfather rattles off a long explanation as he examines the under side of the old tractor.

Jahen interrupts Grandfather's analysis to tell Dan, "He says there is a noise and he is afraid something might break. He says it might be an axle."

Grandfather talks continuously as he probes. He hits it with a hammer in some places and tightens nuts in others. Even though Grandfather is still talking, Jahen ignores the old man's ramblings and he says, "He is very concerned about his tractor. He is always working on it. It is very valuable. There are only three tractors in the entire valley."

"How do the other farmers get by without a tractor?"

"Some have horses to pull their plows," Jahen says, "Others pay Grandfather to use his tractor. Grandfather does very well. He gets paid with lambs, chickens and sometimes money."

As Grandfather works on the tractor, Dan continues to nose around. He goes over to the barn and he finds an area of with brick and stones on the ground and a water nozzle dangling overhead. He looks at Jahen and says, "What's this?"

"That is our shower. There is a bathtub in the house, but it sometimes too much trouble to heat the water. This is easier."

Dan slowly shakes his head, "It might be easier, but it's a whole lot colder."

From the building next door, Grandfather is heard, "Aha." The old man has settled on one area by a front wheel to concentrate his efforts. He persists in talking a steady stream and he slides his tools out from under the tractor.

"He says it is fixed," Jahen says, "We can let it down, now."

Dan releases the chain and eases the front end back down. Knowing how valuable the tractor is to Grandfather, he is extra careful with the old relic. Grandfather washes his hands at the shower and says something else to Jahen. Jahen tells Dan, "He wants us to pick out a lamb for dinner. He said this is a special occasion. We do not have very many visitors. He always treats visitors the best."

"Tell him he doesn't have to do that for me," Dan says. "I can eat the chalow."

"No, no, he likes to do it. It gives him an excuse to eat lamb."

Dan watches Jahen chase the lambs around the pen. Grandfather has a particular one in mind and he points it out to Jahen. Finally, Jahen corrals the right one. Dan doesn't want to watch the lamb get slaughtered, so he goes back in the house. He finds Pari sitting at the table reading a book. He says, "I guess we're having lamb tonight."

"Qorma," Pari says, "Grandfather likes it much. When we have a visitor, it gives him a reason for a treat." Pari closes her book and asks, "Why do you not help slay the lamb? Do you not like to see animals die?"

Dan peeks out the window to see if they are finished, "I'm not crazy about blood, especially my own. No, I just never did like field dressing animals. I guess that's why I didn't become a hunter."

"You do eat the meat, do you not?"

"Yes, I do, but in America we have supermarkets. There are rows and rows of prepackaged food. All of the meat is neatly wrapped and ready to cook. We never have to think about how it got there."

"You are a warrior that came here to kill men, yet you do not like to watch a lamb die," Pari says, "Your feelings are mixed up."

"I don't like to watch anything die, but there is a difference between a harmless lamb and a rabid dog."

"Do you know that if the Taliban find out who you are and why you are here, they will punish many in this valley," Pari says, "They will kill anyone that helps you."

Dan says, "I understand that you are afraid. But don't be. This is my fight and I don't need any help, from anybody."

"You are foolish. You do not know how many Taliban are here. Grandfather says there are more each time he goes to Murzani. You cannot do it alone."

"I don't have to kill them all, but there are two or three that I have to pay back. They are directly responsible for killing my brother in law and four others in my squad. Those are the ones I want."

"Three men?" Pari laughs, "You came here to kill only three men. That will make no difference. There are hundreds in these mountains. You are crazy and you are selfish. Do you not believe in God? God will punish these men."

"In the long run, yes, but I can't wait that long."

Pari goes into Grandfather's room and she returns with the old man's Bible. She drops it on the table and says, "Do you not understand? You may face the same judgement as those you seek. I read in a book that hate is the strongest emotion. Love is strong too, but many times love is not acted upon. Love may get lost for many reasons, such as, people may be too shy or the timing is wrong or there is fear of rejection. But people almost always find a way to express their hate. You have come from the other side of the world to express your hate. Can you not see the madness in your actions?"

Dan temporarily ignores her question and he thumbs through the old Bible. He cannot read it because it is written in Dari, but he knows the message. It has been reiterated by people from all walks of life that he has encountered since he was wounded. He finally answers Pari, "I'm not turning back now."

Pari stomps her foot like a petulant child and she says, "Uh, you are stubborn. Are all Americans as stubborn as you?"

"I guess not," Dan says, "In fact many are more like you. I see that you read a lot of books. Where do you get them?"

"Walid, the man that taught me to read, He has many English books in his newspaper office. He lets me borrow the books, as long as I return them."

"What news does he print? It must be old by the time he gets it."

"His business is very modern. He has a computer. He has too a satellite dish, but he must keep it hidden from the Taliban. If they knew, they would not allow it. I like his shop very much." Pari leads Dan outside to the garden. She hands him a cardboard box and orders, "Pick some good onions and spinach for the quorma. Grandfather likes spinach. If you find anything else that is ripe, go ahead and pick them. Grandfather will take them to town tomorrow and trade for rice and flour and other things we need."

Pari's feisty nature only adds to Dan's enchantment. He helps her get started on the supper then he spends the afternoon helping Grandfather and Jahen with chores around the farm. Pari works hard cooking and doing laundry all day. After supper, Dan helps her wash the dishes. He washes, she dries. When Pari has put the last dish away she says, "What is that smell?" She turns to Dan and asks, "When did you last take a shower?

Dan looks at the ground and sheepishly says, "Well, I guess it has been a couple of days."

Pari disappears for a moment. When she comes back she has a towel and clean clothes for Dan. She says, "Go take a shower. I will wash your clothes."

"But they won't be dry until morning."

Pari pushes Dan toward the door, "That is not bad. There are other clothes to wear tonight."

Dan looks back over his shoulder and says, "What if I wasn't planning on staying overnight?"

Pari smiles and says, "It looks like you must stay here and wait for your clothes. There is soap by the shower and remember to close the door."

Pari washes his heavy fatigues in the kitchen sink. She stares out at the barn and drifts off into dreams of being with Dan while she works.

As the evening progresses, Dan joins the little family at the table. Jahen gets a deck of playing cards from a cabinet. He asks, "Sergeant Ross would you like to play a game?"

"A card game?" Dan replies. "Sure, what's it called?"

Jahen says, "It's called Pasur. It is much fun."

"You're gonna have to show me how to play."

"We will show you how to play. It is easy," Pari says. She takes the cards from Jahen and explains the point system to Dan. She shows him that each player starts with four cards face down and you play with a pool of cards in the middle.

Dan listens to the instructions, but he does not get the whole idea. Instead of asking for further explanation, he figures he can wing it. He does however, come up with an ulterior motive. He asks, "What do you play for?"

Pari says, "What does that mean, play for?"

Dan says, "I mean, what do you get if you win? What is the prize?"

Pari holds arms out and says, "When you win a round you get points. Who ever scores 90 points first is the winner."

"That's it? You just play for points? There has to be a prize. What good are points?"

"It is fun to play," Pari says, "But nobody can beat Grandfather. He always wins."

"Do you ever bet on this game?" Dan asks.

"The old men in town do," Jahen says, "I have seen them. They play for money."

Dan rubs his chin and says, "Okay I'll play, if we make a bet."

Pari shakes her head, "But we never play for money."

Dan says, "I'll play. And if I win, Pari has to give me a kiss... on the lips."

At first Pari is dead set against the idea, but after a moment, she decides it might be fun. She smiles and asks, "And if you lose?"

"If I lose, I'll make breakfast for everyone tomorrow morning."

"What about me?" Jahen asks, "What do I win?"

Dan laughs, "You get to watch the loser pay up."

Jahen deals the cards and the game begins. Dan is still not sure how to play, but he really wants that kiss, so he follows Pari's lead. He watches her play her hands and he makes the same sorts of plays, thinking that copying her strategy will keep him close to her in points. After a few rounds Grandfather proclaims victory, as usual. Pari adds up the scores and determines Dan has finished in last place.

Pari says, "Have fun making breakfast. You may wake me up when it is ready."

Everybody gets a kick out of Dan's misfortune, including Dan, he is enjoying his time with the little family. In fact, it has almost taken his mind off of his reason for being there, but after the cards are put away, Grandfather begins to tell stories in his animated way. He swings his arms and fluctuates his voice as he paints the pictures with his words. Jahen and Pari do the interpreting, but with much less emotion. Dan can tell a lot is lost in the translation. There are stories of friends and relatives who struggled against the Taliban tyranny and the dishonest government. Most of his stories end with his acquaintances paying the ultimate price for their lack of cooperation. Dan learns that most Afghans dislike the Taliban as much as he does. In fact, most of them have even more reason to hate the Taliban. Perhaps Grandfather is trying to deter Dan from his crazy scheme, but instead, his stories have served to further strengthen Dan's resolve. Pari tells Dan that

Grandfather, by the grace of God, has been able to avoid trouble with the Taliban. He has done quite well financially, too. He is saving his money for when Jahen is a little older. He wants to send Pari and Jahen away to the big city for their safety. After hours of conversation, Grandfather and Jahen retire to their bedroom.

Pari and Dan are still seated at the table, she asks, "After hearing Grandfather, are you still going to try to go against the Taliban?"

Dan replies, "Most people outside of this Country have no idea what is going on here. I did two tours here and I didn't know or care. It wasn't until I met you and your family that I realized the oppression and the exploitation you endure. Now, I'm even more obsessed about stopping the Taliban."

"Perhaps it is because you like us, but do you like all Afghan people?"

"Let's just say my eyes have been opened. I'm figurin out the lay of the land. Now, I better start on that breakfast."

"Tonight?" Pari asks, "You do not cook breakfast until morning."

"I have to start tonight," Dan says, "Do you have any corn meal?"

Pari looks through a cupboard and finds the corn meal. She asks. "What are you going to make?"

Dan says, "Mush. That's why I have to start tonight. It has to set up for awile to thicken."

Pari wrinkles up her nose and asks, "What is mush? It sounds strange."

"It's awesome. My grandfather used to make it. It's Depression food. He grew up in the thirties, during the Great Depression in America. Mush is very inexpensive, and good."

Dan puts a pot of water on the stove and measures out the corn meal. He pours the corn meal in the pot and he stands at the stove stirring the mixture. While Dan is looking down at the pot, Pari sneaks up beside him and she lifts up on her tip toes and plants a quick kiss on his cheek, then she quickly backs away. Dan looks up and asks, "What was that for?"

Pari laughs as she talks, "I wanted to lose the bet, but you played so bad, I could not help it"

Dan's jaw drops, "You mean you were trying to lose? No wonder, I finished last. I was copying you. I thought that was my only chance to win." They both laugh as Dan pours the hot mixture in a dish. He covers the mush with a towel and sets it outside in the cool night air. It will congeal overnight and be ready by morning. Dan looks at Pari and asks, "Do you have some extra blankets? I'll make a pallet here on the floor."

Pari brings some blankets from her room and says, "I will sleep on the floor. You take my bed. You are our guest."

"I'm an unwanted guest, so I'll take the floor," Dan says. He takes the blankets and begins to spread them on the floor between the table and the stove.

Pari smiles and says, "You are an uninvited guest, but not an unwanted one." She watches Dan lie down and squirm around to get comfortable. "Do you want anything else?" She asks.

Dan wants Pari, but he knows that is unreasonable. He says, "No thanks, I'm fine. Goodnight."

Pari shares his impractical feelings of desire. She blows out the lights and gets in her bed. Neither Pari nor Dan falls asleep. Pari lies awake in her bed thinking about Dan and Grandfather's stories have reignited Dan's desire to complete his mission. His nightmares are now populated with even more scenes of pain and destruction attributed to the Taliban. However, there are some pleasant thoughts of Pari fighting their way to the forefront of his mind. Unfortunately, the horrific images of his dead buddies cannot be supplanted. Meanwhile, Pari cannot sleep. Her blissful dreams of Dan have compelled her to act. After tossing and turning for more than an hour, Pari assumes Dan is asleep. She grabs her pillow gets out of bed. She tiptoes into the front room and slides beneath the blankets next to Dan. She turns on her side with her back against his warm body. She is pleased when Dan, wraps his arm around her abdomen. She thinks it is a natural reaction by the sleeping man, but she is unaware that Dan is actually awake. He feels her hot pulsating body wedged against his own. He presses his face against her shoulder blade and he feels her heart pounding as though it wants to leap out of her chest. Pari senses Dan's hot breath and stiff whiskers on her back. Her body involuntarily quakes from within. She does not risk letting Dan know she is awake, nor does she let him know how much she wants him. Dan reaches beneath her night gown and slowly runs his hand over her hip and down along her thigh. Her skin is hot and soft and his hand melts into her slender frame. Her body quivers from his touch and Dan cannot help trembling at the sensation. Like Pari, Dan fights to keep his emotions in check and he chooses not to let her know he is awake. Eventually, they both fall asleep in the ecstasy of their embrace. In the early morning hours, when it is still dark outside, Pari hears Grandfather stirring in his room. She quickly slides out of Dan's grasp and she runs to her bed and dives under the covers. A few minutes later, Dan is standing over her bed. Her eyes are wide open. Dan says, "Breakfast is ready. Did you sleep well last night?"

Trying to be coy, Pari smiles and says, "Yes, I slept well. I do not think I moved at all, but there was a cold draft last night. And I have never noticed it before, but this bed can be quite lumpy. How about you? Did you sleep well?"

Dan decides to play along. He says, "Oh yeah, I slept like a baby, although that floor is cold and hard." He laughs at his fallacious response and Pari takes a swing at him with her pillow. Dan stoops down to give her a kiss when he notices Grandfather standing in the doorway. Dan quickly straightens up and says, "Good morning Grandfather."

Grandfather rattles off a few stern words aimed at Pari. She ignores the warning and says, "Grandfather is ready for breakfast. I must get up now. We are going to town today, if you would like to ride with us, you may. Grandfather has to do some trading. We must get ready. Your uniform is probably dry and so are your spy clothes."

"Are you going to town, also?"

"Yes, I want to trade for some different books, I have read these books many times."

Dan looks away with contentment and he stares into space and says, "I can't wait to get to Murzani."

XXI

They all get ready to go to Murzani. Dan and Pari put on their respective disguises. After breakfast the wagon is loaded with fresh produce. Jahen has rounded up two more lambs and he leads them to the wagon. Dan hitches the wagon up to the old tractor. Grandfather does the driving and the others ride in the wagon. Pari and Dan do a lot of talking during the short ride into town. Jahen is bored on the trip, because his sister and Dan act like they are the only ones in the wagon. They practically ignore him completely. He has never seen Pari act the way she does around Dan. She normally acts mature beyond her years. She is the only woman in the house, so she has to fill the role of mother to Jahen. Around Dan, she acts more like the young woman that she is. She laughs a lot, even when it is unnecessary and she is happier than Jahen has ever seen her before. She asks a lot of questions about America and Dan describes his home the best he can. They talk about his family, which makes Dan homesick. The paths through the farmland are narrow and lined with tall crops on both sides, creating a tunnel effect. When Grandfather turns onto the main road, the mud brick buildings of Murzani come into view. Their first stop is near the edge of town. Dan hands the two lambs down to Jahen. Jahen follows Grandfather into a building. There are large stacks of split wood behind the building. Grandfather trades the lambs for wood they will pick up on their way home. There is more trading to do. Next they pull up in front of the dry goods store. They each grab a box of vegetables and go inside. Grandfather does all of the talking, as he trades for oil, flour, rice and sugar. The people in the store are curious about Dan. Jahen tells them that Dan is a cousin from the big city. After loading the provisions in the wagon, Pari whispers to Grandfather that she and Dan will go to the book store. They make plans to meet at the old widow's restaurant after while. Pari hands Dan a stack of books from the wagon and very quietly, she says, "Come with me."

Dan follows her across the street to the bookstore that is also the newspaper office. There is a stand outside the door containing a few copies of the latest paper. Dan glances at the paper. He taps Pari on the shoulder and nods his head toward the stand. He whispers, "Look, that's my picture in the paper."

Pari picks up a copy and she examines the grainy photo. She says, "The headlines mention a missing American journalist. Are you a journalist? Are you missing?"

"Uh, well, I guess so. I mean I didn't tell anyone where I was going."

Her shoulders slump and she holds the paper by her side, "I thought you were a soldier?"

"I am. I mean, I was. It's a long story. They forced me out of the Army when it looked like I wasn't going to get well. But I got well and I had to come back on my own. Nobody knows I'm here and I need to keep it that way."

Pari stares at Dan wondering what other surprises are in store from this man by whom she is infatuated. She says, "Keep your hat pulled down to your eyes. Let's go inside. You are safe in here. Walid runs the paper. He is my friend and we can trust him."

Pari and Dan browse around the store. Pari has read almost every book in there. Dan is surprised at how many of the books are written in English. Dan enjoys her company and listening to her talk about the books or anything else, for that matter. After Pari makes her selections, she speaks with Walid for a while. She introduces Dan to Walid. The two men exchange pleasantries, but Pari does not say why he is there. Although Walid is curious, he does not ask any questions. After stepping out of the book store, Pari sees their tractor and wagon in front of the restaurant. She and Dan make their way over to the wagon. Dan sets the books in the back and he and Pari enter the restaurant. The place is humming. There are five tables of guests. Grandfather and Jahen are sitting and talking with the old widow. Pari and Dan join them. It is hard to get a word in between the two old folks' conversation. Dan reaches his hand out to the old widow. He says, "Salaam. I am Dan."

The old widow smiles broadly and replies, "Salaam. Khoshaal shodom az mulaqat e shuma."

Jahen says, "She said it is nice to meet you."

Dan smiles. He scans the restaurant, examining all of the patrons. Everyone seems harmless, except there are two men with that crazy restless look in their eyes. They are eating at a table in the back corner. It is that same look he noticed the Taliban truck drivers possessed. The entire time he is eating his lunch, Dan notices the men staring at him. The old widow brings out lots of food and drinks. When they have finished eating, Grandfather pulls Dan up by his arm and says something that Dan does not understand. Pari says, "He wants you to go with him. He wants you to help load the wood. We'll stay her while you two work."

Dan tells the old man. "Sure, I'd be glad to help out." As they leave, Dan notices that one of the suspicious characters has left and the other is still watching Dan.

Grandfather fires up the old tractor and Dan jumps in the wagon. They drive down to the big wood pile behind the building. Grandfather stands in the wagon and Dan hands him the wood piece by piece. Meanwhile back at the restaurant, the suspicious character that left returns with a third man. The three men grab Jahen and Pari. They slug the young people in their faces and drag them through the back door into a fenced alley. The old widow tries to stop the men, but they knock her to the floor. She gets up and runs outside, frantically calling for Grandfather. She runs down to the wood pile and grabs Dan by the arm. She points toward the restaurant and yells, "Komak, komak. Pari, Jahen….komak!"

Dan knows there is trouble. He sprints back to the restaurant, but doesn't see Pari. He hears screams from the back of the building. He notices the suspicious character is no longer at his table. He reaches into his boot and pulls out his K-bar. He runs to the back door and surveys the situation. There is a man with his back to the door. He is holding Jahen with his hand over the boy's mouth. Jahen is haplessly struggling to get away. There are two other men holding Pari down. They are striking her in the face and tearing her clothes off. Dan is infuriated to see Pari fighting against the two thugs that dwarf her in both size and strength. Her blood flies into the air with every blow she receives. Dan thinks this may be how Pari's mother died, but it is not going to be her fate. Her screams drown out the sounds of Dan's footsteps as he approaches the man holding Jahen. The man is watching the others assault Pari so intently that he does not see what is coming. Dan locks the captor's neck in the crook of his left arm and in one continuous motion Dan drills the knife blade into the man's sternum. He jerks the k-bar upward, ripping a trough in the attacker's upper abdomen that provides a conduit for his vital organs to spew out of his body. His bloody entrails precede his lifeless body to the ground. He lands with a thud that gets the attention of the other attackers. As Jahen screams with the exhilaration that comes with his freedom, the other two attackers quickly get off of Pari, leaving her partially naked and sobbing on the ground. The two would be killers become aware of their fallen accomplice. They cringe at the sight of his crumpled body lying in a pool of blood. Simultaneously, the two attackers turn to Dan. Each one pulls out a long bladed knife with a curved tip. Dan's mouth falls open in dismay. He recognizes that one of the men is Sergeant Nassir, the ANA traitor whose vision has tormented Dan for months. The traitor laughs and says, "Your American army boots gave you away. Are you a spy?"

Dan replies, "What happened to your Afghan Army uniform, Sergeant Nassir?"

The dumbfounded Nassi says, "Who are you? How do you know that name?"

Dan removes his cap and says, "Does this help?" Without waiting for a reply, Dan turns his back to the two killers. He says, "Surely you recognize my back. It's among you're favorite targets, along with women and children."

The man beside Nassir lets out a loud yell. He lifts his knife above his head and runs toward Dan. The man swings his weapon at Dan's back, narrowly missing. Dan reaches up with both hands and takes hold of the man by the elbow. He flips the insurgent into the air and the man lands flat on his back. As the man lies on the ground wincing in pain, Dan drops to his knees and plunges his k-bar into the man's abdomen. The man is left writhing on the ground and bleeding from the mortal wound. Nassir bolts for the back door which is his only way out, but Dan blocks his passage. Nassir takes a few steps back and smirks. He says, "I remember. You are the rebellious one. I thought you were dead."

Dan crouches to prepare for an attack, "And I hoped you were."

Nassir takes a few steps sideways to get an angle for an attack. He laughs at Dan and retraces his sidesteps searching for an edge. He says, "How many times must I kill you?" Then he swings his long knife at Dan ripping a gash in Dan's left forearm. Dan is unfazed by the wound and like a matador goads a bull into an ill fated charge, Dan holds out his hand and fans his fingers to encourage Nassir to make a run. He confidently thrusts his knife at Dan's belly, only to have Dan sidestep the blade. The traitor's momentum carries him past Dan. Dan twists to his left and releasing months of pent up frustration, he stabs Nassir between the shoulder blades. The traitor falls face down and gurgles his final breaths. His saliva, mixed with blood, oozes from his mouth and pools in the sand. The old widow and Jahen run to help Pari. Dan rips some material from his flowing Afghan disguise and wraps his left arm tightly, in an attempt to stop the bleeding from the deep gash between his wrist and elbow. He gets Jahen's attention and says, "Tell Grandfather to pull the wagon around here by the fence." Although both of Dan's sleeves are covered with blood from his elbows to his hands, he kneels beside Pari and cradles her head against his shoulder. Dan cannot find the words to express his sorrow for what happened to Pari. It could have been much worse. She is battered and bruised, but she is alive. Dan picks her up and he carries her inside the restaurant. He sets her down in a chair.

Pari struggles to speak, "Those men wanted to know who you are. We did not tell them."

Dan presses his cheek against her battered face. He says, "Oh Pari, why didn't you tell them? They are going to find out anyway. I'm sorry this happened to you."

The beating does not diminish Pari's feisty nature. She says, "This is only the beginning. More will come. They will kill you. They will kill all of us."

Dan shakes his head, "I should have never stayed at the farm. I should have left yesterday and never dragged your family into this. From now on, I'm going it alone. You can go back to the farm and I'll never bother you again."

Pari lifts her arm and clutches Dan's shoulder. Her entire body strains as she speaks, "It is too late for that. The killers know all about you and they know who has been helping you. It is my fault, too. Despite my words, I did not want you to leave. I wanted you to stay at the farm."

"You're right about one thing. This is only the beginning," Dan says, "Nassir is the first, but I came here to get at least one more.

The old widow brings a pan of hot water and some clean rags. She begins to work on Pari's face. Jahen comes in to tell Dan that the wagon is in the back. Dan says, "Jahen, find me a stake, a piece of cardboard and a paint brush. Bring them to the wagon."

Jahen stands up straight and salutes. He says, "Yes sir." He immediately begins to look around for the items. Dan drags the dead bodies to the wagon and struggles to load them. Jahen gets a piece of cardboard from the trash and he finds a broken fence post that can be used for a stake. The old widow gets a pastry brush from the kitchen. Jahen gives the items to Dan. Dan dips the brush into the pool of blood that remains at the spot where the first man died. Using the blood for paint, Dan proceeds to write something on the cardboard. He nails the sign to the stake and tosses it in the wagon. Dan gets on the old tractor and pulls the wagon through town. When he gets outside of town, he throws the bodies down on the side of the road that leads to the mountain pass. Beside the mangled and bloody bodies, he uses a piece of wood to drive the sign into the ground. The sign written in blood reads "Amir, you're next".

XXII

The mood on the trip back to the farm is somber to say the least. Grandfather drives the tractor and the others are in the wagon. Jahen rides atop the pile of wood and Dan sits at the rear with his legs dangling out the back. Pari lies with her head resting in Dan's lap. Despite the bumpy ride, the lingering effects of the beating cause her to fall asleep. Dan turns to Jahen and says, "I'm sorry you had to see that, today. You are too young to see those things."

"I have seen men die before," Jahen says, "But never that close. It is not a good thing to see for anybody. Did you learn to fight in the Army?"

"Yes, the Army teaches you how to fight and how to kill," Dan says, "But they don't teach you how to live with it."

Jahen looks at the make shift bandage on Dan's arm. The blood is soaking through the rags and trickling down Dan's arm. Jahen is alarmed and says, "Your arm is bleeding too much."

"I'll sew it up when we back to the farm," Dan says, "You have a needle and thread don't you?"

"Pari has those things."

Grandfather is talking continuously, as usual, but nobody pays much attention to him. He rambles on waving first one arm and then the other, always keeping one hand on the wheel. Frustrated that nobody is paying attention to his tirade, he stops the tractor and turns to his passengers to make his point. Noticeably upset, he continues his outburst. Without understanding a word, Dan gets the message loud and clear.

"He says the Taliban will come," Jahen says, "He says they will come to the farm. He is very afraid. He is afraid they will kill us."

"Tell him that I agree," Dan says, "It's not safe for any of us at the farm. First thing in the morning we will go back to town. You all can stay with the old widow and I'll go to finish my business."

When they get back to the farm, Dan carries Pari to her bed. He lays her down and tries to make her comfortable. He can't help but think about how beautiful she is. Even with the fat lip and the cuts and bruises, Dan thinks she is the most beautiful girl he has ever seen. He leans down and kisses her forehead.

Pari sees blood on her blanket. Her eyes are swollen from the beating, but she does focus in on his wounded arm, she is shocked at the amount of blood that is leaking from the sopping bandage. She says, "Dan, your arm. My sewing kit is in the top drawer. We must care for your arm." She tries to get up, but Dan will not let her. She says, "But you need help, you cannot sew it by yourself?"

Dan grabs her arms and pushes Pari back down on the bed, "You stay here and rest. You're in a lot worse shape than I am. I can do this."

Dan finds the sewing kit in her top drawer. He takes it and leaves Pari resting in her bed. He goes into the kitchen and unwinds the blood soaked rags from his arm. He pulls his stained and tattered spy clothes over his head and throws them in the trash. He really could have done without the disguise. It did not fool anybody. He wraps his belt above his elbow and he cinches it down tight. The blood coming out through the cut has slowed to a trickle. He goes over to the sink and pumps water over his arm to rinse the wound. The water running into the cut stings, but after the initial jolt, the pain blends in with the constant throbbing he has been feeling, all along. Grandfather has been tearing a towel into strips to make clean bandages. The old man reaches down into a cabinet and moves some things around until he finds what he is looking for. He pulls out a dusty bottle of rice wine that looks like it has not been opened in years. He removes the lid and waves the top under his nose to make sure it is still good. He hands it to Dan, who proceeds to pour the wine generously over his arm to disinfect the cut. Grandfather and Jahen watch closely, as Dan pokes the needle through the lip of the cut. Dan can only clinch his teeth to deal with the pain. When he pulls the thread through the first needle hole, Jahen cannot stand to watch any longer. He turns away and sits at the table. Doing his best to cope with the shots of pain that come with each puncture, Dan crudely tailors eight stitches into his arm. A doctor would use twice that many, but the cut is closed. Grandfather nods his head with approval and pours the rest of the wine over the fresh stitches. Grandfather dries Dan's arm with a clean towel and removes the belt before bandaging the wound. Dan goes over and sits at the table with Jahen. After Grandfather cleans the sink, he reaches down

241

into the cabinet a second time. This time he finds another bottle of wine. He pours two glasses and takes them over to the table. The old man pulls out a chair and sits down across from Dan. He slides one glass of wine over to Dan and he downs the other in one long drink. Dan grabs his glass and quickly quaffs down the wine. Being just across the table, Dan can see the lines in Grandfather's face are longer and deeper than Dan had noticed before. Grandfather sets his glass on the table and he leans back in his chair. He slowly moves his eyes, taking stock of everything in the old farm house. He hangs his head for a moment and then he raises his right arm above his head. He turns to his left and he swats at the air, carrying his arm back to his side. Without saying a word he lets Dan know the old place does not mean that much to him. Then he reaches to the center of the table and picks up his Bible. He moves the book closer to where he is sitting. He taps the cover of the Bible with his index finger and he nods. He does not have to speak to convey the value he places on the words in that Bible. Jahen smiles. He walks over to the counter and retrieves the bottle of wine. He refills the glasses and he watches the two men silently share another drink.

The next morning, Dan urges the little family to pack up enough clothes to stay away from the farm for a few days. Dan and Jahen load the wagon and Grandfather gets a few valuables, including his cash fortune and his Bible. He stashes his valuables in a small box and hides it underneath the tractor seat. Although she is plenty able to walk on her own, Dan carries Pari to the wagon and Grandfather starts up the tractor. While the tractor warms up, he makes one last trot through the barn, making sure there is plenty of food and water for the animals. He jumps on the tractor and heads for Murzani. Riding in the wagon, Dan worries about the safety of his new friends. He pulls his knife from his boot. He reaches down and slides Pari's pant leg up exposing one of her calves. Using some small strings taken from his fatigues he ties the knife to her leg. He says, "It's lucky you Afghan people wear loose fitting clothes. Nobody will know it's there. Let's hope you don't have to use it." This trip is much different than the ride to town yesterday. Pari and her family are scared. There is no talking about America. In fact, there is not much talk, at all.

As they get closer to town, they can see a big black plume of smoke bellowing into the morning sky. Walid, the newspaperman runs into the road to meet their wagon at the edge of town. He waves his arms and he gasps for air between words while he speaks to Grandfather. Jahen tells Dan, "He says the Amir and his men set fire to the widow's restaurant. The Amir is holding the old widow hostage in the street. He is pointing a gun to her head and he is threatening to shoot her, unless the men responsible for killing Nassir come forward. Dan immediately jumps down from the wagon and walks down the street toward the Amir. Dan sees an outline of a man holding a rifle to the back of a woman's head. The woman is on her knees and crying. Dan hollers at the Amir, "Let the old woman go. I'm the man you want."

The Amir is unsure who is speaking to him. He asks, "You are an American? But you must have had help. Where are the others?"

Dan keeps walking toward the Amir, "There are no others. There is only me. Now, let her go."

243

"I was told the missing American journalist is responsible," the Amir says, "But I did not believe them." The Amir lifts his leg and places his boot on the old woman's back. He kicks his foot forward sending her sprawling in the dirt, face first. Not far from where the old widow writhes in the street lies Walid's satellite dish, smashed into pieces. The last non verbal link to the world beyond the valley is rendered useless, further isolating Murzani and erasing any concerns the Taliban may have had that their reign of terror can be reported in a timely manner. The morning sun forces the Amir to squint as he looks at Dan. He asks, "Why have you come to Murzani?"

Dan keeps walking straight toward the Amir. With his jaw locked, he remains fixated on the face that has been haunting him for months. He says, "I have come to kill you."

The Amir laughs and says, "Why does an American newspaper man want to kill me?" Dan draws even closer, but the Amir still cannot recognize Dan. The Amir is getting uncomfortable at the rapid approach of the American. He points his AK-47 at Dan and says, "Please stop. I am a religious man. I have no enemies." As the Amir is speaking, ten of his fellow insurgents flood into the street. Two of the men, with their rifles slung over their backs, run at Dan in an effort to stop his advancement. With no regard for his own life, Dan bears down on the Amir. He stares down the barrel of the AK-47 at the Amir's face. He can only think about getting his hands on the man responsible for the deaths of so many of his friends. Even as the first two men try to tackle Dan, he pushes them to the ground without taking his eyes off of his target. Before Dan gets close enough to the Amir, the entire gang swarms around him. Some of the terrorists punch Dan until he falls to the ground, then they proceed to kick him in his head and his body. There are so many assailants, it is difficult for all of them to get a clear shot, but they each do their best to make sure their licks hit home. The Amir pushes his men out of his way, as he breaks through the mob to get a first hand view of the beating. He pushes some of his men away from Dan and he orders the others to stop the beating. He tells them to get Dan on his feet. Dan is bleeding from his mouth and his nose. His face is scraped and dirty. Two of his attackers hold him upright, but he lacks the strength to keep his head from hanging and his chin from resting against his chest. The Amir crouches down to get a look at Dan's face. He grabs a handful of Dan's hair and lifts to get a better look at Dan. He is pleasantly surprised when he finally recognizes Dan. His eyes open wide and he doubles over with laughter. He says, "It seems the shoe is on the next foot Mr. American soldier." Two more Taliban fighters come into the street. They have Pari's hands tied behind her back and they are pushing her toward the meeting between the Amir and Dan. Grandfather trots over to help the old widow get up. He dusts her off and helps her get out of the street.They move over nearer to the smoldering remains of her restaurant. Jahen digs through the charred building and finds a chair. Grandfather uses his handkerchief to dust the soot from the seat and he helps her sit down.

Dan lifts his head when he hears the commotion created by the killers bringing Pari over to the Amir. He leans his head back and looks toward the sky before asking, "What is it with you people and women? You have me. Isn't that enough?"

"If it were up to me, I would kill you both right here and right now," the Amir says, "You see, the man you call Nassir was my cousin. He was a glorious fighter that killed many Americans. In time, you will pay for his death. Unfortunately, our leader wants you alive."

"So what about the girl? Dan asks, "You can let her go."

"Do not worry Mr. Spy. You will get to watch her die before we kill you."

XXIII

The insurgents tie Dan up similar to the way they have bound Pari and they load their prisoners in the back of one of those beat up trucks. The truck is part of a convoy of four travelling south toward the mountains that form the south rim of the valley. There are four guards riding in the bed of the truck along with Dan and Pari. Dan begins to speak to Pari, but is immediately punched in the stomach with the butt of a rifle. He folds over in pain and falls to his knees on the floor of the bed. The road turns into a wide path as the trucks begin their climb up the mountainside. Eventually, the wide path turns into a narrow trail. When the trail disappears and the trucks can go no farther, the band of insurgents takes their prisoners out of the truck and they begin the final leg of the trip on foot. It is a strenuous ten minute walk to their destination. Dan and Pari are pushed and prodded every step by gun barrels digging into their backs. Over zealous jabs cause Dan to fall three times on their forced ascent. With his hands bound behind his back, his face skids on the ground to break each fall. The rocks on the trail tear into the crown of his head and his blood mixed with sweat drips off of his face. After finishing the climb, they arrive at an upper meadow. It is a relatively flat, open area underneath a canopy of tall evergreen trees. The meadow is a respite from the steep, jagged terrain that surrounds the valley. There are at least thirty tents clustered in the small meadow. Dan believes it is the target of the raid the Americans have planned for tomorrow. The prisoners are directed to a part of the camp where three men are talking in front of a tent. The Amir bows to a tall thin man with a long beard that features a blend of black and grey whiskers. His presence is more refined than most of the foot soldiers. His clothes are cleaner and he speaks much better English. He is obviously, the leader of this band of cutthroats. He addresses Dan, "I am Mohammad Omar Nasim Ghafoor. Welcome to our humble abode. I understand you sacrificed yourself. Thinking it would save the lives of others, no doubt."

Dan stares defiantly at the tall man. He answers, "I don't trust you people that much."

The Amir says, "He is not a journalist. He is the soldier that captured me at the hill."

"Is this true?" The tall man asks, "Are you perhaps a spy?"

"I was a soldier, but they didn't want me anymore," Dan says, "Now, I am a war correspondent. That's how I got to this country. But I have come to this valley to kill the men responsible for backshooting my squad in March of this year. I'm sure you're one of those men."

The tall leader ponders the new information and says, "You killed more than twenty of my men and captured our spiritual guide, and they do not want you anymore. It is no wonder the American

Army is so weak." He unfolds a photo that he had stored in a pocket. He compares the photo to Dan's face and says, "There are those that do want you. These pictures have been distributed all over the province. They are looking for you."

Dan is disgusted at the thought. He says, "That's one of our problems. Our Army will spend time and resources looking for one man when they could use those resources to kill people like you."

The tall leader folds the picture and returns it to his pocket. He asks, "How did you get lost?"

"Who says I'm lost?"

The tall leader seems amused by Dan's stubbornness. He says, "Then you were sent to this valley. If it is true, that makes you a spy." He thinks for a moment and asks, "Did you kill Nassir?"

Dan is not interested in matching wits. He is telling it like it is, "I did. He deserved it."

"I knew you killed him," the tall leader says, "I wanted to see if you would lie to me."

Hoping to incite others in the camp, the Amir shouts, "We must kill him now." Some of the other men in the camp gather around and begin to chant in their native language.

The tall leader raises his hands to silence the excited men. He says, "Do not be in a hurry. This man is of great value to us," he speaks to the Amir in the Dari dialect. Obviously, he is giving some kind of orders to the cleric. In turn, the Amir shouts to the men in the camp. A greater number of men begin to assemble. The tall leader leads the prisoners inside his tent. There are thick colorful rugs lying on the ground. Ghafoor sits on the rugs as though he is sitting on a throne. A guard pushes the prisoners to the ground.

Dan persists in pleading for Pari's freedom, "I'm not worth anything. You can't get much in a trade for me. Please let Pari go. She hasn't done anything other than getting beat up by your thugs. Do what you want with me, but let her go."

Ignoring the reference to the girl, the tall leader says, "You are quite valuable, but not in a trade. The Americans are growing weary of their fruitless endeavor in our land. However, a film of a brave young American journalist being tortured and killed may renew their spirit. That will be the impetus for them to continue their hopeless fight."

Dan cannot figure why this nomadic guerilla is so eager to continue fighting. Especially against the American Army which has unlimited resources. He says, "It seems to me you would want the Americans to give up the fight. You can never defeat them."

Ghafoor raises his finger and wags it back and forth, "You do not understand the point. We do not have to defeat them, nor do we want to defeat them."

"Do you want to lose the war?"

"You are a naïve young man," the tall leader says, "If you were going to be alive much longer, you would understand, as I do, that we do not want to win or lose the war. We want the war to continue indefinitely. As long as our governments are at war, I am free to do as I please. The war creates just the right amount of instability for my operations to thrive."

Dan thinks back to Ed Greenbriar's words about the U.S. government's motives. He wonders if anybody wants to win. In a war like this, the people who pull the strings are only interested in power and greed, but to the American infantrymen or the people of a town like Murzani, a war like this is only about killing and death. It occurs to Dan this war, like most others before it, is a byproduct of governmental malpractice and GIs along with the Afghan farmers are buffeted about by the narcissists who orchestrate the madness.

Ghafoor laughs as he continues to speak, "Do you know I was educated in the finest schools in London. Would you believe that I have a large house in Kabul. It is a mansion. I have many maids and three wives. By American standards, I am wealthy like your movie stars. I make more money in one day selling heroine than you make in an entire year." He looks at Pari and says, "This young virgin will make a fine wife."

"She's no virgin," Dan says, "I can attest to that." Pari looks at Dan, knowing he is lying to protect her.

"I think she is a virgin," the tall leader says, as he watches the young people's silent interaction. "Although, you may be telling the truth, I have seen the way she looks at you."

"Good, then you can let her go home. She is no good to you."

"She is not going home," the tall leader says, "If she doesn't want to be my wife, she will be part of your torture." He gets close to Pari and examines her as if he were a cattle buyer perusing livestock on the hoof.

Dan is annoyed by the man's behavior. In his sarcastic tone, he says, "Why don't you look in her mouth? Her teeth are all there."

The tall leader ignores Dan's remark and he moves even closer to Pari. He smiles and asks, "Why does such a lovely creature wear farmer's rags? I can wrap you in priceless gowns. My maids will wait on you hand and foot."

Pari leans back to get away from his advances and she contorts her face to signal her disgust. She yells, "Get away from me."

The tall leader laughs loudly as he returns to his original spot on the rug. In a light hearted voice he says, "This one has fire inside. I like my wives to be more submissive. It is too bad, because you are a most exquisite young woman."

Dan can tell that Pari is uncomfortable. He attempts to change the subject by berating the tall leader, "You are nothing but a user,"Dan says, "You use the farmers to grow your poppy, you use these men to fight your war. How can one man be so greedy?"

"Do you want me to surrender to the politicians?" The tall leader says, "They are no better than me. They levy taxes on the masses and use that money for their own selfish causes and personal gain."

"But they usually stop short of outright murder."

The tall leader laughs and shakes his head. He says, "If you believe that, you are even more naïve than I thought. The history of this world is rich with incidents of governments slaughtering their own people by the millions. It has happened in the East and in the West. Besides, you have endangered the lives of many people in this valley for your own selfish reasons. That is akin to murder. I too have a desire for revenge. I have an opportunity to avenge the deaths of my men that died at the hill. Surely, you can appreciate my motive."

Dan looks at the cuts and bruises that mark Pari's face. He thinks about how he ignored her warnings and how she has paid for his selfishness. Yet despite his getting them into this jam, her eyes project an unconditional compassion for Dan, which causes his heart to break for her. Some of that love that has been on lock down within his soul is clawing its way to the surface. Dan turns back to the tall leader and says, "There was a time, not long ago, that I would appreciate your need to retaliate. I was blinded by hatred, but my eyes have been opened. I learned that revenge provides an empty solace. Killing Nassir didn't ease my mind nor did it provide any closure. The pain never goes away. I'm glad Nassir's dead. He needed to be stopped. Otherwise, he would kill again and again, but there is no relief and the memories are not erased."

"You are soft like all Americans," the tall leader says, "You have no stomach for the fight."

"I can stand the fight, believe me,"Dan says, "But the senseless killing needs to stop. You would feel the same, if not for greed. Your need to perpetuate your lifestyle has left a void in your soul. You have become callous. You are incapable of feeling. Everyone and everything are just nameless faceless pawns for your manipulation."

"That is a perceptive observation from such an unworldly one," the tall leader says, "Are you sure you do not envy me?"

With disdain in his voice Dan says, "Envy? I can almost pity you. Every man is part of something bigger than himself. Your influence reaches beyond the borders of this country. The narcotics industry only begins in these mountains with your slaughter and intimidation. It ends in all corners of the earth in desperation. And along the way, thousands of people are murdered by the distributors and money changers, just so you can lavish in your big house with your maids and your money. Freedom fighter? Huh, you're nothing but a thug. What's worse is that you use these fanatics to do your dirty work, taking advantage of their own desperate circumstances."

"It is not hard to recruit these men," Ghafoor says, "They fight because they are jihadists. I fight because I am a businessman. It works out well for all of us."

"Well I have news for you, Dan says, "Sooner or later everyone has to pay up, but in your case, it really doesn't matter, because you died a long time ago. You're dead on the inside."

"Soldier, journalist and now philosopher, you are a man of many talents, but you are so very wrong. I have a system designed to endure for longer than you or I will live. I have politicians and informants in my organization. I know your Army's plans before they do."

Dan ribs the tall leader, "You didn't know about me, did you?"

Ghafoor cannot stand being mocked, so he returns the sentiment, "You are perhaps the biggest fool of all. You cheated death once and now you risk your life in a hopeless attempt at revenge. Do you not know that self preservation is all that matters? There is no right or wrong, only living and dying. I live well and I will die well. You, on the other hand, will die in the worst way and your death will enhance my cause. You are a gift from Allah. You truly are."

Dan knew what he was getting into when he started his futile quest, but he is upset that he has put Pari in peril. "I'm the gift. Not Pari. Let her go home. I have died a thousand times these last few months. Every time I think about my men getting cut down at Geronimo, I die a little more. You'll be doing me a favor by putting me out of my misery, but I'm asking you to let her go home."

Ghafoor scoffs at the request and says, "The girl will serve as an example of what happens to collaborators. Oh, and her grandfather and brother will pay, as well. But it is a shame to kill such a brave and selfless man such as you. Perhaps, under different circumstances, we could have been friends."

"Circumstances are external. Friendship is born from within men's souls. I pray there is nothing in my soul that is similar to yours."

Hearing those words angers the tall leader. He is no longer amused by the exchange with his adversary. He stands and says, "You seem to think you are better than me, Mr. Spy. I hope your American arrogance eases the pain when your head comes off. If you like to pray, I suggest you start now. I know some things about your religion. Your prophet, Jesus, told the spy in his group that it would be better for him if he had never been born. That is how it will be for the two of you." Ghafoor stands and looks away from the prisoners in disgust. He waves his arm to the guard and says, "Take them away. We will make the torture video after the mission." The guard takes them to another tent. They are thrown to the bare ground with their hands still tied. A Taliban guard is once again posted at the door.

Pari is so mad she shudders. She says, "That man is evil like the thief in Grandfather's Bible. He comes only to kill, to steal and to destroy. He makes me angry. He is not a good example of the Afghan people."

A few minutes later Dan and Pari can hear the tall leader speaking to the assembly of men. The guard steps outside the tent, but remains by the door. He wants to hear his leader while maintaining a close eye on the prisoners. Pari whispers a translation of the tall leaders address. She says, "They are planning to ambush the Americans from your old fort. It will happen tomorrow morning at the mountain pass north of Murzani. They are leaving tonight in groups of fifty men at a time. There will be four groups and they will be hiding in the pass by seven o'clock in the morning. They expect the American soldiers to enter the pass at nine." The guard sticks his head through the door and Pari stops talking.

After the guard turns back to the assembly, Dan tells Pari, "They have done it again. They're always one jump ahead of us. The Americans are planning a raid somewhere south of Murzani tomorrow. Obviously, the Taliban know about the raid. How else could they know Bravo Company is coming through the pass."

"Those poor men," Pari whispers, "They will be massacred."

XXIV

The guard who had been watching the door is replaced by two new guards who enter the tent and they sit across from the Dan and Pari. Their eerie stares give Pari the creeps and even Dan gets tired of looking at their wild eyed mugs. Into the evening and all through the night the camp is bustling with activity. Dan can hear voices, but he cannot understand their words. Nor can he get a translation from Pari, because the guards do not let them speak. As the wee hours of the morning approach, it is getting quite cold in the tent. Dan is able to bear the cool temperatures in his heavy fatigues, but he can see Pari is getting cold. Dan asks for a blanket for Pari, but the guards just laugh at the suggestion. Either they do not understand or they do not care. They only laugh long and hard while mocking Dan in the process. Pari has such disdain for the men, she refuses to speak to them. She would freeze to death before asking them for help. Dan stands and tries to communicate as though he is playing charades. He asks if he can take off his fatigue jacket and wrap it around Pari, but one of the guards pokes his rifle barrel in Dan's chest, sending Dan back to the ground. Finally, Pari falls asleep with her head leaning against Dan's shoulder. Dan tries to sleep, but every time he gets close to dropping off another loud noise outside the tent arouses his mind and keeps him awake. What Dan hears, but cannot see, are groups of fifty insurgents packing up their equipment and traipsing down the mountain trail to the trucks. They have six trucks to ferry the groups over to the pass under the cover of darkness. The tall leader has planned the departures to get all of his men in position for the ambush by daylight. The last group is pulling out of the camp. The two wild eyed guards are replaced by two older men. The first rays of light begin to break through the canopy of tree limbs above. The morning light finds the camp completely empty, except for Dan, Pari and their two constant companions.

The two old men begin to talk among themselves. They both get up and go outside. Pari whispers to Dan, "The old men are deciding what they want to cook for breakfast."

Dan says, "Ask them to make something for us, too."

Pari yells from the tent, asking the old men for some food. One of the guards sticks his head in the tent and laughs. He says something then laughs harder. He joins the other old guy who is making a fire. Dan sits up straight and motions for Pari to do the same. He quietly asks, "Is my knife still tied to your leg?" Pari nods without speaking. Dan whispers, "Swing your leg behind me. Keep an eye on the door. Let me know if they are coming. Dan is able to use his fingertips to pull up her pant leg and expose the K-bar. He rubs the rope bindings against the blade. Soon, he cuts through and frees his hands. He quickly cuts the ropes binding Pari's hands. They both get up and peek outside to see what the old men are doing. Both of the old men are standing by the fire roasting skewered meat over the flames. Their weapons are leaning against a tree a few yards away from the fire. Pari whispers, "You are not going to kill those fat old men, are you?"

Dan shakes his head and says, "I don't want to, but..." His voice trails off. He takes another look through the door and says, "When I jump out there, you tell them to be still or they will die the same as Nassir. Do you understand?"

Pari nods. Dan leaps out of the tent prominently displaying his knife to the old men. In a frantic voice, Pari screams the instructions to the old men. Dan races over to get between the old men and their rifles. Both men freeze in their tracks and hold their hands up.

Dan picks up one of the AK-47s leaning against the tree. He checks the magazine for ammunition and cocks the weapon. He waves for Pari to come over to his location. He hands the rifle to her and says, "It is ready to fire. Hold this gun on those two. Aim it at their bellies and, if they move, pull the trigger." Pari reluctantly holds the rifle while Dan ties them to a tree. "We have to get to Bravo Company before they get to the pass. What is it about ten miles to Murzani?"

Pari says, "You can say it, but our farm is closer."

Dan shakes his head, "No, not the farm. We have to find Grandfather, we need his help."

Pari insists, "Grandfather will be at the farm. Do you not remember the fire? The old widow's place is burned."

Dan takes the rifle from Pari and says, "Come on, let's go." Dan grabs her hand and pulls to get her started. Pari cannot keep up with Dan as he runs down the trail. She is going fast, but Dan is so amped up on adrenaline, he is practically flying. Dan stops frequently to give Pari a chance to catch up. He can see they will never make it in time, unless Pari picks up the pace. There is a farm house a little way up the road. He runs ahead of Pari momentarily to go for help. There is no answer at the door. Dan knows it is unlikely anyone would open the door to a man holding an AK-47. There is an on old horse and a wagon in the barn. The horse has a big barrel belly that weighs him down. He has developed a deep sway in his back that renders him too frail to ride, but Dan thinks the horse may be strong enough to pull the wagon. Dan hitches the horse to the wagon. By this time Pari arrives at the barn, Dan is just about ready to go.

Pari says, "What are you doing? Are you stealing a horse?"

"I'm only borrowing it,"Dan says, "Get in the wagon and hold on."

Dan lifts Pari into the wagon and he hands her the rifle. He grabs the reins and leads the old nag to the road. The horse is reluctant to move, so Dan yanks on the reins to get him started. Dan runs alongside of the trotting horse and Pari yells instructions for the best way to get over to Grandfather's farm. It is after seven o'clock when they finally get back to the house. The old widow runs out of the house to greet them. She gives Pari a big hug and runs back into the house to get Grandfather, who has been heartsick since Pari was taken by the ring of killers. Before she gets to the house, Grandfather is already on the front porch. When he sees that Pari is safe, he falls to his knees with joy. He folds his hands and looks to the sky in prayer. The old widow gives Dan a hug, also. Dan has just finished a seven mile run and he is gasping for air. He bends over with his hands on his knees. Jahen comes out of the house with a bucket of water. He follows instructions and pours the water over Dan's head. Dan cups his hands over his face and wipes the excess water over his head and through his hair. The water feels good. Combined with the cool morning air, the wet splash helps reenergize Dan. While he is laboring to overcome the effects of the long run, Dan looks over to see the heartwarming reunion between Grandfather and Pari. Dan has no time for reunions. He has to warn Bravo Company.

The problem is the Taliban have the road through the pass sealed off and there is no time to trek over the mountains. That would take days. Dan only has only minutes to try to stop the massacre. Getting through the pass in broad daylight, with two hundred insurgents poised to destroy anything on the road, will be difficult. Dan opens the barn door and checks the tractor for gas. He finds a full can of fuel and begins filling the tank. Jahen is watching Dan's every move. He asks, "What are you doing?"

As the fuel drains into the tank, Dan says, "We have to get this thing ready to roll. Tell Grandfather that I need him to drive us through the pass. Tell him to bring his fortune. If things don't work out, we're not coming back."

Pari is now standing in the door of the barn. After hearing what Dan said to Jahen, she adds, "If things do not go well, there will be no reason to return. There will be nothing left."

Dan starts the tractor and backs it out of the barn. As the tractor sits idling, Dan hitches the wagon and Jahen throws some feed on the ground for the chickens, before climbing on the stack of wood that never got unloaded from the wagon. Dan throws a bale of hay next to the wood. It will make a seat for the old widow to ride on. Next, he tosses some blankets in the wagon and he helps Pari get aboard. He yells to Grandfather, "Come on. Let's go." The old man mounts up. He takes one last look at the old farm that has been the only home he has ever known. He drops his head and throws the tractor in gear.

It is a quarter after eight as the motley group approaches the pass. The tractor's engine whines as though it could give out at any moment. Grandfather's implements are just about as worn out as he is. The hitch and the wagon tongue grate against one another, sending out an unsettling combination of clanks and squeaks. The wagon axles creak and moan with every bump in the road. Dan and Pari lie down and cover up. Jahen places some pieces of wood on top of the blankets to keep them still in the wind. Grandfather steers the old tractor as it putters through the pass.

As they enter the pass, Dan sneaks a peek at the canyon walls. He sees countless insurgents stationed up and down the mountain sides. The way they are deployed on the high canyon walls, there may as well be a thousand of them. That is how much of an advantage they will have against an unwitting convoy of trucks on the road. They are in perfect position to annihilate Bravo Company. Dan looks out through the spaces between the wooden slats that make up the sideboards of the wagon. He sees some of the Taliban yelling at Grandfather, in fact, many of them begin running into the road and chasing after the tractor. They are hooping, hollering, waving rags and spitting, but they are not shooting their rifles. Dan suspected that the insurgents would not shoot for fear they would risk giving away their positions. They have to think the advanced scouts from Bravo

Company will be within earshot. Still, Dan is concerned that the killers may try to knock Grandfather from his seat and allow the tractor to crash on its own. That scenario would force Dan to fight it out, but the odds would be long for him and the little family against the bloodthirsty mob. The killers are now stirred into a frenzy. They are chanting in unison as they run alongside the tractor. They are coming in waves from the edge of the road. When one bunch gets tired of keeping pace with their quarry, another bunch takes over, further subjecting the travellers to ridicule and intimidation. For Dan, the thought of the little family getting beaten to death is unbearable. He and Pari are lying face down on the deck of the wagon. He clings to her with one arm wrapped around her back. Although she is shaking, she is comforted by his firm grip. She prays to Jesus for his intercession on their behalf. She thinks only divine intervention will deliver them from the killers. She also prays the Dan will never let go of her. It is mid morning and the sun has yet to warm the canyon, like it will later in the day. Beneath the blankets, Dan feels the heat radiating from Pari. He is restless enough to throw the blankets off and try to stop the men from hurting Grandfather, but there is no sense in making a move, unless it becomes unavoidable. Dan knows that if he were to show himself, it would mean certain death for everyone in the wagon and Bravo Company would still be ambushed.

The old widow and Jahen ride in plain view of the insurgents, yet they show no fear, at least none that is evident from the outside. Grandfather refuses to make eye contact with his hecklers, choosing to keep focused on the road ahead. The teeming attackers continue to spit and throw stones at the old man. He keeps one hand on the wheel and uses the other to reach into a pocket for his handkerchief. Showing no emotion, he wipes some spit from his face. He knows he could be cut down at any moment, but he remains calm. He pushes the gas pedal as far as it will go, asking the old tractor for every ounce of speed it has. Finally, the unfriendly escort drops off. Their jeers and chants fade into the distance. It turns out, all of the anxiety was unnecessary, because for some reason, the insurgents allow the old man through. Dan thinks the ambushers must have orders to wait on the bigger fish before they begin their murderous spree. Besides, there will be plenty of time to punish Grandfather for his collaboration.

Dan peers between the slats to see open country. Knowing they have cleared the canyon eases the tension, but Dan and Pari must remain hidden until the wagon is towed beyond the vision of anyone in the canyon. Pari lets out a big sigh. It is as if she had been holding her breath all the way through the pass. She is still shaking even after it is obvious they are in the clear. Jahen pulls the blankets off of the hideaways. The bright sunlight and cool morning breeze are a welcomed splash in the face for Dan. Pari is still quivering and not talking. After experiencing the events of the last two days, she is bordering on a state of shock. In an effort to calm her nerves, Dan lifts one of the blankets over her shoulders and he closes it around her body. The old widow helps Pari take a seat on the hay. She sits back down beside Pari offers her hand to comfort the trembling young woman.

Dan sits up and strains to look down along the undulating slopes of the road. Way out in the distance, he thinks he sees a cloud of dust that could be Bravo Company trucks heading toward the crossroads.

Jahen says, "The plan to get through the mountains worked. But how did you know they would let us go?"

Dan turns to take another look back. He says, "I didn't. At least not for sure, but I had a feeling they would not want to give themselves away. They want Bravo Company. They have become blind to everything else." He looks around the wagon and continues, "I guess they think you all are too scared to talk to the Americans, or maybe they know Captain Craig would never listen to your warnings."

XXV

A few minutes later, Grandfather pulls the old tractor off of the road to make way for the lead vehicles in the Bravo Company column. The column is comprised of eight trucks and four humvees. The vehicles kick up a cloud of dust as they crawl up the road toward the pass. Dan jumps from the wagon and approaches the lead truck. The truck stops about fifty yards from Dan and a soldier yells, "Stop! Do not come any closer."

Dan holds his hands in the air and hollers, "Combs, is that you Combs? It's me, Dan Ross."

Sergeant Combs cannot believe his eyes. He gets out of the truck and says, "Ross? What the hell are you doin out here? I thought you were back in the States."

Dan keeps his hands over his head, but he walks toward his former compadre. He yells, "I came back to get Nassir and that Amir, but right now, I have to get to Captain Craig. You guys are heading for trouble."

Once Combs is sure it really is Dan, he runs over and shakes his old buddy's hand. He is dumbfounded, "What do you mean, you came back? I heard you were out of the Army?"

Before Dan answers, a voice can be heard blaring through Combs' radio, "Combs, come in Combs. This is Blake. Why have you stopped? What's the trouble?"

Combs replies, "Lieutenant Blake, this is Combs. You and the Captain need to get up here right away. You're never gonna believe this."

"We copy,"Blake says, "Be right there."

Two humvees come roaring up to the front of the column. One is carrying Blake and the other is the command vehicle. Captain Craig and Lieutenant Ashby emerge from the command vehicle, while Blake runs over to greet Dan. Blake reaches out his hand and he says, "Dan Ross. So you are the Ross that's missing from Apache. The photos we got weren't very good. They did look like you, but I didn't think it was possible. I thought you were in a wheelchair." The lieutenant is thrilled to see his friend is well and he gives Dan one of those Army bro hugs. Blake is shocked to find Dan wondering the high desert with Afghan farmers. Blake looks at the farmers in the tractor and he says, "What in the hell is going on? How did you end up out here?"

"Like I told Combs, I came here to do a job. It's a little personal business that I came to take care of,"Dan says, "But you guys are heading into an ambush in that pass. I have to talk to Captain Craig."

Dan, Combs and Blake walk over to speak with Captain Craig. Dan gets close enough for the Captain to recognize him. With a shocked expression, Captain Craig gasps, "You."

Dan flashes a broad grin and says, "That's right Captain, It's me, Dan Ross."

"You're the Ross everybody's looking for?" Captain Craig asks, "I thought you were paralyzed?"

Unable to suppress his desire to smart off to his former commanding officer, Dan keeps smiling and says, "I'm all better, now Captain." Dan savors the absolute surprised look he has inflicted upon Craig, but only for a moment. He looks down the column of trucks and then he turns back to Craig. The grin disappears and he says, "Captain, I'm here to warn you that you're heading into a trap. There are two hundred Taliban fighters laying for you in the mountain pass."

Captain Craig gets that glazed over, confused look in his eyes. The look he gets every time he is presented with an unexpected situation. Craig has never been one to make great decisions on the fly. He asks, "How do you know that?"

"We just came through the pass in that wagon. I saw them with my own eyes," Dan says, "They have taken high positions along the walls of the canyon. They have RPGs and everything. I saw it all. They have enough fire power to wipe out three companies."

Craig is never eager to discount Army intelligence. He says, "That can't be. Our intelligence has them on the far side of the valley. That's almost twenty miles beyond the pass."

Dan says, "Big surprise. The Taliban have out smarted us again. Don't you have any scouts out there?"

"No scouts. I didn't want to tip my hand."

"Tip your hand? I'm tellin you Captain, the deck's already stacked against you."

Blake says, "Why did they let you through the pass?"

"I was hidden on the floorboard of that wagon. They couldn't see me."

Doggedly clinging to his notion that Intel is infallible, Craig asks, "How can Intel be that wrong? There's no way."

"They aren't wrong,"Dan says, "The Taliban camp is on the far side of the valley, but they know you're coming. They have informants. They have government and military informants and some of those informants may be on our side."

Blake can see the Captain is disturbed by that remark. He asks, "How do you know so much about the Taliban?"

"I spent all last night watching them prepare for the ambush,"Dan says, "Well, I didn't actually see them, but I heard them."

Craig scoffs, "Where were you? Why didn't you let us know sooner?"

"I wanted to, but they took us prisoner. We were tied up inside one of their tents."

Craig is getting more confused. He asks, "Who's we?"

Dan points to the wagon, "The girl and me."

Craig looks over at the wagon and shakes his head, "Did the Taliban kidnap you from Apache?"

"No, I stowed away on a convoy to get here. The Hajis took me prisoner after I killed Nassir."

Blake asks, "Nassir? You mean the ANA sergeant that turned on you guys at Geronimo?"

Dan nods, "That's right. He's dead."

Here it comes, the patented Captain Craig bad idea. Craig says, "That's it then. Let's turn back. There's no sense in risking this Company, until we have all of the facts. The operation is off. Blake, get Battalion on the radio. They can tell the Air Cav to stand down."

Dan cannot let them turn back, "No no no, you can't turn back now. You've got them right where you want them, this time. They've bottled themselves up in that pass. If you call off the mission, everybody in that valley will be in danger of retaliation."

Blake steps between Dan and the Captain. He joins Dan's attempt to convince Craig to carry on. He says, "Dan's right, Captain. If the Talibs are concentrated in that pass, we have them trapped for a change."

"I agree,"Lieutenant Ashby says, "We can redirect the air stikes to hit the pass and we can change the Air Cavalry's landing zone to seal off the canyon. There will be no way out for the insurgents."

"Listen to them Captain,"Dan says, "This is your big chance. They fooled us with the attack on Geronimo, but the tables are turned. This really will be the end of the Taliban in this sector."

Craig hags his head and rubs the back of his neck, "I can't do it. The Colonel has to authorize all attack plans and he'll never believe a far fetched story like this. Besides, he wouldn't make those changes without confirming what you have told us. These things take time and coordination."

Dan gets disgusted and says, "You mean red tape, don't you Captain?"

Lieutenant Blake says, "Actually Captain, once engaged in this sort of action, you have the authority to redirect resources and alter strategies, as the situation requires. We've been engaged from the time we stopped for that old tractor."

Craig looks at Blake and says, "Is that the West Point book, Lieutenant?"

Blake answers sternly, "It is, Captain."

There is complete silence. All eyes are on Captain Craig, as the others await his orders. After a long pause, Captain Craig says, "Allright Ashby, you and Blake get on the radio and redirect the air strikes and the air cavalry landing zone. Give them the coordinates and tell them we attack in twenty minutes." He turns to Sergeant Hayes and says, "Get the other platoon leaders up here. We have to get this thing coordinated."

The officers huddle around the command vehicle and finalize the revised plan. Pari and Grandfather wander over to Dan and Combs. Pari asks, "What happens next? Grandfather wants to know if we'll be safe here."

"You'll be safe here,"Sgt Combs says, "Just stay here and don't go any closer to the pass."

After some heated words with whoever is on the other end, Blake gets off of the radio. He tells Captain Craig, "They say they can't redirect the air strikes without confirmation of actual enemy fire. It's because they have been misled into attacking phantom targets before."

"I can't send anybody in there without at least some preliminary strafing,"Captain Craig says, "That would be murder. The lead vehicles will catch hell. Call them back and talk some sense into them."

Blake returns to the radio. He pleads for an exception, but he gets nowhere. He throws the handset down and says, "It's no use. No enemy fire, no air strikes."

Dan runs over to the officers' huddle and says, "I'll draw their fire. I'll drive the lead truck into the pass."

Pari screams, "No, no, Dan you cannot." She runs over to Dan, she wraps her arms around his waist and buries the side of her head in his chest. She says, "Let the Army do it. They did not want you, they do not need you. This is their job, not yours."

Dan peels her arms off of his body. He cradles her chin in the palm of his hand and says, "I have to do this. If I don't, the people in the valley will be murdered and it would be my fault. Look, I came here to do a job. It was a selfish, petty job, but then I met you and the people in the valley. I realized they are good people, just like the people in southern Illinois, where I came from. They've had more than their fair share of heartache. They deserve a little taste of freedom."

"That's out of the question, Ross," Captain Craig says, "It's not going to happen. You're not authorized. You're not even in the Army anymore."

"In that case, I don't have to take orders anymore," Dan says, as he runs over to the lead truck, he looks back at the Captain and adds, "Besides, I'm missing, remember? You don't even know I'm here." Dan looks at Combs and says, "Hey Combs, get your men out of this truck. I'm taking over."

"Doesn't this go against your motto?" Combs asks, "Whatever happened to not letting other people's problems become your problems?"

Dan lets out a little laugh and says, "Yeah, well, I guess I'm in the wrong business for that."

Combs tilts his head to one side, "What, the newspaper business?"

Dan slowly shakes his head back and forth in disagreement. He says, "Life." After a brief pause Dan says, "Now get everybody out of this truck."

As soldiers are jumping down out of the truck, Dan yells over to Blake, "Hey John, stay about one hundred yards behind me. Once those planes show up, come in there fast."

"Don't worry, Dan," Blake says, "We're right behind you."

Dan puts a foot on the first step of the truck and is ready to jump into the cab, when Pari breaks free from Grandfather's clutches and she runs over to Dan, again. She is crying hard, but she has given up on trying to stop Dan from his suicide mission. Dan reaches down with one arm. He wraps it around her waist, lifts her off the ground and gives her a long goodbye kiss. One of the soldiers exiting the truck taps Combs on the shoulder and asks, "I wonder why is Sergeant Ross making out with that Afghan farm boy?"

Combs can only shake his head at the remark. As the extended embrace continues Dan takes his free hand and pulls the farmer's cap from Pari's head. Her long mane of wavy black hair falls off of her shoulders like a flag unfurling from its encasement. Whooping, cheering and catcalls erupt from the soldiers all the way down the column. Combs finds the inquisitive soldier and says, "Are you still wondering?" Combs turns to the rest of his squad and yells, "Now, hurry up and get aboard that other truck. You men get ready to move out."

Dan holds on to a scarf that comes off of Pari's head. He ties it around his neck like a bandana before nestling into the driver's seat. The rest of the officers have rejoined their platoons and the vehicles are ready to move out. Pari has returned to the wagon with her Grandfather, her brother and the old widow. She lifts her arm and gives a deflated wave to Dan. Combs jumps in the humvee with Blake and pulls up behind the truck Dan is driving. Dan sticks his head out of the window and takes a quick glance down the column and throws his truck into gear. At the speed the trucks travel, it's a ten minute drive to the pass, but it seems much longer to Dan. Some of his favorite memories of growing up begin to stir within him, he remembers the little things, like his mom always in the kitchen when he got home from school. She was always so excited to see Katie and him. She wanted to know everything that happened at school. He remembers helping his dad work on that old minivan. Dan would hold the light while his dad would cuss and spit, trying to keep that old thing on the road. As he gets closer to the mouth of the pass, he thinks about Pari and that weak goodbye wave. It was as though her arm weighed a ton the way she labored to hold it in the air. He remembers the terrified expression on her bruised face, he still feels guilty about the beating she took. He also remembers Paul, face down in the dust and rubble at the COP. He has spent four months working to get here. He is finally in position to get even with the butchers that killed his squad members. Dan looks in the rear view mirror to reassure himself that Blake is not that far behind. He lays his foot into the gas pedal, revving the engine and making plenty of noise to announce Bravo Company's arrival at the pass. He worries that even after the first shots are fired, it can take ten minutes for the air support to deliver the first bombs. What he does not know is that Blake reported enemy fire almost ten minutes ago, so the planes should arrive any second. Dan drives the lead truck well into the pass when rifle rounds begin glancing off of the reinforced armor and rocket propelled grenades are exploding on all sides of the truck. Dan keeps plowing through the pass at a steady pace in spite of the barrage of enemy fire. He looks in the rear view mirror to find Combs and Blake some three hundred yards to his rear. Behind Blake's humvee, Dan can see the last of the Bravo Company column has entered the pass. All of the vehicles are taking heavy enemy fire as the insurgents attempt to find their range and home in on their targets. Dan reaches into his boot and gets his K-bar for one last time. He props the knife against the gas pedal to keep the truck at a constant speed. He unties the scarf from his neck, the one he got from Pari, and he rigs the steering wheel. After securing the wheel with the scarf, the truck should remain on a steady course down middle of the road, even after he lets go of the wheel. He prepares to jump out of the truck, but the crossfire catches up with Dan when two rockets hit the truck simultaneously. One rocket hits behind the cab. The other rocket hits the front of the truck beneath the engine compartment causing it to flip into the air and explode. A thick plume of black smoke rolls into the sky. Blake and Combs watch the smoke bellow upward. Ignoring the bullets bouncing off of their own humvee, they take a moment to mourn their friend as the oily smoke rises into the sky.

Blake barks out orders to Combs, he yells, "Get everybody out of theses trucks, Sergeant. Tell them to take cover behind the boulders on the right side of the road. Let's bail out."

Moments after Blake and Combs vacate the humvee, it is hit by a rocket and explodes in a fiery ball. Likewise the truck behind their vehicle is destroyed in a similar fashion. In the background, behind all of the smoke, Blake sees the first wave of jets firing rockets and dropping bombs. In an impressive spectacle, four jets approach the pass from the east and four others from the west. The planes deliver their deadly payloads and crisscross above the road in an interweave formation. The bombs and missiles are coming from both directions and they are hammering the mountain sides with an unbearable onslaught. Waves of jets replicating the crisscross formation decimate the Taliban positions. Men are heard screaming from hot shrapnel wounds and severed limbs. As a final wave of jets finish pummeling the Taliban positions, Bravo Company infantrymen flood into the pass and begin scaling the mountains on both sides. At the same time the Air Cavalry troopers have landed on the far end of the pass and they are sealing off any exit routes that were previously available to the insurgents. At first, the scene is bedlam as the insurgents attempt to fight their way out. They put forth a valiant effort, but the GI's are too much for them. Within minutes the Taliban are cornered in a small section of the pass. The foot soldiers begin the arduous task of rooting out the last of the guerilla fighters. For the most part the road is secured and only sporadic rifle fire can be heard from the upper elevations of the mountains.

Grandfather has pulled the wagon into the pass. With tears pouring from her eyes, Pari jumps out of the wagon and runs up the road yelling, "Dan, Dan, Dan, where are you, Dan?" She begins crying. Some soldiers try to hold her back, but she breaks through their grasps and finds the remnants of the truck Dan was driving. The burned out shell is still burning with tall flames stretching high into the air. There are scattered pieces of wreckage strewn along the road. She breaks down and falls to her knees. Blake comes from behind and kneels down beside her. He does not speak, he just puts his hand on her back and stares at the flames. After a few moments, Pari breaks the silence with some questions for Blake. She asks, "Why was he so driven? What makes a man lay down his life for a strange people in a strange land? Why would he give so much for people he did not know, people that live on the other side of the world from his home?"

Blake stares at the flames and mulls those questions for a few moments before replying, "I guess he found something worth dying for. In some ways he's lucky. A lot of men die out here without ever finding it."

Dan's two closest friends stand up and continue to stare at his fiery grave. The searing heat forces Blake to take Pari by one arm and lead her a few steps back away from the glowing metal remains. Pari and Blake are unaware that Dan is lying unconscious on the other side of a boulder not twenty yards from where they are standing.

They are also unaware that Ghafoor has slipped through the dragnet the American soldiers have employed to round up the insurgents. He is slithering along the base of the canyon walls using the fallen boulders for cover. He is armed with an AK-47 that has only a handful of rounds left in the magazine. Ghafoor is contemplating his options. His empire is in tatters. It has crumbled around him like the stones falling from the canyon walls. The lion of Murzani has been declawed. There is little hope of evading the droves of soldiers pouring into the pass and he knows his capture will result in certain execution. Ghafoor is resigned to go down fighting. He figures there is enough ammo to make one more big splash. He is no jihadist. He never believed in the promises of great rewards in heaven, but at this point, those promises are all that is left. The ultimate manipulator desperately attempts to influence the deity. He hopes one last depraved act will punch his ticket to the land of coutless virgins.

Dan is starting to gather his senses. He awakens to a literal splitting headache. His head wounds are superficial, but very bloody and sharp pains knife through his brain. After being blown to the side of the pass by the truck explosion, his wound was self inflicted. He dove behind the boulder for cover and was watching the first few planes deliver their bombs, when he realized that his fatigues were on fire, so he did the whole stop, drop and roll thing. He slammed his head on a rock and knocked himself out cold. Those events have left him struggling to get his bearings. He sits up and leans his head on the top of his shoulders. He rolls his head in a circular motion to loosen his stiff neck. As he spins his head around he spots Ghafoor poking his head over a boulder and looking at the road. Dan moves slowly, trying not to let Ghafoor see him. Dan looks around a boulder to see what is commanding the tall leader's interest. To his horror, he sees Ghafoor level off his rifle and take aim at Pari and Blake. Ghafoor has found his final targets and he wraps his finger around the trigger. Dan jumps to his feet and runs toward Ghafoor, yelling out a gutteral, "No." The tall leader swings his weapon around toward Dan, who is only a few feet from Ghafoor and closing fast. Ghafoor is aiming from his hip. Blake draws his sidearm, but cannot shoot at the insurgent without hitting Dan. Pari covers her ears and screams. Dan leaps toward Ghafoor like a big cat pounces on its prey. Ghafoor squeezes off his last few rounds at point blank range. The first burst misses Dan. He latches onto the barrel of the weapon and deflects it upward. The final bullet from the rifle enters Ghafoor's neck below his chin. The bullet exits through the top of the tall leader's head, scattering pieces of his scalp onto the adjacent boulder. Dan lands on top of the lifeless insurgent and tumbles to the ground.

Blake fears the worst. He runs over to find Dan struggling to untangle himself from the dead insurgent. Dan holds his arm out for Blake to pull him up. Dan says, "This dude was their leader. His name is Ghafoor or something."

Blake says, "I recognize the name. You're right. He's the head honcho." Blake puts his arm beneath Dan's shoulder and helps him walk over to Pari. Pari runs to meet Dan and she wraps her arms around him. Overcome with happiness and tears, Pari can barely speak. She wipes the blood from his face with another of her scarves. She manages a big smile and says, "You worried me to sickness. And your head, what happened?" Dan does not answer, he hugs her without talking. Pari continues to sob uncontrollably, but now, she is overcome with joy. Dan picks her up in his arms and carries her through the bustling battle staging area. There are soldiers scrambling to secure the mountain pass. There is still plenty of smoke and dust filling the air and limiting visibility. There are voices overheard from radios reporting the action in the higher elevations. There are Taliban prisoners slouching in the back of a truck under constant surveillance by armed GIs. There are more soldiers carrying the wounded insurgents on stretchers. There are medics working feverishly to administer any life saving aid they can muster. There are med evac helicopters still miles away, but the whoofing of their engines can be heard above clamor of the busy scene. Dan keeps moving with Pari in his arms. He doesn't ever want to let go of her.

Dan reunites with Grandfather and the old widow. He sets Pari down on the back of the wagon and he takes a seat next to her. The old folks each lay a hand on Dan to express their happiness that he is unhurt. Grandfather begins to rattle off one of his long tirades, but is interrupted by the old widow. They banter back and forth. Nobody pays too much attention to them, nor does Pari bother to interpret for Dan. After resting for a few minutes, Dan and Pari take another walk around. There is one area designated for the dead insurgents. There are rows of blood soaked bodies laid out for identification. Some are missing arms or legs or both. There are more than one hundred amassed so far, with more coming all the time. Pari looks away from the morbid sight, but Dan is drawn to two bodies in particular. One is Ghafoor. The other has incurred more than a few wounds, but his face is recognizable. Dan has found positive proof that his quest is over. Blake is standing nearby, so Dan points to the dead body and says, "Hey John, you know this one here don't you?"

Blake nods with a thin smile, "Yeah, that's that Amir. The one we captured at the hill."

Dan says, "Yeah, only he's not getting away this time."

Lt. Blake silently nods in agreement. Combs appears from out of the crowd to ask, "Lieutenant Blake, what do you want us to do with all of these prisoners? The Air Cavalry just brought in another group."

"I'll be right with you, Sergeant,"Blake says. He turns to Dan and Pari and says, "Duty calls. I'll see you guys after while."

As Blake gets back to work, Dan takes Pari back to the wagon. Grandfather and the old widow are immersed in conversation as they watch the soldiers manage the aftermath of the one sided melee. Dan thinks about Ghafoor lying in the dust on the side of the road. He looks at Pari then tilts his head the direction of the dead leader and says, "He told us he would die well. I'm not sure what dying well is, but I'm guessing that's not it."

"He received what he deserved,"Pari says, "He reaped the same as he sowed."

Her words make Dan think of Father Donovan, back home. Dan wonders what the old priest would think of the events of the last few days. Surely, he saw this sort of thing in Vietnam. Dan hopes it is not a deal breaker on that road to salvation that Father Donovan likes to talk about. Jahen, who had been running around and talking to soldiers, returns to the wagon. Pari hollers, "Jahen, stay out the way of the soldiers. They have much work to do."

Jahen smirks at the order from his bossy sister. He says, "Dan you are a brave man. All of the soldiers are talking about your bravery. They are proud that you drove that truck into the pass and I am too." Dan does not respond to Jahen. He just stares at Pari. Jahen is put out that Dan is ignoring him. After a while, Jahen asks, "Are you going back to America, soon?"

Pari perks up and listens closely for the answer.

"I'm going back to America just as soon as I can,"Dan says, "And I'm taking you with me."

Jahen's eyes swell and he smiles broadly. He says, "What?"

Immediately after Jahen's response, Pari asks, "What?" She looks at Dan with a confused expression.

"That's right,"Dan says. He looks at Pari while he continues to talk to Jahen, "I'm taking you and Grandfather, oh, and I'm taking Pari, too." He studies Pari's face to see her reaction.

Jahen is ecstatic. He goes over to tell Grandfather the news. Attempting to gauge her feelings about going with him, Dan does not take his eyes off of Pari. Grandfather goes off on a long tirade of spirited chatter. He waves his arms and points toward the valley.

Pari softly says, "Grandfather will never leave this valley. He is going to move to Murzani and use his fortune to rebuild the old widow's restaurant. He says he is tired of the farm. He is ready for retirement with the comfort of an old woman."

Dan asks, "What about you and Jahen? What did he say about you going to America?"

Pari says, "Oh he is happy that you want to take us to America." She attempts to be coy with Dan, once again. She says, "But you did not ask me. Do American men make all of the decisions, without first asking?"

Dan sheepishly replies, "Well, some do.... I uh, just thought..."

Pari cuts him off before he can finish. She asks, "Are women in your country treated like objects?"

Dan should have been more prepared for her feisty response, but he wasn't. He says, "No, not all…"

Again, Pari cuts him off and she asks, "What makes you think I want to go to America? What will I be there? What will I do?"

"You will be my wife,"Dan says, "And you can do whatever you want."Pari smiles, then her smile turns into laughter. She cannot hide her jubilation any longer and she leaps into an embrace with Dan. As the lovers kiss, Jahen can only shake his head.

The mountain pass gets even busier as a squadron of helicopters fly in from the north. The choppers have to land outside the pass. The road is cleared to make an uncluttered path to truck the wounded men to the med evac helicopters. The back end of a larger helicopter opens and a humvee rolls out. It is Colonel Willis. He has flown down from FOB Apache with plenty of help to process the wounded and the prisoners. Dan and Pari sit side by side on the back end of the wagon with their legs dangling off of the ground. They watch the incredible amount of activity as the soldiers wrap up the battleground with well drilled efficiency. After a few more minutes, First Sergeant Hayes comes over to the wagon. He says, "Hey Ross, Colonel Willis would like to see you over at the command vehicle."

"You bet Hayes," Dan says, "I'll be right over." Although he doesn't like the tone of the first sergeant's voice. He thinks he may be in trouble. He thinks they may arrest him. But Hayes always has sounded like that. He has always been all business. As Dan approaches the command vehicle, he sees Colonel Willis, Captain Craig and a few other officers talking. Colonel Willis is the first to speak as Dan joins the meeting. In a tone of voice Jerry used to use when scolding Dan, the Colonel says, "You gave us quite a scare young man. We thought you were kidnapped."

Dan looks down. "I'm sorry about that Colonel."

"It sounds like you had quite an adventure the last few days. It will be something to tell your grandchildren about, I suppose." Dan gets a little nervous with all the brass staring at him. The Colonel continues, "Do you remember when you first got to Apache I said, *Don't be a cowboy?*"

Dan silently nods his head. He looks up at the sky and that voice in his head says, "Okay, here it comes. They're going to lock me in the stockade and throw away the key."

The Colonel steps a little closer to Dan. He likes to use his burly presence to intimidate people when he is making a point. It works. Dan is sweating more than he was when he drove the truck into the canyon. The Colonel says, "Well, you went John Wayne on me. If you were still in the Army, I'd have to court martial you. But since you're a civilian, all I can do is say, thank you and well done."

That's the last thing Dan expected to hear. The Colonel shakes his hand, as do all of the other officers in attendance, including Captain Craig. The Colonel says, "If there's anything we can do for you, before you go back home, just let me know."

"There is something Colonel,"Dan says, "Can the Army clear it so I can take those two Afghans home with me.?"

The Colonel takes a step back and asks, "Are you serious? Why in the world do you want to take those two Afghans home?"

"Well, I'm going to marry the girl and this is no place for her little brother to grow up."

The Colonel strains his neck to look over at the wagon. He wants to see what girl Dan is talking about. He says, "I guess we can arrange that. In fact the chaplain at Apache can preside over the wedding ceremony."

"I appreciate that, Colonel,"Dan says, "But there's a priest back home that would be upset if I got married by anybody but him. He's retired Army, too."

Willis nods and says, "Well. It's a great day for this Battalion. I'm proud of each and every soldier in this outfit" He looks at Dan and says, "You'll make sure we look good in the papers, right Ross?"

Dan shakes his head, "I'm out of the newspaper business, Colonel. But my editor deserves the whole story, except for that part about me taking a shower in front of a bunch of farm animals. Anyway, I'll let him write the story."

"I'm sorry, what did you say about farm animals?"

"Oh, nothing, don't worry, the 329th will look real good in the papers."

The meeting breaks up and Dan starts back over to the wagon when he hears Captain Craig's voice. "Hey Ross," the Captain says, "Wait up. I'd like to talk to you."

Dan turns around and says, "Sure Captain. What's up?"

The two men walk side by side as they talk. Captain Craig says, "I want to personally thank you for what you did today. You saved a lot of lives, perhaps the whole Company."

"No need to thank me. I just happened to be in the right place at the right time."

"Do you ever think about how you got here, or why?" Captain Craig asks, "You were practically the only survivor from your squad that day at Geronimo. There has to be some divine power that guided you. You overcame all kinds of obstacles and objections. In defiance of any sort of reason, you miraculously ended up here in position to save this company today."

Dan never thought about it before talking with the Captain, but this might be what his Katie and the nurses and doctors were talking about. This may be why he was spared that day. This may be one of those big things God had planned after the attack at Geronimo. Dan never bought into the God theory, but maybe there is something to it. For the first time in months, Dan has to prompt his brain to recall the events at the COP. It is as though he has finally been able to compartmentalize those images. They will always be there, but now, instead of the involuntary preoccupation that has plagued him, he has some freedom to choose when and how he will remember his friends that died that day. It is not the deaths of Ghafoor and his cohorts that freed him. It might not even be the fact that Bravo Company has survived and the people in the valley are unshackled. Maybe it was that bump on the head, but Dan is beginning to get the message that his family, Father Donovan and just about everyone else he has encountered the last four months implored him to consider. Pari and Grandfather are examples of that message and being around them is most likely what drove it home. Jesus carried the message over two thousand years ago and most people on earth still ignore his words.

The message that set Dan free is that there is injustice in the world and there always will be, but if you can live without being consumed by hate, you will not miss out on everything there is to love in this life.

He is deep in thought and the Captain has to grab his shoulder to get his attention. Dan says, "Oh, I'm sorry Captain. I drifted away there for a second."

Craig says, "There is one more thing, Dan I'm going to revise the record on the attack at Geronimo. Any inferences of wrong doing, on your part, will be stricken. It's a bitter pill to admit mistakes, but it's better late than never."

Dan stops walking as does Craig. Dan looks at the Captain and says, "You don't have to do that. It doesn't make any difference now."

"It may make not make any difference to you," Craig says, "But it matters to me. You had to do something about that day at Geronimo and so do I."

Dan shrugs, "You do what you think is right, Captain."

Craig continues, "I'm also going to ask Colonel Willis to replace me as CO, as soon as he can. I realize that battlefield command may not be my strong suit. Besides, it's time for me to settle down with my wife and family. My daughters are almost teenagers. They are getting to the age where they need a dad to be home more often." Dan is mystified that the stoic, red ass captain is baring his soul to a young man with whom he has had so many disagreements. The two men shake hands and Captain Craig takes his free hand and overlays the clasp. Craig says, "Thanks again, for everything. Good luck with your new family."

By the time Dan gets back to the wagon, Grandfather has said his goodbyes to Pari and Jahen. Dan hugs the little man and the old widow. Even though the old folks do not understand a word he is saying, Dan speaks to them anyway, "You'll be hearing from us. We'll write."

Pari listens to final instructions from Grandfather. She nods her head, while she helps the old widow get in the wagon. Grandfather fires up the tractor and starts for home. The widow woman is his only passenger. Pari's puffy eyes swell even more and tears roll down her cheeks. She waves goodbye, watching her Grandfather disappear into the mass of humanity.

Jahen tugs on Dan's fatigues and asks, "Can I be an American soldier someday?"

Dan says, "We'll see. But the first thing we have to do is get you enrolled in school. In America, you have to go to school every day." Jahen turns his lip at that thought.

Pari smiles and puts her arm around Dan's waist. She says, "You are already sounding like a parent. I like that."

Blake pulls up in a humvee and says, "There's a helicopter leaving for Apache. I'm supposed to put you guys on it."

Dan, Pari and Jahen hop in the humvee with Blake. After the short trip to the landing area, they exit the vehicle amid the swirling dust kicked up by the helicopter blades. Dan yells over the screaming aircraft engines, "John, when you get back to the States, make sure you come up to Quincy to see us."

Blake shakes Dan's hand and he gives Pari a hug. He nods and says, "I'll make a point of it." Blake stands next to the humvee and watches them board the helicopter. He waves goodbye, as the chopper lifts off and disappears in the morning sky.

XXVI

Eight months later the parade grounds at Fort Polk, Louisiana are
once again prepared for an official military ceremony. It is a warm
spring day. The sun is out and there are no clouds in sight. The
decorative landscaping is bursting with new blossoms. There are high
ranking officers that made the trip down from division headquarters at
Fort Drum. There are soldiers decked out in their dress uniforms.
There are rows of folding chairs lined in front of the raised platform
that was built for this event. The flags, raised to the top of their masts,
are rippling in the breeze. Immediate families of soldiers are seated in
the first few rows. Behind them, there are more folding chairs and
permanent grand stands spilling over with extended families, friends
and military personnel. The top brass, including Captain Craig, are
seated behind the podium. After some preliminary proceedings like the
invocation and introductions, the division commander makes his way
to the podium amid the shuttering of a host of camera lenses. As the
General steps up to the podium, he acknowledges the polite ovation
from the audience. The two stars on each of his shoulders spray

reflections of sunlight into the blue sky. He fumbles with a pair of reading glasses, but once they are in place, he begins with remarks explaining the reason for the ceremony and then he reads a prepared proclamation. The sound system amplifies his voice so it can be heard throughout the post. He looks down at the document and recites these written words, "By this citation, the president of the United States of America, authorized by Act of Congress, July 9, 1918, takes pleasure in presenting the Silver Star to these soldiers of Bravo Company, 329th Battalion, 10th Mountain Division, for conspicuous gallantry during combat operations in support of freedom in Afghanistan, on March 30, 2011. In the face of extreme duress and a hail of enemy fire in broad daylight, these soldiers displayed courage in keeping with the highest standards of valor. Through their distinctive accomplishments, they brought credit upon themselves, 10th Mountain Division and the United States Army."

After the proclamation is read, Captain Craig stands and joins the General at the podium. He reads the names of the recipients one by one, beginning with those being honored posthumously. Upon announcing each of the deceased honorees, family members make their way onto the platform to accept the medal from the General. Even though it has been a year to the day since the memorial service, there is still an outpouring of emotion. There are soldiers positioned to help weak kneed mothers up the steps. Craig begins by announcing Specialist Albert Sandoval. Little Al's parents rise and make their way to the podium. The General shakes their hands and presents a medal to Mrs. Sandoval. The Sandovals step to the back of the platform and stand facing the audience. As the proceedings continue Cuz's widow is helped to the platform to accept the medal and join the Sandovals at the back of the platform. Next, Chi Chi's mom ascends the steps that lead to the temporary stage, holding a handkerchief to her eyes to soak up some of the tears She accepts the medal from the General on behalf of her fallen son. The next man to be honored is Eric Simms. Hambone's father walks behind a soldier helping his wife up the steps. The couple finds their way to the general and they line up with the others on the platform.

Craig continues by saying, "Corporal Paul Larson, deceased." Katie stands holding her seven month old baby boy. A soldier holds her arm to support her climb to the stage.

The General looks at the baby and asks, "What is this fine young man's name?"

"Paul" Katie replies with tears in her eyes.

"That's a good name," the General says. He fastens the medal on the baby's shirt.

Dan closes his eyes and pictures each of the deceased men's faces as they are honored. He cannot help but smile when he thinks of Hambone's antics or Chi Chi's dancing. They were all friends that Dan will never forget.

The living recipients are the next ones called and Craig starts with, "Corporal Albert Jones." Big Al quickly steps up to shake the General's hand and receive the medal. Next the Captain calls Pete Lester. Although he is still limping from the shrapnel wound, Pete makes his way up the steps unassisted. He accepts his medal and is followed closely by Z, who is getting around well.

Finally the Captain announces, "Staff Sergeant Daniel Ross, retired." Dan stands up and grabs Pari's hands. Dan insists on Pari going with him to accept the medal. After all, she endured more hardship at the hands of the Taliban than Dan and she did so with more grace than Dan, as well. She resists for awhile, but she does not want to make a scene, so she finally goes along. After ascending the steps, Dan shakes the officers' hands and shifts his weight from one foot to another, rocking back and forth, as the General pins the medal on the breast of his uniform. He steps back in line with the other recipients and removes the medal. He holds it in the air to show his folks, before pinning it on Pari's dress.

The End

James Williams is a guy who took forty years to decide what he wanted to do with his life. Born in the "Show Me" state, Missouri, he has lived in Texas since he was very young. Williams graduated from the University of Houston-DC with a degree in accounting, but he never worked a day as an accountant. His Missouri stubbornness prevented him from staying at any job for more than three years at a time. Consequently, he has had fourteen different full time jobs in the thirty years he and Julie have been married. Williams always had a wanderlust spirit, but the pressures of providing for his wife and four kids required him to keep his nose to the grindstone. Writing was the farthest thing from his mind, except for silly poems and songs he wrote for the kids when they were little. Never a big reader of fiction, Williams confined his reading to the newspaper and history books, but he had a knack for telling stories. So on a whim, he decided to write a novel. Williams lives in Tomball, Texas and now that he knows what he likes to do, you can find him at work on his next book.

CPSIA information can be obtained at www.ICGtesting.com
Printed in the USA
LVOW04s0055301114

416232LV00018B/1971/P